'I loved Mollie – she is rebellious … thoughtful and funny.'
thetbrpile.com

'A girl's eye view of early feminism … exciting, vivid … with the impulsive
and daring Mollie.'
Lovereading4kids.co.uk

'A historical novel with a contemporary edge.' *Sunday Business Post*

The book is set in Dublin, 1912, when Home Rule was being lobbied for, and
women were arguing that the vote should be for all. The plot revolves around
the irrepressible Mollie becoming both politically aware and active. The family
servant, Maggie tartly sums up her own shaky existence, 'I may very well be
part of the family, but it's a part that can be sent packing without a reference.'
I … curled up on the couch and did not put it down.'
Historical Novel Society Review

'For junior feminists … a must-read.'
The Irish Times

'Carey brings to life Mollie's struggles in a way that makes the book strikingly
relevant to the teenagers of today. A historical novel with a contemporary edge.'
Sunday Business Post

'A cracking book.'
Irish Independent

The Real Rebecca

'Definite Princess of Teen.'
Books for Keeps

'The sparkling and spookily accurate diary of a Dublin teenager. I haven't laughed so much since reading Louise Rennison. Teenage girls will love Rebecca to bits!'
Sarah Webb, author of the *Ask Amy Green* books

'This book is fantastic! Rebecca is sweet, funny and down-to-earth, and I adored her friends, her quirky parents, her changeable but ultimately loving older sister and the swoonworthy Paperboy.'
Chicklish Blog

'What is it like inside the mind of a teenage girl? It's a strange, confused and frustrated place. A laugh-out-loud story of a fourteen-year-old girl, Rebecca Rafferty.'
Hot Press

Rebecca's Rules

'A gorgeous book! ... So funny, sweet, bright. I loved it.'
Marian Keyes

'Amusing from the first page ... better than Adrian Mole!
Highly recommended.'
lovereading4kids.co.uk

'Sure to be a favourite with fans of authors such as Sarah Webb and Judi Curtin.'
Children's Books Ireland's Recommended Reads 2012

Rebecca Rocks

'The pages in Carey's novel in which her young lesbian character announces her coming out to her friends and in which they give their reactions are superbly written: tone is everything, and it could not be better handled than it is here.'

The Irish Times

'A hilarious new book. Cleverly written, witty and smart.'

writing.ie

'Rebecca Rafferty ... is something of a *Books for Keeps* favourite ... Honest, real, touching, a terrific piece of writing.'

Books for Keeps

Rebecca is Always Right

Fun ... feisty, off-the-wall individuals and a brisk plot.'

Sunday Independent

'Be warned: don't read this in public because from the first sentence this story is laugh out loud funny and only you'll make a show of yourself ... this book is the funniest yet.' *Inis Magazine*

'Portrays a world of adolescent ups and downs ... Rebecca is at once participant in and observer of, what goes on in her circle, recording it all in a tone of voice in which humour, wryness and irony are shrewdly balanced.'

The Irish Times

ANNA CAREY is a journalist and author from Dublin who has written for the *Irish Times*, *Irish Independent* and many other publications. Anna's first book, *The Real Rebecca,* was published in 2011, and went on to win the Senior Children's Book prize at the Irish Book Awards. Rebecca returned in the critically acclaimed *Rebecca's Rules*, *Rebecca Rocks* and *Rebecca is Always Right*. *The Making of Mollie* (2016) was her first historical novel and was shortlisted for the Senior Children's Book prize at the 2016 Irish Book Awards.

MOLLIE
on the MARCH

Anna Carey

THE O'BRIEN PRESS
DUBLIN

First published 2018 by The O'Brien Press Ltd,
12 Terenure Road East, Rathgar, D06 HD27, Dublin 6, Ireland.
Tel: +353 1 4923333; Fax: +353 1 4922777
E-mail: books@obrien.ie
Website: www.obrien.ie
The O'Brien Press is a member of Publishing Ireland.

ISBN: 978-1-78849-008-5

10 9 8 7 6 5 4 3 2 1
23 22 21 20 19 18

Layout and design: The O'Brien Press Ltd.
Cover illustrations: Lauren O'Neill

Printed and bound by Nørhaven, Denmark.
The paper in this book is produced using pulp from managed forests.

Published in:

DUBLIN
UNESCO
City of Literature

To all the women still marching for our rights in Ireland today.

Acknowledgements

Thanks to everyone at the O'Brien Press, especially Emma Byrne and my ever-patient and supportive editor Susan Houlden; Helen Carr for being generally encouraging; Lauren O'Neill for another wonderful cover; everyone who generously spread the word about Mollie, especially Marian Keyes, Claire Hennessy, Nina Stibbe, Sarra Manning and Sarah Webb; Nicola Beauman of Persephone Books; the historians without whose work I couldn't have written about Mollie's adventures, Rosemary Cullen Owens, Margaret Ward and especially Senia Paseta. Any historical errors are, of course, entirely my own; the extended Carey and Freyne families; and Patrick, for making me laugh and keeping me going.

HISTORICAL NOTE

This book is set in Dublin in 1912. At the time, Ireland was part of the United Kingdom, but there was a big demand in Ireland for what was called Home Rule. This meant that Ireland would be part of the UK, but would have its own parliament in Dublin.

In 1912, the only people who could vote in general elections in the UK were men (and not even all men – only men who owned or lived in property of a certain value). Lots of women, however, were campaigning for the vote, and they were known as suffragists or suffragettes. In June 1912 several members of the Irish Women's Franchise League broke windows of various government buildings as an act of protest.

25 Lindsay Gardens,
Drumcondra,
Dublin.

21st June, 1912.

Dear Frances,

I AM NOT IN PRISON

I know this sounds awfully dramatic, but I last wrote to you just after Nora and I had broken the law as daring suffragettes, and since then I've rather been caught up in revising for exams and things. So I thought you might have been worrying about us. But I am happy to say that we are still free.

Or at least, we are not in prison, like the brave suffragettes who broke windows all over Dublin last week. I know Nora and I are very lucky not to be languishing in a jail cell right now, but I must admit that I don't feel very free. We still have a couple of exams left to do, and when I'm not studying my mother keeps making me do all sorts of stupid chores. This is particularly unfair as Harry, who also has exams, doesn't have to do his usual task of helping Maggie with cleaning the boots. (This is literally the only thing he ever has to do, and it's barely a chore at all as he actually LIKES mucking about with boot blacking, and besides, at this time of the year, there's hardly any cleaning to do because the streets aren't muddy, just dusty.) What with the studying AND all the mending I barely have a moment to think. In fact, I'm worried I might come down with a brain fever from overwork. Though when I told Mother this before school this morning she just laughed cruelly.

'I don't think there's much chance of you working yourself into any sort of fever,' she said, callously. Then she must have felt a bit guilty because she said, 'But I suppose I could let you off the mending this afternoon. Just this once.'

'Thank you so much,' I said, very sarcastically, but she didn't seem to realise I was being sarcastic because she said, 'You're welcome.'

So anyway, that's why I'm upstairs lying on my bed writing to you right now, instead of downstairs sewing buttons onto Father's shirts, which is what I was meant to be doing this afternoon. Father is stuck in the office working on some dull bill or other so I am not missing the latest installment of his epic novel. Hopefully he will read it tomorrow evening.

I haven't told you much about his novel recently, have I? It's still very exciting. The brave hero Peter Fitzgerald is pretending to be a German spy, but unfortunately he can't really speak German so he has to say '*ja*' and '*nein*' to everything and hope for the best. That means 'yes' and 'no', in case you don't know. Those are pretty much the only German words I know – they teach German in my school, but you have to choose between it and French and I chose French. I think it would be good to learn both, then if you had to pretend to be a spy (or if you actually were a spy), you would have more options. I've always thought being a spy sounds awfully exciting. Phyllis has accused me of spying on her often enough so maybe I have a natural talent for it. In fact, perhaps I should learn Russian too, just in case. Russian spies are always cropping up in books.

Anyway! I am so sorry you won't be coming to Dublin this summer. You could have joined in my and Nora's suffrage activities! I don't know if we will paint any more postboxes though. Just painting one postbox was terrifying enough. But we will do something, especially as the Prime Minister is coming to visit Dublin next month, and there will definitely be some sort of protest then. And in the meantime, we will try and go to more meetings. Of course Phyllis is refusing to take us to any, especially since the brave women from the Irish Women's Franchise League got arrested for breaking windows.

'Anything could happen now,' she said. Remember, we had both been at that big meeting in the Phoenix Park a few days after the women got arrested. Loads of protestors turned up and yelled horrible things at the suffragette leaders, and the police had to step in when the mob started pushing and shoving them. That was bad enough, but Phyllis seemed to think that things would only get worse.

'And,' she said, 'I won't be able to keep an eye on you and Nora if things get dangerous.'

As if we couldn't take care of ourselves! She's being so unfair. She needs us at meetings, if you ask me. If it weren't for us, she'd have been caught holding a banner at that Phoenix Park gathering a few months ago. After all, me and Nora were the ones who told her that Mother's friend Mrs. Sheffield was passing by. And what thanks did we get for that? None! She didn't even buy us a bun in the Phoenix Park tearoom afterwards. We had to buy our own. She's so ungrateful. I told her this and she didn't even have the good grace to look ashamed of herself.

'I never asked you to come to that meeting,' she said. 'And you needn't look so martyr-ish. You only found out about the movement in the first place because you were sneaking around spying on me.'

This was true, I suppose. But still!

'Besides,' Phyllis went on, 'you've talked me into taking you to enough things already.'

I was going to remind her that when she actually took us to the biggest suffrage meeting that ever there was, her stupid friend sold our tickets and we had to sit in the vestibule outside the concert hall for about five hours. But I didn't get a chance to mention it because she immediately marched off into the drawing room where Mother was sitting with Aunt Josephine. I think she only went in there to avoid talking to me, as no one would ever join Aunt Josephine voluntarily. Poor Mother doesn't have a choice, because Aunt Josephine just turns up at the house whenever she feels like it, whether she's invited or not (which she hardly ever is).

Phyllis should remember the movement needs all the support it can get at the moment because the IWFL heroines finally had their trial yesterday. Phyllis wanted to go along to support them, but Mother had made an appointment at the dressmaker to get some new summer frocks fitted, and Phyllis couldn't think of a convincing excuse to get out of it. But her friend Mabel went to the court and she came over yesterday evening to tell Phyllis all about it. I already knew that Mabel had planned to go to the trial so when she called to our house and Phyllis took her straight upstairs to her room, I knew what they'd be discussing. And so — and this is NOT sneakish, Frances, I wasn't spying on them — I followed them and knocked on the door.

'Go away,' said Phyllis, without even bothering to open it.

I opened it myself and stuck my head in. 'Please let me hear what happened at the trial,' I pleaded. 'You know you can trust me not to breathe a word.'

'Oh go on, Phyl, let her stay.' Mabel gave me an apologetic smile. 'I still owe her for that business at the big meeting.'

If you recall, it was Mabel who sold our tickets to someone else.

Phyllis sighed.

'Very well,' she said. 'But promise me you'll just sit quietly on the floor and won't interrupt.'

'I wouldn't dream of it,' I said, and I sat down on the floor in a very dignified manner.

'So, Mabel,' said Phyllis. 'Tell us all.'

Mabel took a deep breath.

'Well,' she said, 'the bad news is they got two months.'

Two whole months! In a horrible dank prison, full of black beetles and other horrid things. I thought of the terrible bits about prison in *No Surrender*, that book about English suffragettes.

'They won't force feed them, will they?' I said.

'It depends on whether they go on hunger strike,' said Mabel.

I hoped they wouldn't, for their own sakes. They do awful things to women who go on hunger strike. They shove mashed-up food down their noses and throats with a rubber tube, which sounds like utter agony. I read that some women can barely speak after they are released.

'How did they seem?' said Phyllis. 'In the court, I mean.'

'Jolly cheerful, actually,' said Mabel. 'Mrs. Sheehy-Skeffington had two huge bouquets of flowers with her. And they all seemed pleased so many of us were there to support them. I heard someone say there were nearly two hundred suffragettes in the gallery.'

'Gosh,' I said.

'Even the judge seemed quite sympathetic,' Mabel went on. 'He said they were ladies of "considerable ability" and he didn't seem particularly keen on having them there at all. But I suppose once they had been caught and admitted what they'd done, he had to give them some sort of prison sentence.'

'So there weren't any Antis in the court?' asked Phyllis.

Mabel shook her head. 'I didn't see any,' she said. 'Everyone seemed terribly supportive. And the ladies themselves were simply marvellous. When they were being led off, Mrs. Palmer cried "Keep the flag flying!" And we all cheered and cheered.'

'Oh, I do wish I could have gone, instead of standing in a stupid dressmaker's being poked with pins for hours,' said Phyllis longingly.

'And Mrs. Sheehy-Skeffington gave an awfully good speech,' Mabel continued. 'She pointed out that a man had got a shorter sentence that morning for beating his wife than they'd been given for breaking a few windows. And then she reminded us all that they might be going to jail, but that the rest of us were free and we had to remember that the Prime Minister is coming over in July.'

'There aren't any fixed plans for his visit yet, are there?' said Phyllis. 'I mean, no special meeting or anything.'

'I don't think so,' said Mabel. 'Mrs. Mulvany was saying something about making banners and posters and things to greet him on his way into town from Kingstown. But I don't think anything's been decided yet.'

As soon as I heard this, I decided that me and Nora must find some way of taking part in the protests. I'm not sure the IWFL would let us hold an official IWFL banner (I know Phyllis wouldn't), but I don't see why we couldn't march along behind one. Or even make one of our own.

I knew better than to mention this straight away, though. Phyllis would only tell me it was too dangerous. She's always convinced something really awful and violent will happen, and as far as I can tell it never does. Even the rowdies at that last meeting weren't too frightening (though I suppose the police did step in before they could go too far). Whatever happens I am ready to face it for the cause. Besides, as you know, I can run pretty fast, so if the Antis did start throwing cabbages and things I'm sure I'd be able get away before I got hit by one. At least, I hope so.

~

I am sad that you won't be coming over here this summer, but how exciting that you are getting to visit America! Will you get to go to the place where *Little Women* is set? I remember Professor Shields telling us that it's somewhere in New England. I love that book, even though the March sisters are a lot more devoted to their mother than I am to mine. They never really complain about her making them sew on buttons. Maybe Americans are all more saintly than we are. Please find out and report back.

Part of me wishes that we were going away somewhere exciting and novel for the whole summer like you, but another part of me is glad that I won't miss out on any suffrage activity, especially with Mr. Asquith coming over. And we will get to go on our usual holiday to Skerries in August, which isn't particularly exciting but is always good fun, especially when the weather is nice. We can swim in the sea and go and look at the boats and spot seals. Harry says he's going to hire a boat and row over to one of the islands off the coast all by himself 'to get away from all you women', but I bet he won't. It's just more of his usual boasting. I don't think he even knows HOW to row a boat.

I suppose I should go and learn some French verbs now, not that I want to. Oh, writing about verbs reminds me, in your last letter you asked how Grace Molyneaux had been carrying on since she threatened to tell Nora's parents about me and Nora being suffragettes. Well, I am pleased to inform you that she has kept her word about not telling. In fact, now that the exams are about to begin she is in a complete frenzy, because this is her last chance to win the Middle Grade Cup, with which of course she is totally obsessed. She spends all her lunchtimes with her nose in her special study notebook which she guards with her life.

She probably will win the stupid cup at this rate, which will make her worse than ever (if that's possible – perhaps it's not). I still hope Daisy Redmond gets it. Daisy studies because she likes learning things, not so she can lord it over everyone else like Grace does. And Daisy's been working very hard even though her mother has been very sick recently and she hasn't been able to see her because she (Daisy) is a boarder and her parents live in Waterford. So she definitely deserves something good happening to her. But anyway, in the meantime Grace seems more interested in studying than tormenting me and Nora, which can only be a good thing.

I am going to send this letter first thing tomorrow. Good luck in your own exams! I hope I do well in mine, if only because if I don't Mother and Father will probably force me to study all summer and then I won't be able to do any suffragette things.

Best love and votes for women
Mollie

30th June, 1912.

Dear Frances,

This is not going to be a long letter because I want to
make sure you get it before you head off to America. I
am pleased to say that I am FREE. Yes, I have survived
my exams, and they weren't actually that bad apart from
Historical Geography, where I made an utter hames of
explaining how a glacier is made. But the rest were all
right, and in fact I actually did very well in English, so
hopefully my parents will remember this success next term
when they're going on about how I need to study more.

Harry, of course, made a huge fuss about his own exams,
demanding tea and toast at all hours of the evening 'to
fuel my brain' during his studies. And what's worse is that
he actually GOT it. No one brought me any brain fuel
when I was studying, but then I suppose I didn't ask for it,
because I'm not a baby like him. Honestly, you'd think he
was working to become a doctor or something, the way he
carried on, instead of just a boy doing some summer tests.
He's finished now too. He and his friend Frank came round
to our house for a celebratory tea today after their last exam,
though in fairness to my mother, I must say that she gave

me a celebratory tea yesterday after my exams had finished. For once, Harry did not get preferential treatment.

For both teas there was a special lemon cake made by Maggie. Maggie is a much better baker than any of the rest of us. Mother sometimes says she worries that Maggie will get fed up of working for our family and will go off and start her own bakery and make cakes all day, which I must say sounds like a better job than sweeping our floors and chopping vegetables for our dinners. But when I said this to Maggie – adding that of course I would miss her very much if she went off to make cakes – she said that it was a nice idea, but she'd never have the money to start her own bakery. Which is rather unfair, but on a shamefully selfish level I am quite glad she won't be leaving us any time soon, because I do love her.

Sorry, I got distracted there. I find this often happens when I'm trying to tell a story. I start off writing about one thing and then I think of something else, and before I know it I've gone off on what in geometry class we call a tangent. I will try to stick to the point for the rest of this letter. Although now I'm not entirely certain what my point was.

Oh yes! I was talking about Harry and Frank. Well, there is quite interesting news on that front which is that Frank is coming to stay with us. Yes, he will be staying in our house for just over a week in July. His parents are going to visit an elderly aunt who lives somewhere in Kerry and apparently she (the aunt) can't abide having children in the house. Frank's father tried to explain that Frank wasn't exactly a child anymore and was quite capable of being quiet, but the aunt didn't care. She sounds worse than Aunt Josephine. Frank says that his parents want to stay on her good side because apparently she is quite rich, and they hope she'll leave them something when she dies, though they will never admit this to Frank. So they decided that he could stay with another (nice) aunt and uncle in Meath. And Frank wasn't particularly looking forward to it as his cousins are all much, much younger than him.

When Harry heard this, he asked our parents if Frank could stay with us instead and they said yes. I told Nora this yesterday and she looked at me in an extremely irritating way.

'So he'll be there for ten whole days,' she said. 'Maybe he will finally declare his love.'

I hit her with a pillow. (We were sitting on her bed at the time.)

'Shut up Nora Cantwell, you vile creature,' I said. 'He won't do anything of the kind. And I hope you'll drag your thoughts out of the gutter while he's staying in the house.'

'I was only teasing,' said Nora. 'To be perfectly honest I think it's more likely that you'll declare your love to him.'

So of course I had to hit her with a pillow again, and she fell off the bed, which shut her up. That was a few days ago, and she hasn't come out with any more rubbishy nonsense since, so I hope she has decided she's not going to subject me to vulgar teasing. She does still keep giving me significant looks whenever Frank's name is mentioned, but she's been doing that for a while anyway so it doesn't really bother me anymore.

It will be rather strange having Frank in the house all the time, though, especially as it's the holidays so we'll be free all day. (Well, free when Mother isn't expecting us to do tedious chores, and by us I mean me and Phyllis and Julia because Harry does barely anything.) But Frank's not coming until the week after next (I think) so I suppose I have plenty of time to get used to the idea.

And there is even more good news: Grace Molyneaux didn't win the Cup! Daisy Redmond won it instead. I was very happy about this, not just because I hate Grace (although I must be honest, I do a bit). But Daisy deserved it AND when she got the prize she was very happy and didn't lord it over the rest of us at all, which we all know Grace would have done.

Unsurprisingly, Grace was not a good loser. When Mother Antoninas announced the winner Grace looked so horrified I actually felt sorry for her for a moment. (I was quite surprised by that, but it turns out that sometimes seeing your enemies humiliated and miserable gives you a strange sort of wormish feeling in your stomach and you can't enjoy it at all, even if you thought you would beforehand.) After the prize giving was over and we all went to the refectory for milk and buns, Grace ran away to the lav and when she came back she looked like she'd been crying. Even Nora looked a bit uncomfortable when she saw that.

'I know I wanted this to happen,' she whispered to me and Stella. 'But she does look rotten.'

But just as we were all starting to feel sorry for Grace, she marched up to Daisy and unintentionally reminded us why we'd been yearning for her downfall. At first I thought she was going to congratulate her successful rival, which would have been very gracious for Grace (living up to her name, for once). But no! She folded her arms, tossed her curls and hissed, 'I suppose you think you're very clever.'

Daisy looked quite startled.

'Not particularly,' she said.

'You know they only gave you that cup because they felt sorry for you,' said Grace. 'Because of your mother.'

I knew Grace was capable of dealing low blows, but this was very low, even for her. Daisy's face went very white and she ran out of the room. For a moment no one said anything, but then Stella ran over to Grace. I've told you before that Stella can be a tigress when roused, especially for a good cause. Well, if looks could kill, Grace would have been lying stone dead on the refectory floor.

'You utter beast,' she said furiously. 'Didn't you know Daisy got a telegram this morning? Her mother's much worse. Daisy's going straight home after lunch. Sister Henry's taking her to the station. And the only reason she hasn't left already is because there isn't a train until three.'

Grace obviously has some human feeling left because she looked pretty guilty when she heard that.

'Well, how was I to know?' she said. And before Stella could say anything else to her she marched over to a seat in the corner of the room with her plate of buns. Her faithful follower Gertie went after her. But May Sullivan, who you probably remember has been hanging around them since she started at the school earlier this year, didn't follow them.

In fact, ever since the day when Grace threatened to tell our parents about our suffrage activities and Stella showed us how ferocious she could be when it comes to important things, May has been spending more time with other girls in the class. She's become friendly with Nellie Whelan and Mary Cummins, who are jolly decent and who are both supporters of our suffrage cause. When Grace marched off, Nellie had already taken a seat next to Johanna Doyle, and May went over there and asked if she could join them. I really think she might have finally had enough of Grace. Hopefully when we come back in September she will have totally escaped her former friend's clutches.

It seems so strange that we won't see lots of our classmates for months and months (well, two months). I know we'll see some of the girls who live in our part of Dublin, and poor Nora will probably be forced to see Grace at some stage, seeing as she's her cousin, but all the boarders will be scattered all over the country and in some cases beyond – there are a few girls who come over from Scotland. I shall miss Stella terribly, she has been simply marvellous this term. I can't believe I ever compared her to a white mouse. It was awfully sad saying goodbye on the very last day. Nora and I had to promise to write every week, which of course we will.

'And do let me know …' Stella's voice dropped to a rather loud whisper. 'If you do any suffragette things. I'll be cheering you on from Rochfortbridge.' That is the name of the nearest town to Stella's family house. At least, the house they live in at the moment. Her father is a bank manager and they have lived in quite a few places. I'm not sure why bank people seem to move around a lot but they do. It's rather like being a diplomat – you get posted to exotic environs.

'If we commit any more crimes for the cause,' said Nora

solemnly, 'we will wear our suffragette scarves in your honour.'

Stella, in case you've forgotten, knitted wonderful scarves for me and Nora in the IWFL colours. It was nice of Nora to promise to wear them, but I couldn't help thinking it might be a bit warm if we do anything in July. Anyway, the more I think of it, the more I feel I don't actually want to break the law again. Every time I think of Mrs. Sheehy-Skeffington and the other ladies languishing in their prison cells I feel a bit sick. And then I feel a bit cowardly because really, I should be prepared to do anything for the cause, including breaking the law. But I don't want to go to prison if I can help it.

Our IWFL heroines are not on hunger strike like the poor English suffragettes, so thankfully they haven't been force fed or anything like that. But it must be extremely horrid to be locked up in a nasty jail, all because they were fighting for their rights – for all of our rights, I should say. I shall pray for them tonight. (After all, Jesus did talk about visiting prisoners being a good thing, so praying for them can't be wrong, can it?)

I hope your journey to America goes safely. It sounds very exciting to me. I do understand why you feel a bit nervous – I bet I'd keep thinking about the *Titanic* too – but really, how likely is it that TWO ships will be hit by icebergs in just a few months? Now I've written that sentence down it doesn't look very consoling, but you know what I mean. Ships cross the Atlantic all the time and practically all of them get there safely, so I'm sure you will too. Phyllis's friend Mabel went to visit relatives who live in Boston a few months ago. (They are very grand, much more so than anyone we know here, and live in a giant sort of house Phyllis called a brownstone, which I imagined being rather like a castle, but which according to Phyllis is just an ordinary big terraced house.)

Anyway, Mabel got there and back quite safely, and Phyllis says she had a jolly good time on the boat so I am sure you will too. Apparently Mabel's cabin was very nice and there was a dear little round porthole, through which she could gaze out at the vast ocean, though she felt rather guilty whenever she caught a glimpse of the poor people down in third class, which wasn't nearly as comfortable. I don't think they even have portholes down there. Maggie's cousin Bridie went to America a few years ago by third class and she arrived safely too – but she hasn't come back and Maggie says she never will.

'What has she got to come back to here?' said Maggie, when I asked about Bridie the other day. 'She's got a good job in a nice little hat shop in New York now.'

'Do you hear from her often?' I asked, handing Maggie a tea towel. She was putting away some dishes in the kitchen at the time. Maggie shook her head.

'She's not a great one for writing,' she said, carefully drying her favourite teacup. (It has strawberries on it, and Julia gave it to her for her birthday a few years ago.) 'But she sends me a card every Christmas so I know she's still alive and well.'

'Do you think she might ever get home for a visit?' I said.

'Goodness, no,' said Maggie, putting the cup on the dresser shelf. 'She'd never be able to afford the journey here and back. No, she's over there forever now.'

It seemed awfully sad that Maggie's cousin will never see her family again, but Maggie pointed out that lots of people leave Ireland and never come back.

'So there's no point in crying over it,' she said. But I still think it's sad. I know I complain about my family a lot, but I couldn't bear the thought of going to the other side of the world (well, almost) on my own and never seeing any of them again. Even Harry (not that I would ever admit that to him). I suppose I wouldn't mind if Aunt Josephine went to America and never came back, but I don't think that's very likely to happen.

Do write before you get on the boat, and if you don't have time, maybe you could write me a letter once you're actually on it – Mother said that sometimes you can send letters from steamships because little boats call in and take letters back home. Imagine getting a letter that was sent from the middle of the Atlantic Ocean! What would the postmark be? Mother was a bit vague on the details so she may be all wrong about this, but if it turns out you can send letters from the middle of the sea, please do send me one.

Also, I've been thinking of what you said about getting post once you're in America, and I have come up with a solution. Why don't I keep writing letters here and then send them all to you when you're back in England? If I try sending them to all the places you're visiting in America then I would probably keep missing you, but this way you will eventually have a full report on all the doings in Dublin. Of course, there may not be much to write – probably not anything as exciting as the last few months. But I will keep writing to you anyway, while you're off in Boston and New York and New Orleans and all those other exciting places. And then you can read them all when you come back and have a record of summer in Dublin in 1912.

Much love and votes for women – and bon voyage, as we say in French class,
Mollie

4th July, 1912.

Dear Frances,

I know you are on a boat right now and I wish I was there
with you because something awful has happened. In fact,
it's so terrible I can barely bring myself to write about
it. Don't worry, no one has died or been horribly ill or
been arrested (no one I know, anyway). But it is still pretty
dreadful.

GRACE IS STAYING IN NORA'S HOUSE.

FOR AT LEAST TWO WHOLE WEEKS.

Remember when Harry had to come home from our
cousins in Louth because one of them had scarlet fever?
Well, Grace's brother goes to boarding school in Louth
and clearly there is some sort of terrible scarlet fever
epidemic up there because he (the brother) arrived home
for the holidays this morning and promptly came down
with it as soon as he walked in the door, as far as I can tell.
And Grace had been away visiting an aunt for the day and

her parents had to telephone the aunt (so it turns out the Molyneauxs did have a phone after all, I always thought that was just Grace showing off) and tell her that Grace couldn't come home.

~

But the aunt can't look after Grace all summer so she has to stay with her other relatives and that means the Cantwells! And she will have to SHARE NORA'S ROOM.

~

Nora ran around to my house as soon as she could after hearing this terrible news. When Maggie showed her in I thought someone had died, she looked so pale and sick and miserable.

'What's happened?' I said. I remembered that her brother George had been due to come home from his school in Westmeath that morning. Maybe there had been an awful train crash. 'It's not George, is it?'

'Oh no,' said Nora. 'He's fine. He's at home now, being fed with cakes. And it's all very well for him,' she said, looking as if she were going to burst into tears, 'because his summer hasn't been completely ruined!'

And then she told me about Grace.

I feel so sorry for her. It's bad enough for me sharing

a room with Julia, but Julia's all right really. At least, she is when she's not going on about how I don't say my prayers for long enough. Imagine how awful Grace will be. And what makes it worse is that the room only has one bed and Nora's parents have got hold of a camp bed (how, I don't know. Nora thinks it might have been used by her journalist uncle when he wrote about the war in South Africa), and Grace and Nora will have to take turns to sleep in it! Nora rightly pointed out that she shouldn't have to give up her bed to Grace but Mrs. Cantwell didn't agree.

'She told me I should have more sympathy for a poor girl who couldn't go home for weeks,' said Nora in a disgusted voice. 'And that she thought it would be nice for me and Grace to spend some proper cousinly time together. She went on about how sad it was that we weren't friends.'

'What did you say?' I said.

'I told her that it wasn't sad at all,' said Nora. 'Neither me nor Grace particularly wants to be friends, so why should my mother care? But she started going on about how we'd regret it when we're older and that relatives are very important and it was all very boring.'

'Maybe George will have to look after her,' I said. 'After all, she's his cousin too.'

But Nora shook her head.

'I asked Mother about that,' she said. 'And she said she

couldn't expect George to look after a girl.'

We shared a sorrowful look.

'No chance of getting your mother to come to the next IWFL meeting, then,' I said. 'What's Grace like with George? Is she awful to him too?'

Nora made a face.

'She only sees him in the holidays, of course, but I think she considers him one of the grown-ups,' she said. 'Even though he isn't. So she's all nicey-nice to him. And that means I'll be the only one in the house who sees her true colours. Imagine.'

It truly was a horrid prospect.

'Well, you can come over to my house whenever you like,' I said. I patted her on the arm because that's what you're meant to do when you're comforting people, but it didn't cheer Nora up.

'I'm not sure I'll be able to,' she said gloomily. 'Mother keeps going on about what a wonderful opportunity this is for me and Grace to become great pals. She's going to organise lots of outings and things for us.'

'Oh dear,' I said.

'It's just because she and Aunt Alice have always been awfully close,' said Nora. Aunt Alice is Grace's mother, and she and Nora's mother are sisters. 'She can't understand why I don't want to be friends with Aunt Alice's daughter. Especially when,' and here Nora did a not-very-accurate impersonation of her mother's voice – "Grace is such a wee darling".' Nora's mother is from Belfast and she sometimes says things are 'wee' when she means 'little'.

As I have said before, grown-ups always think Grace is wonderful. But maybe having Grace under her roof for weeks will change Mrs. Cantwell's mind. Grace is staying with the other aunt overnight and is arriving in Nora's house tomorrow. So as I write this letter, poor Nora is being forced to get her room ready for Grace, which means putting practically half of her clothes in the attic so there's room for Grace's things, as well as making up the stupid camp bed, which is full of springs that keep pinching her fingers and which almost collapsed when she sat on it earlier.

I mentioned the dreadfulness of all this to my family this evening, but, worryingly, my parents didn't feel very sorry for Nora at all. I thought they were a bit more tender-hearted than that, but apparently not.

'When I was at school I had to share a dormitory with five other boys,' said Father. 'We all have to muddle along with people we don't like.'

Mother agreed.

'I'm sure it will be good for both of them,' said Mother. She looked at her four offspring. 'Sometimes I think you modern children are terribly spoiled.'

Spoiled! When I spend half of my time trimming hats

and learning French verbs and sharing a room with Julia. Maybe Harry and Phyllis and Julia are spoiled (well, Harry definitely is), but I'm certainly not.

Anyway, I will of course keep a record of how Nora gets on with her unwelcome guest. I hope you are having lots of fun on the boat. Thanks awfully for sending me your American itinerary – I have marked all the places you're going to go in my atlas and put the dates next to each one so I will be able to imagine you in each location. I believe there are a lot of dangerous wild beasts in America so I hope you are being careful – I don't want you to get eaten by a bear or a wild cat or a possum or anything.

Best love and votes for women,
Mollie

P.S.

Later

I mentioned the wild beasts of America to Phyllis before I went to bed and when I told her I hoped you wouldn't get eaten by a possum she laughed and laughed and said a possum was a little animal about the size of a big rabbit or a very small dog.

'Some dogs are dangerous,' I protested. 'And savage. Just think of the Menace.'

As I am sure you remember, the Menace is a dreadful little woolly dog belonging to Mother's friend Mrs. Sheffield. His real name is Barnaby, but he is one of nature's menaces, hence his nickname. I must admit he's never actually bitten anyone, as far as I know. But he always looks as if he wants to and he barks a LOT.

'Well, I can assure you that Frances is in no danger of being eaten by a possum,' said Phyllis, in a very patronising and annoying way. She did, however, deign to admit that bears really are dangerous, but when I showed her your itinerary she laughed again in a superior fashion and said it was very unlikely you would meet one in New York or Boston.

'But what about the bits in between?' I asked. But she told me that you will presumably be travelling by train rather than roaming on foot through the woods and she had never heard of a bear getting on a train, which is a good point. Still, you're going to be in the countryside at some stage. Do keep your eyes open for bears and lions and things.

5th July, 1912.

Dear Frances,

I have been keeping a close eye on the papers in case there is anything about your ship hitting an iceberg or indeed any other naval incidents, and I am very glad to see that there have been no disasters so far. You must be practically there by now – or have you actually arrived? Anyway, I hope your voyage across the mighty ocean was fun and exciting (in a non-dangerous way). I wish I had some exciting news to report from Dublin, but alas all is doom and gloom because Grace is now ensconsed in Nora's room and she is being every bit as bad as we feared she would be.

She arrived this morning. Nora had begged me to call over for moral support so I went while Mrs. Cantwell was on her way to Amiens Street station to collect Grace, who was getting a train from Belfast. George had gone off to play tennis, as free as a bird.

'In just half an hour she'll be here,' said Nora miserably. We were in her room, trying to move the camp bed as far away from Nora's bed as possible. 'These are my last moments of freedom.'

'Not that way,' I said. 'You won't be able to open the chest of drawers.' We moved the camp bed towards the window.

'Ow!' squeaked Nora. 'I caught my finger in the stupid springs again.'

Her finger was red and a bit swollen so we left the bed where it was and went to the bathroom, where Nora ran her finger under the cold tap.

'I'm already in agony and she hasn't even got here,' she muttered.

'Maybe it won't be so bad.' I forced myself to sound cheerful. 'After all, she won't want to hang around with you either.'

'She will if it's what Mother wants,' said Nora. 'She always does what grown-ups expect her to. It's why they all think she's wonderful.'

You'd think some grown-ups would find her annoying, the way she's always smirking at them and sucking up to them, but they never seem to care about that. Nora was drying her hands when we heard the front door open and Mrs. Cantwell called, 'Nora? We're home.'

'Coming, Mother.' Nora sounded as if she was being called to the gallows. I followed her downstairs, where Grace, smiling with unnatural brightness, was hanging her hat and coat up in the hall.

'Hello, Nora.' She sounded much more friendly than

I'd ever heard her before. Then she noticed me coming behind Nora and her smile flickered for a moment. But only for a moment. 'And Mollie too!' she cried. 'How nice.'

'Hello, girls.' Mrs. Cantwell turned to her daughter. 'Nora, why don't you show Grace up to your room?'

'She knows where it is,' said Nora. I say 'said', but really it was more like a grunt.

'Yes,' said Mrs. Cantwell firmly, 'but I'd like you to show her where she can put her things.'

'All right.' Nora barely repressed a sigh. She had started up the stairs when Mrs. Cantwell said, 'And I think you can take the first turn on the camp bed tonight, can't you, Nora?'

I gave Nora a warning look. I knew – and I totally understood – that she wanted to protest, but I also knew that if she started off Grace's visit by making a fuss, her Mother would probably be even more on Grace's side. Nora knew this too, and she said, 'All right. Come on, Grace.'

'Wonderful,' said Mrs. Cantwell brightly. 'And while you're doing that, I'll ask Agnes to get us some tea and cake.' She went off to the kitchen and Grace followed me and Nora up the stairs. As soon as the kitchen door closed behind Mrs. Cantwell, Grace said, 'I really think you could be a bit more cheerful, Nora. No one likes a gloomy girl.'

Nora swallowed and said, in a very stiff voice, 'Here's my room.'

'Gosh.' Grace put her bag on the floor. 'It's much smaller than I remember it being.'

'That's probably because the last time I let you in here was at my ninth birthday party,' said Nora. 'You were smaller then too.' She pulled open the bottom of the chest of drawers, which was now empty. 'You can put your things there.'

'What about my frocks?' said Grace. Nora marched over to the wardrobe and flung open the door. It was half empty because Nora had been made to pack away lots of her clothes and put them up in the attic. ('Where they'll probably be eaten away by moths,' she'd grumbled earlier. 'And it'll be all Grace's fault.')

'That's not very much room,' sniffed Grace.

'Well, that's all the room there is,' said Nora. 'Is there anything else you need to know?'

Grace plumped herself down on Nora's bed.

'This bed's not terribly comfortable, is it?'

Nora gritted her teeth.

'You're more than welcome to have the camp bed,' she said. Grace gave an incredibly annoying tinkling laugh.

'Oh no, this one will do,' she said. 'I suppose I don't have a choice.'

'Neither of us do,' said Nora. 'We'll leave you to unpack.' And she grabbed my hand and pulled me onto the landing, slamming the door behind her.

'Is everything all right?' called Mrs. Cantwell from the drawing room.

'Fine,' Nora called back. 'I just banged the door by accident.' She looked at me and pointed silently towards the bathroom. We went in and closed the door.

'If I ran away from home today,' said Nora, 'how long do you think it would take before I could get a job and earn some money to keep myself? It'd only have to be for a few weeks, until Grace goes.'

I sat down on the edge of the bath.

'I don't think you could get a job,' I said.

'Why not? Lots of girls our age work,' said Nora.

'Yes, but in jobs that aren't very nice,' I pointed out. 'And besides, you'd have no references.'

'I could forge them,' said Nora. 'It can't be that hard, my handwriting looks very grown-up. And I'd rather scrub floors than stay in the same room as that little beast.' But she didn't sound very convincing. Grace might be one of nature's worst creations, but sharing a room with her isn't nearly as horrible as the sort of job most working girls our age end up doing. When Maggie and her sister Jenny were fourteen, they were both working as scullery maids. I knew, and so did Nora, that we were lucky we weren't ever going to be forced to do a job like that. Scrubbing floors is no joke when you have no choice in the matter. Besides, if someone who spoke like Nora asked for a job as a scullery maid, they'd think she was playing some sort of odd joke.

'Come on, Nora,' I said. 'Let's go down. We might as well eat some cake.'

Nora sighed.

'All right then,' she said.

When we walked into the drawing room the tea and cake were already laid out.

'Just in time,' said Mrs. Cantwell. 'Where's your cousin?'

'Unpacking,' said Nora. The cake was a sponge one and looked jolly good. 'Can I have a slice of cake, please?'

'Wait until Grace gets down.' Mrs. Cantwell lifted the cake stand out of Nora's reach. Nora threw me an outraged look, but unfortunately Mrs. Cantwell noticed. 'And don't make faces at Mollie like that. I know you're not happy about sharing your room —'

'It's not the sharing my room part,' Nora interrupted. 'It's the sharing it with Grace. I wouldn't mind if it was any of my other cousins.'

Mrs. Cantwell sighed and pushed her spectacles up her nose.

'Nora, think what it's like to be Grace right now,' she said.

'I'd rather not,' muttered Nora.

Her mother ignored her.

'She can't go home for weeks on end,' Mrs. Cantwell continued. 'The family were meant to be going to a hotel

in Killarney next week but of course that's all off now.'
She poured out tea for herself, Nora and me. 'And I know
you might find this hard to believe, but she's probably not
very happy about sharing a room with you. Imagine if you
had to go and stay with someone you knew perfectly well
didn't like you.'

I have to admit it was a pretty grim prospect. I was
starting to feel a bit sorry for Grace. Nora put a lot of
milk and a large lump of sugar in her tea, but didn't say
anything.

'So please,' said Mrs. Cantwell, 'try to get along with her.
Can you promise me that?'

Nora looked like she was genuinely considering it, until
Mrs. Cantwell spoiled it all by saying, 'After all, she's such
a sweet wee girl. I know you don't get on very well at
school, but maybe you'll like her more once you've spent
some time together outside of lessons.'

Nora glowered at her mother.

'I'm quite sure I won't,' she said.

'Well, you're going to have to,' snapped Mrs. Cantwell,
clearly losing her patience. 'Ah, hello Grace, darling.'

Grace was standing in the doorway with an expression
on her face that could only be described as simpering.

'Am I too late for cake?' She tossed her curls as she
spoke. (She does this a lot and grown-ups seem to think
it is 'winsome'. If I did it, I'd probably hit someone in the

face with one of my plaits, and no one would think it was winsome at all.) She practically skipped across the room to the table. 'Oh goodie, there's some left.'

'We haven't been allowed to eat any of it,' said Nora flatly. 'So obviously there's some left.'

Grace gave another dreadful tinkling laugh. I've never heard her do this at school. She probably knows she couldn't get away with it there. Someone would eventually give her a slap. But in the bosom of her family she could toss her curls and giggle as much as she liked. She was like a child in a pantomime, the sort who always have dreadful names like Little Gertie or Baby Betsy, even though you know they're probably about twenty-five really. Later I told Nora I couldn't believe that Mrs. Cantwell didn't see through this little-girl act, but Nora reminded me that this is how Grace always behaves with her grown-up relatives. Aunt Alice, Nora said, encouraged it.

'But she wouldn't dare do it at school,' said Nora. 'The staff wouldn't stand for it.'

I imagined Mother Antoninas's reaction to Grace flicking her hair about.

'They definitely wouldn't,' I agreed.

Mrs. Cantwell, however, seemed inexplicably charmed by Grace's manner.

'We were waiting for you, dear.' And of course she gave Grace the first slice of cake.

'Mmmm!' said Grace. 'How delicious, Aunt Catherine.'

I thought Mrs. Cantwell would have to see through her now but no, she just smiled and said, 'I'm glad you're enjoying it.'

The cake was indeed delicious, but I couldn't really enjoy it with Nora on the other side of the table looking like she was about to either burst into tears or growl at someone. All in all it was a dismal tea. Nora just sat there brooding, while Grace prattled on at Mrs. Cantwell, who seemed somehow delighted with her. I couldn't really think of anything to say, so I concentrated on eating the cake. Every so often Mrs. Cantwell would try to involve me and Nora in the conversation, and I did my best, but it was hard going. I was very relieved when the clock on the mantelpiece eventually struck four o'clock.

'Thanks awfully for tea, Mrs. Cantwell.' I leapt to my feet. 'I'd better be getting home now.'

'Maybe you and Nora and Grace could go on a little outing tomorrow,' suggested Mrs. Cantwell. 'To the park or the Botanic Gardens.'

'If my mother says it's all right,' I said. And then I said goodbye. I felt like an awful heel running away and leaving Nora with Grace, but I really did have to go home. Nora walked out into the hall with me, closing the drawing-room door behind her.

'Are you sure I couldn't find a job somewhere?' she

whispered miserably. But she knew it was a ridiculous dream. I tried to think of something comforting to say.

'Just think of Jane Eyre,' I said. 'She had to live with horrible cousins too.'

'Yes, and she only got away from them by going to boarding school,' retorted Nora.

'Not a very nice one,' I said.

'Even a boarding school where you have to eat burned porridge and your best friend dies seems like more fun than sharing with Grace.' Nora's face was the picture of misery.

'Thanks very much,' I said. 'If you'd rather I died of consumption …'

'You know what I mean,' said Nora. I left the poor thing standing forlornly at the front door, with the prospect of days and days of Grace ahead of her. It seems so unfair, especially when I remember that we will have the charming and civilised Frank as a guest, while Nora has to put up with Grace prancing around the house.

Of course I didn't talk about Frank's visit to Nora this afternoon as (one) it would look as though I were gloating and (two) she would probably say something annoying again about me being in love with him. I do wish she'd forget about all that nonsense. It just struck me that the only good thing about Grace staying there is that Nora might be too preoccupied with her to think of any annoying remarks about me and Frank. But that is a rather selfish thought, when even as I write poor Nora is probably having to get ready for bed in the same room as Grace. I bet all Grace's nighties are covered in frills and ribbons and she will look patronisingly at Nora's perfectly serviceable plain cotton and broderie anglaise. I will let you know when I write more tomorrow.

Best love and votes for women,
Mollie

Saturday, 6th July, 1912.

Dear Frances,

Sadly the first night with Grace was just as bad as Nora
had feared. I was right about the nightie – apparently
Grace went to bed in 'something that looked like a
wedding dress', as Nora put it. This morning I was lying
on a rug in the sunny back garden reading *A Tale of Two
Cities* (It's jolly good, all about the French Revolution.
There is a miserable but strangely attractive lawyer called
Sydney Carton who is in love with a rather boring girl
called Lucie and also some terrific French revolutionaries
who are frightening but exciting), when Nora came out of
the kitchen door.

'Maggie let me in,' she said, throwing herself down on
the rug beside me.

'Where's Grace?' I asked.

Nora rolled onto her back and covered her face with
her hat.

'Urrrrrrrgh,' she said. At least, that's what the noise that
emerged from beneath the hat sounded like.

'You haven't pushed her in the river or anything, have
you?' I wouldn't quite put it past her.

'Unfortunately I have not,' said Nora. 'I left her in the kitchen, helping Agnes make a cake. I suppose I should thank my lucky stars that she wants to hang around a hot stuffy kitchen on a day like this.'

'What does Agnes think of Grace?' I said.

'Oh, she loves her,' said Nora bitterly. 'Grace has been doing her usual good girl act. "Oh Agnes, how clever you are, could you show me how to grate a lemon?"'

'Well, maybe she really does want to know how to make a lemon cake,' I said. 'And it's probably quite nice for Agnes to feel appreciated.'

'I appreciate her!' said Nora indignantly, sitting up and putting her hat back on her head. 'You know I do. I just don't suck up to her the way Grace does with all grown-ups.'

Grace only fusses over grown-ups when she wants to impress them. She wasn't particularly nice to the women who scrub the floors and windows at school. But I wasn't surprised that she had been nice to Agnes. She clearly wanted to get everyone in the Cantwell household on her side – apart from Nora, of course.

'Did your mother mind you leaving her with Agnes?' I said.

Nora looked slightly guilty. 'Well,' she said, 'Mother doesn't exactly know I've gone.'

'Oh Nora!' I cried. 'You could have just told her you

were going out while Grace was happy in the kitchen.'

If Nora's parents discovered that she was sneaking off without saying a word to them, they might start keeping a closer eye on her movements and then that would put a stop to all our potential suffrage activities for the next few weeks. So far, Nora and I have managed to work out a system whereby we each tell our parents we're going to the other's house. And we do it just infrequently enough to avoid suspicion. But one ill-timed escape like today could cause Mrs. Cantwell to start questioning Nora's regular outings to my house.

'I'll go back in a minute, she won't even notice,' said Nora. 'I just had to get away and breathe the fresh air of freedom for twenty minutes.'

'Can't you get away later today?' I asked. 'Does she still want us to take Grace to the Gardens?' But Nora shook her head.

'It turns out George is playing a match at the tennis club today, and Grace says she wants to cheer him on, so we all have to go,' she said. She looked at me hopefully. 'It's some sort of club tournament. I don't suppose you want to come too?'

I didn't particularly want to sit around the tennis club watching Nora's brother play tennis, but Nora looked so miserable I had to tell her I'd ask my mother. Even though a part of me hoped she'd say no.

'Anyway,' I said, you still haven't told me what she was like last night.'

'Well, first of all,' Nora began, 'she went to bed at eight. And when Mother said that was very early she got all wide-eyed and said, 'But Aunt Catherine, doesn't Nora go to bed then?' And of course Mother said I should go up with her and get her settled in and that maybe I should go to bed too. At eight! In the holidays!'

Even Julia doesn't go to bed that early in the summer holidays and she's only twelve.

'And then, when we were in my room, she kept fussing over the curtains and saying it was too bright, and I said of course it was, after all it was broad daylight outside, and she said in her house they have decent thick curtains and the sunshine can't get in.'

'How rude!' I said.

'And THEN,' Nora said, getting more and more worked up, 'when she finally fell asleep she kept tossing and turning and making hideous snorting noises and I had to lie there on that wobbly little camp bed, and I couldn't go to sleep even if I'd been tired! Which I wasn't, of course, because it was practically the middle of the day.'

'So what did you do?' I asked.

'I got my book and read until it was too dark to see properly,' said Nora. She has been reading a book called *Lady Audley's Secret*, which she says is very exciting. (She is going to lend it to me when she's finished.) She found it hidden away on top of the bookshelf in their dining room so she's not sure her parents would approve of her reading it, but she is reading it anyway. The thought of poor Nora trying to read her book in the increasing gloom made me feel so sorry for her that I have decided I will try my hardest to persuade Mother to let me go to the tennis club. I am going to do so now (though a part of me is hoping that she will say no so I don't have to go ...)

Later

Well, I didn't have to try very hard because it turns out that Mother heartily approves of the tennis club.

'I went to their last fundraising fête,' she said. 'I was thinking we might join. It could be a very nice place for you children to spend some time over the summer.'

'I'm not going to play,' I said hastily. I didn't want to be forced out on the tennis court. 'I'm just going to watch Nora's brother.'

'Well, maybe you'll get a taste for it,' said Mother, but I was pretty sure I wouldn't. We play tennis at school sometimes and I am not very good at hitting the ball. Well, I can hit it all right, but hardly ever strongly enough to bounce off the grass, and everyone in my class knows this and so they always stand up near the net to catch my feeble shots and then lob the ball straight back over my head. Nora is quite a decent player, but she says she's not interested enough in the game to play properly. Her parents joined the club a few years ago so they can all play there, but George is the most enthusiastic tennis player in the family.

Mother said I should change my clothes before going to the club.

'You can't turn up in that old thing,' she said. 'There's a grass stain on the seat.'

'No there isn't!' I said indignantly, but it turned out that there was. So it was probably for the best that Mother made me change into my new-ish pale blue frock (new to me, really a hand-me-down from Phyllis). I don't see why I had to change my stockings, though, they were perfectly all right. But Mother insisted they looked 'grubby'. And she made me wash my face and neck and behind my ears, even though I'd washed myself perfectly well that morning. Really, she made me feel like a dirty little street urchin.

I think she was worried I'd disgrace her in front of Mrs. Sheffield and her other friends who are members. But Mrs. Sheffield spends all her time with Barnaby, so she can't be too fussy about cleanliness. He's always jumping into puddles and rolling around in mud (when it's raining) and dust (and worse things than dust. He's particularly interested in horse dung) when it's dry. They have to put him out in the garden at least once a week and clean him with a garden hose.

So what with the new-ish frock and the stockings and my white kid shoes, I was a vision of cleanliness when I knocked on the Cantwells' front door. Agnes let me in as Nora came down the stairs.

'What happened to you?' Nora barely attempted to restrain her laughter. 'You look like something off a chocolate box.'

'Mother made me change,' I said glumly. 'She thought I was too scruffy to appear in front of the tennis club ladies.'

'Well, you'll still look scruffy next to Grace,' Nora whispered. 'She's practically head to toe frills.' And so she was. A few minutes later the three of us were on our way to the tennis club, Grace wearing a spotless straw hat decorated with small pale silk flowers, a cream linen blouse with a pale blue ribbon around the neck and lace at the collar and cuffs, and a beautifully made cream skirt with a ruffle around the edge. It all looked pretty ridiculous for a Saturday afternoon if you asked me, but Grace was clearly very pleased with herself and made me and Nora walk on the outside of the pavement in case any passing vehicles threw up dust.

'What about them throwing up dust on us?' said Nora.

'No one will notice,' said Grace, looking disdainfully at

Nora's buff coloured skirt and pale green blouse, which I thought were jolly nice. Nora clenched her fists and glowered at Grace (who didn't notice, of course) but she didn't say anything. She is making a very brave effort to control her temper. I don't know how she does it to be honest, I'd have pushed Grace under a lorry by now.

We managed to make it to the tennis club without anyone either being pushed under a lorry or indeed covered in dust (well, no more than usual on a sunny summer's day). George's match was taking place on a court on the far side of the club, which was very busy and had a festive air. It felt more like a garden fête than a sports tournament. There was even a table with some jugs of lemonade and a tea urn, staffed by some harassed-looking women who, it turned out, were on the tournament committee.

'Shall we get some lemonade?' Nora suggested. I thought this sounded like an excellent and refreshing idea after our hot walk. The lemonade, however, wasn't good enough for Grace, who wrinkled her nose after just one sip and said, 'You'd think they'd be able to come up with better lemonade than this.'

'I'll drink it if you don't want it,' said Nora, who had already drained her own glass of the delicious beverage.

'No, I need a drink after the walk,' said Grace, and she quickly drank it down. 'Where's your brother's match?'

'Court one,' said Nora. 'Though I'm not sure where that is.' George has been a member of the tennis club for a few years, but Nora has never shown much enthusiasm for it.

We wandered around until we found George whacking a ball against a wall near the court. I never quite know what to say to George. He's only a year older than Nora and not particularly intimidating – he even looks a bit like her, with his reddish hair, though he's a lot taller. And he's quite friendly – much nicer than Harry, to be honest. But because he's in boarding school I only ever see him in the holidays, so I never really have time to get used to him. It's not because he's a boy (though I know it would probably be easier to talk to him if he were a girl). It's more that he feels like a sort of stranger who sometimes turns up in Nora's house. I once asked Nora was it odd when he came home, and she said it generally was for the first couple of days. After all, he went off to prep school when he was nine, so for nearly six years she hasn't seen much of him for most of the year.

'But then after a while it sort of goes back to normal,' she said. 'Usually one of us will push the other one off a chair or something like that. Then we can joke with each other again.'

I was quite pleased to hear it. Much as I might dream of the idea of Harry going off to boarding school (presumably one as far away as possible, like another country), the idea of us being like strangers to each other when he returned did make me feel a little sad (only a very little bit, mind you. A part of me thought it would be a very satisfactory state of affairs).

Anyway, George greeted us quite cheerfully. Grace said hello to him in her familiar simpering way, but I was relieved to notice that he didn't seem to care for it.

'What time is your match at?' Nora asked.

'It's in ten minutes.' George threw a tennis ball in the air and caught it again. 'But you know, you don't have to watch if you don't want to. It won't be that exciting.'

I couldn't help thinking that George is a lot more humble than Harry, who would definitely have bragged about how wonderful his match was going to be.

'I'm sure it'll be thrilling, Cousin George,' said Grace sweetly.

George and Nora exchanged looks and I realised George definitely wasn't impressed by Grace's goody-goody act.

'I wouldn't go that far, um, Cousin Grace,' he said drily. He glanced over at the court, where another boy in tennis whites was already waiting, bouncing a tennis ball on his racket. 'Anyway, I'd better warm up.' And off he went.

'I'm going to … refresh myself,' said Grace, and headed off in the direction of the tennis pavilion.

'Refresh myself indeed!' said Nora. 'Why can't she

ever say she's going to the lav? We all know that's what she's doing.'

'Well, at least we've got rid of her for a few minutes,' I said.

'Did you hear her?' said Nora. 'Calling him Cousin George! Like something out of a Victorian novel. I wouldn't dream of calling her Cousin Grace.'

'Well, if it's any consolation, I don't think George was charmed by it,' I said. 'You probably won't have to worry about him siding with Grace.'

'Old George isn't so bad,' said Nora. 'Oh look, the match is about to begin.'

The tennis match was actually pretty exciting. George must play a fair bit of tennis in his school because he's jolly decent at the game. The sun was beating down on the court – I don't think I could have run for longer than a couple of minutes in that heat – but George was full of energy.

Grace arrived back halfway through the first set. To my surprise, all she said when she returned was 'What's the score?' When we told her, she watched the match with great attention. And it can't have been just because she wanted to suck up to George afterwards by telling him how brilliantly he'd played, because when his opponent – a boy called John McDonagh – hit an excellent serve, Grace said, 'that was marvellous,' with real admiration in her voice. I'd never seen her like this before. I couldn't decide what the difference was and finally I got it: for once, she wasn't thinking about impressing anyone.

The match lasted quite a long time, but in the end George won and we all cheered very loudly as the umpire cried 'Game, set and match to George Cantwell.' When he walked off the court, dabbing his brow with a white towel, he was immediately surrounded by his tennis-club pals.

'I didn't realise he was so good,' said Nora. 'He must have been practising awfully hard at school.'

'I wish I could play a game,' said Grace, and for once she sounded sincere.

'Maybe you can,' said George, who had suddenly emerged from the crowd of admirers. 'You know they're allowing non-members to play best-of-three games on the third court? Just schoolboys and girls. You don't have to have special tennis clothes.'

'Are they really?' said Grace.

George nodded. 'It's just for fun, to give people a chance to try the game. It's girls until four and then boys until six. Though you have to be at least fifteen.'

'I was fifteen last month,' said Grace. I had vague memories of Gertie and May giving her cards.

'There you go, then,' said George.

'Do you really think I could play?' Grace sounded positively wistful.

'Well, they might be fully booked,' said George. 'But it's worth a try.'

'Where's the third court?' Grace asked.

George pointed at the far end of the club grounds.

'Down there,' he said.

And without even making a smart remark at any of us, Grace ran off.

'Goodness,' said Nora. 'I didn't realise she was so interested in tennis.'

'I suppose she's been devoting all her attention to the Middle Grade cup in recent times,' I said. 'She hasn't had time to think about sports until now.'

'Well, I'm going to get a lemonade,' said George. 'Want one?'

Nora and I exchanged glances. We both knew that if her mother found out that she'd lost Grace at the tournament, she would not be pleased.

'No thanks,' said Nora. 'I think we should probably see what Grace is up to.'

'I was thinking the same thing,' I said. And off we went to court three, where we found Grace deep in conversation with a willowy young woman in white who was holding a notebook and pencil.

'We've got a free spot after this game,' the willowy woman was saying. 'Someone got sick after eating too many buns.'

'Oh goody, what luck,' said Grace, which sounded a bit heartless as regards the poor bun eater, but in fairness I'd probably have been thinking the same thing if I were her.

'It'll probably be in about twenty minutes,' said the young woman. A ball sailed over our heads. 'Well, less if they keep whacking the ball out like that.'

Grace looked over at us.

'We can stay that long, can't we?' There was a look in her eyes that could almost be described as pleading.

Now, after the way Grace had been carrying on, I wouldn't have blamed Nora if she'd insisted on going home straight away. After all, they'd gone to the club to see George's match, and now that was over they weren't required to hang around the place any longer. But she must have been feeling noble – or maybe a part of her saw that this was a way of keeping Grace occupied – because she said, 'I suppose so.'

Grace looked relieved but, being Grace, she didn't say thank you. She just turned back to the tall young lady and said, 'Then please put my name down for it. Grace Molyneaux.' And she spelled her surname carefully. The young lady grinned. She reminded me of Phyllis, for some reason.

'Don't worry, I won't mistake you for anyone else,' she said. 'I'll call you when it's time.'

She went over to talk to the umpire, who was looking

rather harassed. An argument seemed to have broken out between the novice players on the court, who bore a strong resemblance to each other. I had a feeling they were probably sisters. The umpire decided in favour of the smaller one, and the game recommenced. Nora turned to Grace.

'Are you sure you're going to be able to play?' she said. She indicated Grace's frilly garments. 'After all, you're not exactly dressed for games.'

'You don't think they'll stop me playing, do you?' Grace actually looked worried. 'That lady would have said if there was a problem with my clothes.'

'Oh, they'll let you play,' said Nora. 'I was just thinking you might get your things dirty. Or torn.'

'Oh, that,' said Grace. 'I don't care about that.'

And the thing was, I believed her. The frills had only been to impress grown-ups. But clearly Grace wanted to play tennis even more than she wanted to look sweet in front of Mrs. Cantwell. If left to her own devices with no adults to suck up to, I bet Grace would be a very different person.

~

For a while we stood at the side of the court and watched the game. It mostly involved the ball being hit straight into the net, followed by an argument. Then when the argument was over and play had continued once more, one of the players would hit the ball right out of the court.

They never seemed to get it going back and forth between them for more than two shots.

'Well, you can't be any worse than those two,' said Nora as the game came to a contentious close (the small one insisted the ball she'd just hit wildly over the net had landed inside the line and was not, in fact, out. But she was wrong).

'Grace Molyneaux and Catherine O'Reilly!' called the tall young woman.

Grace took a deep breath. 'Wish me luck,' she said, and strode out onto the court, where the tall young woman handed her the tennis racket that the loser of the previous match had flung on the grass in rage.

'I wouldn't dream of it,' muttered Nora.

Grace rolled up the sleeves of her lace-trimmed blouse, gave the tennis racket an appraising shake, and tossed it lightly in the air before grabbing it firmly by the handle.

'Goodness,' I said. 'She looks fearfully professional.'

'Especially in comparison to her opponent,' said Nora. A rather vague-looking girl wearing spectacles and a pale blue dress was walking onto the other side of the court, holding a racquet as if she'd never seen one before. The tall young woman tossed a coin to see who would serve first, and Catherine O'Reilly won.

'I bet this'll be like the last game,' muttered Nora. 'The ball will probably end up three streets away from the club.'

But it wasn't like that at all. Catherine O'Reilly tossed

the ball into the air, and as it came down she raised her racquet with what looked like an effortless but extremely powerful gesture and slammed the ball across the court. That was surprising enough, but what was even more shocking was the fact that Grace dived across the court and managed to wallop the ball back to her opponent. But the other girl – who didn't look at all vague now – immediately hit it straight back to Grace, who flung herself in its general direction and managed to get it back over the net. Catherine O'Reilly ran towards it but didn't get there in time.

'Fifteen love!' called the willowy young lady.

'Goodness!' exclaimed Nora. 'Grace isn't bad.'

'I think that's the first time you've ever said anything nice about her,' I said.

'Well.' Nora shrugged her shoulders. 'She's decent at tennis. I can't deny it.'

Grace was crouched like a tiger on her side of the net, looking at her opponent with narrowed eyes. A lock of hair fell over her face and she pushed it back with an impatient gesture. You wouldn't think it was the same girl who'd been prancing about tossing her curls the day before.

'How on earth did she get so good?' I said, as Grace returned the bespectacled Miss O'Reilly's serve with a powerful stroke. The heat didn't seem to be affecting her powers of play.

'I dunno,' said Nora. 'Her grandmother on the other side — her father's mother, you know — lives in the country and I think they have a tennis court in the garden. So she's probably been practising in the holidays.'

'And she never said a word at school,' I marvelled. 'I suppose she was concentrating on winning cups for lessons.' The competition was genuinely rather gripping. Grace didn't win the first game, but she did win the second. In fact, the two players seemed to be pretty evenly matched, and as the last of the three games began, they were both looking a bit red in the face from their exertions. And yet they played on with great enthusiasm in what turned out to be another close contest.

'Deuce!' said Nora, as Catherine O'Reilly missed one of Grace's skillful shots. 'Oh dear, she'll be insufferable if she wins.'

The words were barely out of her mouth when the bespectacled girl served an immensely powerful stroke. Grace rushed towards it but it was too late — the ball had bounced out of the court.

'Advantage, Miss O'Reilly!' cried the willowy young woman. Miss O'Reilly pushed her spectacles up her nose and prepared for her final serve. If we'd been at school, I wouldn't have put it past Grace to do something to put her off — as we know, she has no honour — but she just bounced for a moment on the balls of her feet and waved her wrists around to loosen her joints. Miss O'Reilly served, and Grace's racket caught the ball and hit it straight back to her. A rally ensued, with each player darting around their sides of the court with what seemed to me, a girl who is not very good at tennis, miraculous speed. And then Grace hit the ball over the net with such force that it zoomed past Miss O'Reilly's face – narrowly missing her spectacles – and landed just outside the court boundaries.

'Out!' cried the umpire.

'Miss O'Reilly is the winner!' cried the willowy young lady.

I thought Grace was going to chuck her tennis racquet on the ground like the loser of the last game. But she shook Catherine O'Reilly's hand and handed her racquet back to the young lady, who smiled at her and said, 'That was jolly good, by the way. And well done for losing with such good grace. I do like to see fair play on the court. You're not a member here, are you?'

Grace shook her head. 'I came to see my cousin,' she said. 'George Cantwell. He's a member.'

'Oh yes, I saw one of his matches earlier,' said the young lady. 'You really should think of joining. A lot of girls play during the summer.'

'Really?' said Grace.

The lady nodded.

'The senior tournament is tomorrow so the courts will be in use all day, but if you'd like to join the club you could call in on Monday or Tuesday. Ask for me if you can't find me. Miss Casey.'

Grace's expression was thoughtful as she bid Miss Casey goodbye and walked over to me and Nora.

'Hard luck,' I said. Which is probably the nicest I've ever been to Grace. Of course Grace didn't say thank you. Instead she turned to Nora.

'Your family are members of the club, aren't they?' she said. 'I mean, the whole lot of you, not just George.'

'Officially,' said Nora.

'Well, surely I count as a member of the family?' said Grace. 'I want to go to that girls' session. And if they say cousins aren't allowed I could say I'm your sister or something.'

Nora didn't look very happy at this idea of anyone thinking Grace was her sister. Grace being her actual cousin was bad enough.

'You'll have to ask Mother and Father,' she said. 'Or you could always ask your parents to let you join by yourself.'

'Don't be ridiculous,' said Grace. 'It would be a waste of money just for a few weeks.' Grace lives in Rathmines and gets the tram to school every day, so the tennis club won't be very convenient once the glorious day arrives when she returns to her own home. 'Anyway, I don't see why I should have to,' Grace continued. 'Not when my aunt and uncle are members already.'

I can't believe I'd almost been feeling sorry for her just a few minutes earlier. I glanced over at the clock on the tennis-club pavilion. We'd been there for over two hours.

'I really should go home,' I said. But no sooner had the words left my lips than something small, fluffy and terrifyingly strong appeared as if from nowhere and jumped up on me, putting its filthy dusty paws all over my clean frock.

'Barnaby!' I shrieked, for of course it was the Menace.

Mrs. Sheffield hurried up, holding a broken leather lead. 'Barnaby, you wicked little animal,' she said, breathlessly. 'I'm so sorry, Mollie. We got him a new lead and it simply wasn't strong enough.'

As I am sure you remember, the Menace has such super-canine strength that as a rule he has to be taken out in a specially-made harness rather than a usual dog-collar and lead. But as Mrs. Sheffield now explained to us, the buckle on his harness had come loose and was being repaired.

'And I really thought this collar and lead would be enough to hold him until his harness came back,' she said, slipping the broken lead under Barnaby's collar and tying it in what I hoped was a good strong knot. 'But he's such a, well, such an enthusiastic dog.'

That's one word for him, I thought. But I didn't say anything. I just looked down at my nice fresh clothes, which were covered in dusty paw prints. At least, I hoped it was just dust. I looked at the Menace, who was now sitting peacefully beside Mrs. Sheffield, staring up at me with his button eyes as if butter wouldn't melt in his mouth. I stared back at him, but he didn't blink. I don't think he ever does, actually.

'Well!' said Mrs. Sheffield brightly. 'Hello, Nora. Are you having a nice day?'

Of course Mrs. Sheffield has known Nora for years, not just because Nora is often in my house when Mrs. S visits Mother, but also because of the tennis club. Though she has clearly given up on Nora as a tennis-playing cause.

'Yes, thank you,' said Nora.

'And who's your little friend?' asked Mrs. Sheffield, smiling at Grace.

Any sensible girl of fifteen would have resented being called our 'little friend', but of course Grace smirked back at Mrs. Sheffield and tossed her curls, which were dustier and messier than they had been before the match but still impressively bouncy. She looked like a different girl to the one who'd been ferociously dominating the tennis court just a few minutes earlier. And despite the fact that I was covered in Barnaby's paw prints, I did not forget my manners.

'This is Nora's cousin, Grace,' I said. 'Grace, this is Mrs. Sheffield. She's on the tennis-club committee.'

Grace's face lit up.

'Oh how lovely to meet you,' she said. 'I just played my first match here. Well, not a match really, just a short game. They're letting non-members have a go.'

'So you're not a member?' said Mrs. Sheffield. She's always on the lookout for new tennis players in the summer.

Grace shook her head. 'I just came to see my cousin,' she said. 'George, you know.'

'Ah yes, he's one of our most promising players,' said Mrs. Sheffield. 'And did you enjoy it?'

Grace beamed. And for once, her smile actually looked genuine. 'I loved it,' she said.

'She's jolly good,' said Nora, which was the second time I'd ever heard her say something nice about Grace. Twice in one day!

'Is she now?' Mrs. Sheffield turned back to Grace. 'So are you thinking of joining the club?'

'Well, I'm only staying here for a few weeks,' said Grace. 'I live over in Rathmines usually. But I do wish I could play while I'm staying with Nora. It's such a nice club. And I really want to improve my game.'

Mrs. Sheffield looked thoughtful.

'Well, the Cantwells are members, and you're a Cantwell ...' she said.

Nora interrupted. 'She's a Molyneaux, actually.'

'She's still your cousin,' said Mrs. Sheffield. 'I think we can include you in their membership, can't we? A nice little girl like you would be an asset to the club.'

She smiled at Grace in the sort of way most people would smile at a baby in short frocks. And Grace, being Grace, just beamed back. By the time Mrs. Sheffield went off to the pavilion, Barnaby trotting at her heels (He looked back at me as they walked off, and if those button eyes could speak, they'd have been saying, 'you got off easily this time'), it had been agreed that Grace's name would be added to the Cantwells' membership and that she could come along to the schoolgirls' sessions for as long as she liked.

'An asset to the club,' said Grace smugly, as we walked back along the dusty road.

None of us really cared who was on the outside of the pavement now. Grace was still hot and damp after her match, and I was filthy after the Menace's attentions. Even Nora, who hadn't played tennis or been jumped on by an annoying dog, was looking a bit scruffy. All of our stockings were sagging. There's something about that sort of weather that makes everyone look a bit bedraggled after a while.

We were all too hot and tired to say much, but when Grace quoted those words of Mrs. Sheffield's, Nora couldn't stop herself saying, 'She hasn't seen you play yet.' She didn't sound like her heart was in the insult, though.

Grace obviously thought this too, as she didn't even

respond to the jibe. When we reached the corner where I turn off to go to my house, Nora told Grace to go on ahead and she'd follow her on in a moment, and Grace just said, 'All right,' and headed down the road. But just to remind us that even the boiling heat can't stop Grace being Grace, she paused, turned back and said, 'You'd better try and clean yourself up before your mother sees you, Mollie. You look an absolute fright.'

'Charming,' I said, as Grace strolled off in the direction of Nora's house. 'Mother can't be too angry with me, though. After all, it was because of her friend's dog.'

'I'm afraid grown-ups aren't always fair about that sort of thing,' said Nora (truthfully, as it turned out). 'Though you never know. Miracles do happen. Look what just happened with Grace!'

'You're still stuck with her tonight,' I said.

'Yes, but will I be stuck with her the day after tomorrow?' said Nora. 'If she joins the tennis club and spends all her time there, they can't expect me to hang around there with her. I'll be free.'

'You didn't sound very enthusiastic about her joining the club when we were back there,' I pointed out.

'Well, you know what she's like,' said Nora. 'If I'd encouraged her to join, she might have decided not to, just to spite me. I wouldn't put anything past her.'

Somewhere nearby, a church bell started to ring.

'I'd better go,' said Nora. 'Or Grace will eat all the cakes. Call over tomorrow after Mass, won't you?'

I said I would and she ran off. I do hope she's right and that Grace will devote herself to the tennis club during her stay. It would make things so much nicer for us. Though clearly Lady Fortune is not smiling on me at the moment because when I got home Mother took one look at my dirty clothes and went absolutely wild.

'It was Barnaby's fault!' I protested. 'He burst his bonds and jumped on me.'

But Mother didn't seem to care.

'You should have stopped him,' she said, unreasonably.

'No one can stop Barnaby!' I wailed. 'Even Mrs. Sheffield knows that. She apologized for him!'

But Mother was determined to be unfair.

'I don't suppose Nora and that cousin of hers came home looking like that,' she said, and I couldn't deny it, but that's only because Barnaby doesn't know them well and so was unlikely to pick them as his unfortunate victims. (I told Mother this and she said I was being ridiculous and that Barnaby was just a dog and didn't choose victims, but she obviously doesn't know him as well as I do.)

Anyway, I couldn't argue with her anymore so I went up and changed and now I am lying on my bed in my old yellow frock with the little white flowers on it (the one that makes me look like I am coming down with some sort of wasting disease – yellow does *not* suit me) writing to you. I'm sure Mother's going to make me mend some socks or help Maggie with the dinner or something like that in a minute so I must enjoy my freedom while I can.

And speaking of freedom, I am keeping my fingers firmly crossed about Grace being occupied by the tennis club. It would make things much easier if she's out of the way. Nora and I haven't even had a chance to discuss what we might do for Mr. Asquith's visit yet, and there is just over a week to go! We must think of something soon.

By the way, I looked up a picture of an American possum in the nature book, and although they are small they have giant pointy teeth and look absolutely terrifying! They definitely look like they could eat a person; it just would take them longer to eat all of you than it would take a bear. So I think you should still watch out for them.

Best love and votes for women,
Mollie

P.S.

I am writing this bit very late because I stayed up finishing *A Tale of Two Cities* by candlelight (Julia was fast asleep), and the ending was so sad I feel too agitated to go back to sleep. The last time I cried so much at a book was when you-know-who died in *Little Women*. (I don't want to mention the name of the dead person because I remember how much it upset you when you read it.) It was awfully good, but it might not be the best book to read on holiday because you might feel a bit embarrassed if you start crying on a train.

I am going to read a book that Mabel has given me next. Well, she gave it to Phyllis, who handed it to me along with a note from Mabel. It was a belated apology for selling our tickets to the big meeting, and in her note Mabel said she had read the book herself when she was on that trip to her cousins in America. Hopefully it will be a bit more cheerful than *A Tale of Two Cities*.

Monday, 8th July, 1912.

Dear Frances,

I am writing this sitting in the back garden, but right now
you are in the United States of America! I got your letter this
morning – it was so exciting to see an American stamp. I've
only seen one or two before. It's funny to think of you being
so far away. I mean, I know we've hardly ever been in the
same country since you went away to school, but somehow
it makes a difference knowing you're now thousands and
thousands of miles away. (At least I think it's thousands, I
am not quite sure and it's hard to tell from my atlas. I know
London is four hundred miles away from Dublin, though, so
Boston must be at least three times that.)

I am glad that the voyage went so well. (Of course I
knew you hadn't hit an iceberg, or anything, because it
would have been in the papers.) I'm sorry you were so
sick, though. I'm quite certain I'd have been sick too.
I'm sure I've told you about the time the summer before
last when we went out in a boat on one of our trips to
Skerries and as soon as we were out of the harbour my
tummy began to feel most peculiar. And even though
Phyllis told me to stare very hard at the horizon it didn't

make any difference at all and I had to lean out of the boat and be sick when we were sailing around the cliff of Red Island. And then when we got back to blessed dry land I felt all dizzy, as if the ground were moving around like the sea. And that was after just an hour on the ocean waves! I can only imagine what I'd be like for a whole week. Though perhaps, like you, I'd start to get my sea legs after a few days. How very brave of you to eat a strawberry ice, I couldn't eat anything but dry toast after my own bout of seasickness.

Anyway! You are on land for weeks and weeks now so I suppose you will have plenty of time to get your land legs back. And the rest of your voyage does sound like good fun. I can't imagine what it must be like to play games and go to a dancing class on a ship in the middle of a gigantic ocean. Every time I think of it I feel a bit ill. I definitely couldn't have done any dancing on that rowing boat (not that there'd have been any room).

I wonder if you've seen much of Boston yet? I am so excited that you are going to go to the town where Louisa May Alcott lived! I can't wait for you to tell me all about it. I couldn't quite picture the town in *Little Women* because I don't really know what American towns look like. I just know that they must not look much like Irish ones because they have houses made entirely of wood, which sounds very odd to me and makes me think of garden sheds.

It all sounds thrilling, especially as you are going to ride some of the way there in a motor car. I have never been in a motor car but I long to have a go in one. I imagine that even familiar streets would look quite different if you were speeding through them in a motor. I mentioned this at home once and Harry, who always feels the need to act all superior even though I know for a fact that he has never been in a motor car and would love to have a go, informed me that it would only be the same as an express tram and I could travel in one of them any morning I liked. He is so annoying.

If I had any way of ensuring you'd actually get this letter, I'd send it just so I could urge you to read a wonderful, wonderful book called *Anne of Green Gables* (though you probably don't need any entertainment with all those new and exciting things to see – and all those possums and bears to avoid). It's the book that Mabel gave to me via Phyllis.

'I had heard it was a kids' book, but my cousin told me it was awfully good and it was,' she wrote in her note. 'And it's been published over here now so I got you a copy.'

I woke up very early this morning (our room is always terribly sunny in the morning, I wish the curtains were thicker) and started reading it because I couldn't get back to sleep. And it's more than awfully good. It is magnificent! Honestly, Frances, I think it's the best book I've ever read

in my life, even better than E. Nesbit and *Jane Eyre* and the
Sherlock Holmes stories. It's about an orphan girl called
Anne who has had a very hard life and then she goes to
live with these old farming people who are brother and
sister. And they don't want her at first because they wanted
a boy to work on the farm but then they start to like her.
(I haven't got very far yet so maybe they send her back to
the orphanage in the end, but I really don't think that will
happen.)

It's set in Canada (originally I thought it was America
but it's not) and it makes Canada sound very beautiful. But
the best thing about the book is Anne herself. Oh Frances,
I've never read a character who seems so like a real girl.
Things go wrong for her sometimes and people around
her often think she's being ridiculous, but she doesn't get
too downhearted and she uses her imagination to make
everything better. Which in a way is what we're doing
with the suffragette movement – we imagine that things
can be better rather than the stupid way things are now.

Anyway, I absolutely love Anne Shirley of Green Gables
and I take back everything I have ever said about Mabel. I
totally and utterly forgive her for getting rid of our tickets.
If you did happen to come across the book, I'm sure it
would keep you amused when you're riding the railroads
(as I believe they say in America)! Or maybe you could
read it in your cousin's motor car, though Father, who

once rode in a motor all the way from town to Rathmines, says that you can't really read in one because you get sick.

I forgot to mention it before, but I got a letter from Stella on Friday. She is very bored all by herself in the middle of the countryside and says she is knitting a cardigan but even that isn't enough to keep her entertained. (It certainly wouldn't be enough to entertain me, and Stella likes knitting even more than I do. She can get strangely excited over new ways of knitting socks.) I wish she could stay in Dublin over the summer, but I suppose her parents don't get to see her for most of the year when she's at school. She wants to see them too, of course, and she does love her home (which sounds like it's about twice the size of our house), but she says she wishes they lived a bit closer to school so she could come up to town for the day and see her chums.

I was thinking of asking Mother and Father if Stella could visit us after Frank's visit, but I might leave it for a bit as Mother is still annoyed with me for, as she puts it, 'letting that dog jump all over you'. As if I had a choice! That Menace is haunting me. I walked past the Sheffields' house on my way to see Nora yesterday morning after Mass and the dreadful creature was sitting in the bay window. When he saw me he jumped up and put his paws up on the glass and started barking his head off. He didn't stop until I turned the corner at the end of the road. (He's

so loud you can hear him all the way down the street.)
I don't know how they put up with him, he must drive
them demented with his noise.

When I arrived at the Cantwells', Nora answered the
door because Agnes had her day off today (and as Nora
said later, Princess Grace will never lower herself to open a
front door for anyone).

'Where's her majesty?' I whispered.

Nora rolled her eyes.

'In the back garden with George,' she said. 'Badgering
him about the tennis club. The poor thing keeps trying
to get away but she keeps stopping him with more stupid
questions. '

'What did your parents say? About her joining the club,
I mean?'

Nora's face brightened.

'Oh, they love the idea,' she said. 'I knew they would.
The only thing is that she can't go until Tuesday. They're
having the grown-ups' tournament today, remember? And
then tomorrow we have to go to Bray to visit some cousin
of Mother's. So I'm afraid we're saddled with her today.'

'Maybe she'll stick with George,' I said hopefully, but
Nora said there was no luck there.

'He's helping out at the grown-ups' tournament later,'
she said. 'Fetching people's tennis balls or something, I don't
know. I'm never quite sure what tennis people get up to in

that place. Anyway, Grace can't tag along with him.'

'So what'll we do with her?' I asked, and Nora was shrugging her shoulders when the Cantwells' drawing-room door opened and Mrs. Cantwell came out.

'Mollie!' she said. 'How nice to see you.'

She's not usually so enthusiastic about my visits, but I suppose she hoped I'd be able to stand between Nora and Grace as a buffer if things got too tense.

'Hello, Mrs. Cantwell,' I said dutifully.

'I was thinking,' said Mrs. Cantwell, 'why don't the two of you take Grace to the Phoenix Park?'

'On our own?' Nora sounded surprised, and I didn't blame her. We're not usually allowed to go all the way to the park on our own, mostly because you have to take at least two trams or buses, so it's quite a complicated journey.

'I think I can trust you girls to look after yourselves,' said Mrs. Cantwell. 'And of course to look after Grace.'

I don't know why she kept talking about Grace as if she were a delicate little baby who had to be looked after. Or rather, I do. It's because Grace always acts like a delicate little baby and it's very, very annoying. Nora told me that apparently she was quite delicate when she was an actual baby so people did fuss over her a lot, but she's perfectly all right now.

'Can we have some money for the tearoom?' asked Nora hopefully.

'You can have sixpence each spending money, and your fares,' said Mrs. Cantwell. 'You too, Mollie.' Which was jolly generous considering I'm neither a daughter nor a niece. The weather was lovely today – less baking than yesterday, with a nice light breeze in the air – and the thought of wandering around the park was rather a nice one. Sometimes there's a band playing during the summer, and lots of people playing games. Of course, Nora had to push her luck.

'Can we go to the zoo, too?' she asked.

Mrs. Cantwell just ignored her and went back into the drawing room, saying, 'Go and get your cousin.'

'It was worth a try,' said Nora, and we went out to the back garden, where George was saying, 'Well, I'm not sure if there are any professional lady tennis players.' He looked very happy to see us.

'Hello, Mollie!' he said. 'Sorry to rush off, but I'm late for the tournament. Bye, Grace.' And without another word, he practically ran back into the house. Grace didn't seem to realise he'd been trying to get away from her.

'I can't wait to go to the club on Tuesday,' she said, as she and Nora gathered together their hats and outdoor shoes. 'George was saying he's sure I'll fit in beautifully.'

Nora rolled her eyes. As we made our way towards the tram stop, Grace kept going on and on about how wonderful at tennis she was going to be and how she would soon be the junior star of the tennis club.

'I hope that O'Reilly girl who beat you yesterday doesn't show up,' said Nora innocently.

Grace's face darkened. 'I hope she does,' she said. 'I'll show her how to play tennis.'

I was going to say it looked to me as if she already knew, but I kept my mouth shut. The tram was surprisingly crowded and we couldn't get seats together; I ended up squashed next to a woman carrying a large basket that I suspect had a dog in it even though she said it didn't when I asked. She looked quite annoyed at me for even asking so I looked away from her and out of the window and tried to think of interesting ways to protest Mr. Asquith's visit. I remembered what Phyllis had said last month about the Countess Markievicz turning up at a political meeting in England, driving a coach with four white horses. We couldn't exactly do that – for one, we don't have a coach or horses, and we couldn't drive them even if we had them. But we could do something dramatic. Apparently Mr. Asquith is going to the Theatre Royal during his visit. Perhaps, I thought, as Dorset Street sped by outside the windows, we could somehow work our way into the good graces of the theatre company and then, when we had got ourselves on stage (I am not sure how we would do this), we could leap out in front of the footlights and unfurl a giant banner saying VOTES FOR IRISH WOMEN. I mean, we could easily make one out of an old sheet and a bit of paint.

Or if that didn't work (and I have a feeling that getting ourselves onto the Theatre Royal stage is easier said than done), maybe we could try and catch Mr. Asquith when he arrives in the country? We could find out what boat he is arriving at – apparently it's going to be at Kingstown – and we could easily get a train out there from Amiens Street station. Then perhaps we could hire a rowing boat and row out into the bay, holding the banner. I know I always get seasick even in a rowing boat, but I'm prepared to make a sacrifice for the cause. I was wondering if it would do more harm than good to the movement if I actually did get sick in the boat while holding the banner, when the woman sitting next to me got off the tram with her basket and Nora ran over and took her place. I told Nora about my ideas and she was particularly impressed by the last one, which she said was a stroke of genius.

'Especially because I know what a terrible sacrifice it will be for you to set foot in a boat,' she said. 'It is a very noble gesture. I wonder how much it costs to hire a rowing boat.'

'It was only a couple of shillings when we hired one in Skerries,' I said. 'I bet we could get that much money together in a couple of weeks.' I thought of the sixpences Mrs. Cantwell had given us just half an hour earlier. Nora must have been thinking the same thing because she said, 'We definitely can. Some things are more important than buns,' in a very noble voice. And then I realised we had reached the point where we have to change trams so there was a bit of a scurry to grab Grace and get off in time. Luckily we didn't have to wait long for the next tram, but unluckily we all got seats together and Grace started talking very loudly about the strange smells one always encountered on trams.

'This is why Father is definitely going to buy a motor car,' she said in a voice so piercing it must have been heard upstairs on the tram. Many of the smells were clearly coming from our fellow passengers, some of whom looked very unimpressed by Grace's speech. I was relieved when we finally reached the gates of the park and joined the crowds making their way down the road that leads to the zoo as well as the playing fields.

'Gosh, it really is crowded,' said Nora. And I was about to suggest leaving the main path and cutting across the grass when I saw a very familiar figure walking on the pavement on the other side of the road, dressed in grass-stained cricket whites.

'Frank!' cried Nora, waving frantically in his direction. Frank's face broke into a wide smile when he saw her, and I found myself wishing I'd worn my blue cotton blouse with the little stars embroidered on the yoke instead of the slightly scruffy old linen one I was wearing. I always seem to meet Frank when I'm looking particularly grubby. Of course, I thought, as he worked his way through the crowds towards us, Frank was looking quite scruffy himself, but I didn't mind about that, so maybe he wasn't too horrified by my scruffy appearance either. I am probably thinking too much about the state of my clothes. Although I really don't want him to think I go around in filthy rags all the time. All right, I really am thinking about it too much. I'll stop now.

'Hello, girls,' he said, shaking first my hand and then Nora's. He turned to Grace, because I suppose he couldn't ignore her. He's always so polite. 'I'm sorry, I don't think we've been introduced ...'

Grace, of course, simpered at him. And there was something about her smirking expression that made me feel strangely uneasy.

'I'm Grace Molyneaux,' she said. For a terrible moment I thought she was going to curtsey, but she just shook his hand instead. 'Nora's cousin.'

I remembered that I had told Frank quite a lot about Grace and I hoped that he wouldn't say anything about having heard all about her because she would guess that he hadn't heard anything good from me or Nora. But he just said, 'How do you do? I'm Frank Nugent,' and I thought Grace was going to pull a muscle in her face, she was smirking so much.

'Frank is a friend of my brother Harry,' I said.

'I'm a friend of the entire Carberry family,' said Frank. And he smiled at me in a very nice way.

'Have you been playing cricket?' I asked, and no sooner were the words out of my mouth than Grace let out an extremely irritating peal of laughter.

'Oh Mollie!' she cried. 'What a question. What else do you think he was doing dressed like that? Putting up wallpaper?' And she laughed again at her supposed wit. I felt like kicking her but managed to restrain myself. I was pleased to note, however, that Frank didn't seem particularly amused by her *bon mots* (that's French of course. It literally means good words, in case you don't know).

'A few chaps from school decided to organise a match,' he said. 'Cricket's not my game, really, but it's good fun. Especially when they hand out the lemonade afterwards.'

Sports groups seem very keen on giving people lemonade. I suppose I can't blame them. I imagine it's the only way they can get lots of people to take part. It would take a lot more than a glass of lemonade to make me run around a field and try to hit balls with what is essentially a narrow stick (this is also why I have not been tempted by the girls at school who want to try hurling). Though of course maybe if I were any good at sports, apart from drill and dancing (which doesn't really count) and running quite fast for short distances, I might feel differently.

'Do you play tennis, Frank?' asked Grace in her sweetest voice. 'I've just joined the club.'

Frank asked if she meant the club near our house and Grace confirmed that she did.

'You should join too,' she said.

'I haven't played it much,' said Frank. 'Though it is fun. Maybe I could give it a try.'

'What an excellent idea,' she said. 'The more the merrier!'

I doubt she'd say that if me and Nora wanted to join.

'But I must get going now,' said Frank. 'Very nice to meet you, Grace.'

Grace simpered again. It really is the only way to describe the expression she makes every time she wants to impress someone. I hoped Frank remembered everything I'd said about what an awful, mean glory-hunter she is and wasn't taken in by her smirks.

'And I'm sure I'll see you all soon.' Frank turned to me. 'Not long now before I trespass on your family's hospitality.'

'Everyone's looking forward to it,' I said. Which is actually true. The whole family likes Frank. I'm probably not even the only one of us counting the days until he arrives (four, as it happens).

With a cheery wave, he bade us farewell.

'What a nice boy,' said Grace. 'I hope he does join the tennis club.'

'Come on,' I said. 'Let's go to the tearoom.'

We set off across the grass, Grace still jabbering on about how George had given her his second-best tennis racket and what fun she was going to have at the club. She was halfway through some boring story about the time she beat her other cousin at some sort of family tournament in her grandmother's house when I saw another familiar figure making its way towards us.

'Oh no,' I said. 'Not again!'

'Is that the dog who jumped on you yesterday?' Grace peered in the direction of the Menace, who was straining at his harness in his eagerness to harass me again.

I nodded grimly. 'I'm afraid it is.' I can't get away from the dreadful little monster at the moment.

'Mollie!' cried Mrs. Sheffield. 'How nice to see you. And your friends too.'

'I see Barnaby's wearing his harness,' I said.

'Oh yes,' said Mrs. Sheffield. 'I collected it from the cobbler yesterday afternoon. That lead really wasn't strong enough for him.'

Barnaby sniffed my skirt, as if considering another attempt to ruin my clothes. I quickly stepped back.

'By the way, Mrs. Sheffield,' said Grace brightly, 'I'm definitely joining the club. My aunt and uncle are going to put my name down.'

'That's wonderful.' Mrs. Sheffield beamed. 'I do like to see more girls joining. Oh, Barnaby, stop that!' For Barnaby had turned his snuffling attention to Grace. But instead of leaping back from the Menace, as any sane person would surely do, Grace leaned over and patted his woolly head.

'What a lovely doggie,' she said.

Mrs. Sheffield's smile grew even wider, which was, I am sure, just the reaction that Grace had been hoping for.

'He is, isn't he?' she said. 'Though he can be quite a handful.'

And that was when something very peculiar happened. The Menace, who had been sniffing away at Grace's hand, stared at her very hard with his button eyes. This is not unusual for the Menace, of course. But then, still staring her straight in the face, he sat down and offered her his woolly paw.

Grace gave another dreadful tinkling laugh and shook it. 'I think he likes me!' she cried.

'You're very honoured,' said Mrs. Sheffield. 'He hardly does that with anybody.'

That's certainly true. I didn't think the Menace was even capable of shaking paws. He's more likely to snarl at someone's hand than shake it.

'The only explanation I can think of,' I told Nora

later, 'is that he recognised Grace as a kindred spirit.' And Nora agreed that it was the only thing that made sense. Especially as Grace clearly felt the same way about him, because she rubbed his head again and said, 'I wish I had a dog like this.' And for once, she actually sounded sincere.

'Well,' said Mrs. Sheffield, 'you can take Barnaby for a walk whenever you like. He's a lively little companion, isn't he, Mollie?'

I remembered the last time I took the Menace for a walk. If you recall, he escaped from my clutches and ran away, and if Frank hadn't happened to be passing and grabbed hold of him, he might never have been seen again. And even though the Menace is the bane of my existence (well, one of the banes, along with Harry and Grace and the anti-suffragists and Ancient Order of Hooligans), I didn't want him to be lost forever. Of course, I had never told Mrs. Sheffield about the Menace getting away from me so I just said, 'Yes, he's very strong.'

'I'm sure I'd be able to handle him.' Grace gave me a disdainful look. And the Menace looked up at her with what almost looked like … respect. If those button eyes were capable of showing such an emotion, of course.

To my astonishment, Grace clearly meant what she said and wasn't just saying what she thought a grown-up wanted to hear. In fact, she actually arranged to call to Mrs. Sheffield's house and take the Menace for an outing in a few days' time. After we'd bid farewell to both Barnaby and his owner (Grace had rubbed his head again when she said goodbye to him, and he'd closed his eyes in what looked like pleasure), Nora said, 'You do realise that that dog is an absolute savage and a menace to civilised society, don't you? We won't be able to come with you if you walk him.'

'I wouldn't expect you to,' said Grace. 'I can look after him perfectly well on my own. I don't need the pair of you getting in the way.'

She's probably right. Based on previous experience, I wouldn't be much use if he misbehaved. By that stage we had reached the tearoom, and the next few minutes were spent finding a table, ordering cakes (I got a Mary Cake all to myself. When we go to Bewley's Mother always insists on cutting even the tiniest cakes in two and sharing them between us). For a while we ate our cakes in what was almost a companionable silence.

'This is jolly good,' said Grace, swallowing a mouthful of chocolate cake.

'So's this scone,' said Nora. She had a smudge of jam and cream on her chin. 'You know, Grace, I bet Agnes would make a chocolate cake if you asked her to. She makes pretty decent ones.'

'I'll ask her then,' said Grace.

It was all remarkably civilised. Maybe cakes and scones and buns are the key to social harmony? People seem to behave much more nicely when they're sitting around eating together, I thought. Then I remembered how awfully Grace has behaved in the past in the refectory at school. So buns weren't the answer. Maybe, I thought, she'd just be nicer if she wasn't trying to be better than other girls all the time. I was pondering this question (and eating my cake) when a voice behind me said, 'Mollie! Nora! What are you doing here?'

Was every single person I knew in the park today? I suppose it was a sunny July Sunday, but still! I turned around to see Mabel's friendly face smiling at me. She was carrying a bag that, I could see, contained some copies of the *Irish Citizen*, the official publication of the Irish Women's Franchise League.

'There isn't a meeting on today, is there?' I said, forgetting all about Grace's presence.

'No, it was yesterday,' said Mabel. 'But I thought I'd take advantage of the fact that everyone goes to the park when the weather's like this. I've sold quite a few *Citizen*s already.' She looked at Grace and smiled. 'Hello there. I haven't met you before, have I?'

'No,' said Grace. 'I'm Grace Molyneaux. Nora's cousin.'

'This is my sister's friend, Miss Purcell,' I said. I didn't see why Grace should be on first name terms with Mabel.

'Are you a young suffragette too?' said Mabel. 'Nora and Mollie are excellent supporters of the cause.'

And for once, Grace didn't know what to say. On the one hand, she's been nothing but contemptuous of me and Nora for being involved in the Movement, but on the other hand, she always sucks up to grown-up people. And Mabel, though she's only about nineteen, definitely counts as a grown-up. She wears long skirts and she's put up her hair (and unlike Phyllis's wild locks, it actually seems to stay up once she puts it there). It was actually rather funny, watching Grace decide whether it was more important to make a grown-up like her or to show us that she despised our cause. But Grace is nothing if she's not clever. She smiled sweetly at Mabel and said, 'I don't know much about political things.'

'Neither did I when I was your age,' said Mabel. 'But I'm sure Nora and Mollie can set you right, can't you, girls?'

This was another unusual situation. Grace is definitely not used to a grown-up telling her she could learn anything from either me or Nora, and she didn't look particularly happy about it. Usually the situation is the other way around.

'Of course we can,' said Nora, cheerfully. 'I say, Mabel, can I buy a *Citizen*? I've got the money on me.'

'I'll buy it for you.' Mabel took a magazine out of her bag. 'To make up for getting rid of your ticket to the meeting. After all, I got Mollie a book, I should give you a treat too.'

'Thanks awfully,' said Nora, as Mabel handed her

a magazine. Mabel took a penny out of a very pretty embroidered purse and put it into a larger brown one.

'This is my business purse.' She held up the large brown receptacle. 'I can't mix up my own pennies and my Citizen money.'

'I meant to tell you, thanks for the book too,' I said. 'It's absolutely wonderful.'

Mabel smiled.

'I thought you'd like it,' she said. 'I'll lend you the sequel after you finish it. Now, will you be joining us to protest Mr. Asquith's visit next week?'

That's what I like about Mabel. She has accepted that we have a right to take an active part in the suffrage cause, unlike some people I could mention (Phyllis) who behave as though we're just doing it to annoy them. But I knew it wasn't safe to say much about us wanting to attend the protests in front of Grace. Grace is quite capable of finally saying something to Nora's parents, especially since she didn't win the cup. Now she has nothing to lose. So far, all she has known about me and Nora is that we support the cause and have considered taking militant action. But she doesn't know quite how far we've gone. Then again, neither does Mabel.

So I just said, 'We will definitely be there in spirit.' Which is of course true. Though hopefully we will be there in person too.

'Excellent,' said Mabel. 'You're a credit to the cause, girls.'

If Grace hadn't been there, I'd have taken advantage of the fact that Phyllis wasn't around to ask Mabel exactly what protests have been planned (Phyllis still hasn't told me anything, of course) and maybe even tell her about our boat idea, just to see what she thought. But even though I desperately wanted to know all the details, I could only hope that Mabel wouldn't volunteer a word. Imagine if she revealed something secret, believing we were all trustworthy, and then Grace told the police!

'Right,' said Mabel. 'I'd better go and catch all the people who come in here after twelve o'clock Mass and sell them some magazines. Goodbye, young suffragettes. Lovely to meet you, Grace.' And off she went.

And off I must go too, for a while at least – Mother has just called me and asked me to help her sort out some old clothes of Phyllis's to see if any of them will 'do' for me now I've grown a bit. Phyllis was taller than me when she was my age and rather larger in the chest so I'm not sure any of these things will fit but Mother says I won't know until I try all of them on. What fun. I will return to continue my tale later.

Later

It is a sign of how seriously I take my mission to keep you informed of all my activities that I have taken up my pen despite the fact that I am now utterly exhausted. Mother kept me in her room for what felt like hours and hours, making me take off clothes and put other clothes on, over and over again. As I suspected, none of Phyllis's old things fitted me particularly, but that didn't stop Mother insisting that they'd all 'do very well'.

'How?' I demanded, looking down at the printed dress that had looked rather nice on fifteen-year-old Phyllis, but which looked like a floral sack on me.

'We can take this up a bit,' said Mother, holding up the hem.

'But it's too wide!' I said.

'We can take it in here,' said Mother, pulling in the fabric around my chest. It was all very humiliating really, being reminded how short and scrawny I am. And none of this would be happening if my family ever bought me new clothes, instead of expecting me to wear my sister's cast-offs. The only new thing I ever get are hats because even my Mother doesn't expect me to wear a ragged old boater with tatty ribbons that had spent a summer on Phyllis's head three years ago. Oh, and stockings and underthings too. But nothing actually interesting that is seen by the rest of the world. It's so unfair. You're so lucky, being an only child. Actually, when it comes to clothes Nora might as well be an only child too, because of only having a brother. The most unfair thing of all is that Julia, of all people, gets quite a lot of new things because by the time both Phyllis and I have worn something for ages even Mother agrees that it's too worn out to be given to Julia. Middle children never get anything nice.

Anyway! I will stop complaining about my ragged wardrobe and continue my story. When I stopped writing earlier, Mabel had just left the tearoom. Grace looked after her suspiciously.

'What's all this about Mr. Asquith's visit?' she said.

'Didn't you know?' said Nora innocently. 'He's coming to Dublin next week.'

Grace scrunched up her nose in irritation.

'Of course I knew that,' she said. 'But what did that girl mean when she asked if you were going to protest?'

'She's a suffragette,' said Nora.

'Yes, I did guess that,' snapped Grace. 'But what protest is she talking about? I hope there's not going to be any more window smashing.'

'I'm sure there won't be,' I said, though I wasn't totally sure. After all, no one has given me any details of the protests yet. And I don't think Mabel would have mentioned the protests to us at all if anything illegal were planned. 'But you must have known the suffrage campaigners would do something when Mr. Asquith was here. After all, they've protested against Mr. Redmond often enough.'

Grace sniffed. 'And made a disgrace of themselves too,' she said. 'My father read in the paper that they were brawling in the street.'

'They certainly were not,' I said hotly. 'That was just the Ancient Order of Hibernians causing trouble.'

'The Ancient Order of Hibernians would do no such thing,' said Grace. 'My Uncle Thomas is a member.'

I might have known Grace would be related to one of those dreadful Hibernians. Though as soon as I thought this I felt a little guilty, because of course she's related to Nora too.

'I didn't know that,' said Nora.

'Well, he's not your uncle, is he?' said Grace. 'He's Father's brother. Anyway, he and Father told Mother that the suffragettes were asking for trouble, making shows of themselves like that, and she quite agreed with them. And so do I.'

I couldn't think of anything to say that wouldn't set off a row, and right now we can't afford to fight with Grace, not with her staying in Nora's house. So I said, 'Good for you, Grace. Now, I feel like some fresh air.'

'We've only just got here,' said Grace. 'I haven't even

finished my buns.'

'All right,' said Nora. 'You can stay here and we'll get some fresh air. We'll walk around the tearoom.'

'Fine,' said Grace. She and Nora glared at each other, and for a moment I could actually see a family resemblance between them. They're both very good at looking fierce. Then Nora turned on her heel and marched out of the tearoom.

'We'll just walk around the trees outside,' I said to Grace, and hurried after Nora. I found her kicking a stone along the gravel path.

'I can't bear her!' said Nora. 'All that guff about her stupid uncle.'

'Did you know he was an Ancient Hooligan?' I said. But Nora hadn't known anything of the kind.

'I've hardly ever met him,' she said. 'I think the last time I saw him was at Christmas when we visited their house, and he wasn't talking about anything political then.'

'We've got to be careful what we say in front of Grace, you know,' I said.

Nora sighed. 'I know.' She sat down on a bench and kicked another stone. 'But it's so difficult when she starts saying things like that.'

I sat beside her.

'We must rise above her,' I said. 'I know that's easier said than done.'

'It certainly is,' said Nora. 'You should have heard her last night after supper. Boasting about how good at lessons she was.'

'But you know,' I went on, 'maybe ... maybe we could just try to be nice to each other.'

'Nice!' said Nora. 'She's not being very nice to me. Or you, for that matter.'

'I know,' I said. 'But we can't risk her saying something to anyone, not when Mr. Asquith's visit is so close. And,' I added, 'it might make things easier all round.'

'Easier how?' Nora looked sceptical.

'Well ... this bickering and fighting,' I said. 'It's all very well when it's just lunchtime at school. But it's quite exhausting when it's happening all the time.'

'I suppose you're right,' said Nora.

'So why don't we ... I don't know,' I said. 'Offer a peace treaty, like they do in wars.'

'I doubt she'd sign it,' said Nora.

'Mollie! I say, Mollie!'

It was Mabel's voice. I turned around to see her hurrying across the grass towards us. She was quite out of breath when she reached the bench.

'Is everything all right?' said Nora.

'I hope so,' said Mabel. 'Did I leave my big leather purse at your table in the tearoom when you bought your *Citizen*? I just tried to give someone change for a shilling and I realised I didn't have it with me.'

'I didn't notice it,' I said, glancing at Nora.

'Neither did I,' said Nora. 'But we can go back and check.'

'Where's your friend?' said Mabel, as we started walking towards the tearoom entrance.

'She's not our friend, exactly,' I said.

'She's not our friend at all,' said Nora. 'She's my cousin. And I hate her.'

Mabel looked taken aback.

'Goodness, Nora, you sound quite fierce,' she said.

'Actually, Mabel,' I said. 'When we go back in, maybe don't say too much about any suffrage activities. I mean, I don't know why you would, but just in case you felt like saying anything about the protests ...'

Mabel grinned. 'This cousin is not a supporter of the cause, I take it?'

'Quite the opposite,' said Nora.

'Ah,' said Mabel. 'I see. And I suppose that's why you were quite vague about your own protesting plans?'

'Exactly,' I said. I glanced at Nora. 'Actually, we did have a plan but we're not quite sure how practical it is ...'

And I told her about the rowing boat scheme.

'Goodness,' said Mabel. 'That's not a bad idea, you know.'

'Really?' I said. I'm not used to any grown-up (or sort of grown-up) approving of my ideas. Even Mabel, who is more sympathetic than a lot of almost-grown-ups I can think of (Phyllis and Kathleen).

'But I'm not sure you and Nora are the best women for the job,' said Mabel. 'Not that I don't think you're brave enough,' she added hastily. 'But I'd hazard a guess that you're not exactly experienced oarswomen.'

'Well, no,' I said.

'And Mollie gets terribly seasick,' said Nora, unnecessarily. 'But she is willing to sacrifice her tummy for the cause.'

'And her breakfast, probably,' said Mabel with a smile. 'I'm not much good on the water myself. It's a grand scheme, girls. But I think you could serve the cause just as well with something a little more, well, landlocked. Think about it.'

I was quite relieved to hear this. I must admit that the more I thought about trying to hold up a banner while rowing out to sea (and possibly being swept away towards Wales), the more unwell I had felt. So it was good to know that if we decided not to embark on an aquatic protest, Mabel wouldn't consider us cowards.

By now we had reached the entrance of the tearoom, where Grace was waiting for us. To my surprise, she was flicking through the pages of the *Irish Citizen* when we walked in, though as soon as she saw us she quickly put the magazine back where Nora had been sitting.

'Where have you been?' she snapped.

Then she saw Mabel and her expression changed. 'Oh, hello, Miss Purcell.'

'Hello there,' said Mabel, in her usual friendly fashion. 'I don't suppose you've seen an impractically large leather purse anywhere about the place, have you?'

'I have, actually,' said Grace. She held up the purse. 'You left it on that chair.'

'Grace, you angel!' cried Mabel, who may not be as good a judge of character as I thought. She grabbed the purse and put it carefully back in her bag. 'There's a whole pound in it. If you hadn't found it, I'd have had to pay it all back out of my own money.'

'It's nothing,' said Grace. 'It was just sitting there.' But she looked quite pleased.

'Right, I must fly,' said Mabel. 'I've got to meet my Mother in Switzer's at two and I want to get as many of these *Citizen*s sold as I can before then. Bye, girls!'

And she ran off again, leaving me and Grace and Nora alone. There was a slightly awkward silence. All at once the idea of us trudging around the park being rude to each other for hours seemed utterly unbearable. Whatever Nora thought, I was going to try and make peace with Grace. At least, temporarily.

'Sorry we were gone for so long,' I said, awkwardly. Grace sniffed in that irritating way of hers, but I tried not to be annoyed by it.

'I don't expect better manners from a pair of suffragettes,' she said. 'Come on, then. Let's go for a walk down to the Nine Acres.'

And after that I really couldn't bring myself to offer the sign of peace. Mocking the cause, just after Mabel had been so nice to her! I decided that I wouldn't say anything to antagonise her. But I jolly well wasn't going to say anything particularly friendly either.

'Fine,' I said. And off we went. The weather was perfect – there was a nice light breeze so it wasn't too hot. But nobody said very much, and I don't think any of us were having a good time. Including Grace. It struck me, not for the first time, that lording it over everyone and sucking up to adults instead of just having a decent time with girls your own age can't be all that fun.

We trudged down through the trees without talking. The park is lovely, but it got rather dull after a while. I thought of E. Nesbit books and how the children in them are often bored during the summer, but then they find an enchanted castle or a magical Psammead or something like that, and I wished (even though of course I am far too old to believe in such things) that something similar would happen to us. But the most exciting thing that happened was when we saw some rabbits. They were very sweet. But it was cold comfort. Besides, as soon as they saw us they ran away at amazing speed. (They were even faster than the Menace, who I'm sure would have tried menacing them if he'd been anywhere in the vicinity.)

If Stella had been there instead of Grace – or if things were different with Grace – we could have had a jolly afternoon. We could have bought some oranges from one of the sellers and climbed a tree and stayed up there talking about all sorts of things. But of course that wasn't possible. Finally, just as the pleasant weather was starting to feel uncomfortably muggy, even under the shady trees, Nora said, 'We should probably turn back now. It'll take simply ages to get back to the gates.' I half expected Grace to object out of spite (I wouldn't have put it past Nora to do the same thing if their positions had been reversed), but she must have been feeling too hot and tired to fight with anyone because she just said, 'All right.'

And so we trudged back again. The weather was definitely muggy now, and by the time we reached the tram stop we were all hot and a bit smelly. I realised that I had been bitten by midges (and whenever I am bitten by midges the bites always swell up so I look as if I am covered in hideous boils – Mother put some calamine lotion on them when I got home but they still look absolutely awful). The tram was very crowded and stuffy, but Nora and I managed to squeeze into a seat together.

'Well!' said Nora. 'What an utter waste of a trip to the park.'

'It was, a bit,' I said. 'Though I couldn't help thinking that maybe …' I trailed off.

'Maybe what?' said Nora.

'Maybe if we really did make peace with Grace, these outings wouldn't be so bad. They might even be fun.' Even as I said the last words I knew they didn't sound very convincing.

'Mollie Catherine Carberry!' Nora's face was a picture of shock. 'A truce before the visit is all very well. But are you actually suggesting we make friends with that monster?'

'Well, not when you put it like that …' I said.

'Have you forgotten how awful she was to Daisy when she won the Cup?' said Nora. 'And how she threatened to tell on us until Stella stopped her? Have you forgotten how beastly she's been about the cause?'

I had actually briefly forgotten about how dreadfully she'd behaved to Daisy. But even so.

'Maybe she can be reformed!' I said. 'Oh Nora, you can't pretend that fighting with her all the time is making you very happy.'

'I'd rather be miserable than suck up to Grace,' said Nora. She folded her arms and glared at me in her fiercest fashion. 'I'm disappointed in you, Mollie.' And she turned away from me and stared out the window, even though there was nothing to see out there but a filthy old coal van.

It was bad enough squabbling with Grace, but the thought of being at odds with Nora too was simply too much for me.

'All right,' I said. 'No overtures of friendship. I promise'

'Good,' said Nora, in a less fierce voice. I glanced at the far end of the tram, where Grace was squashed in between a sturdy man in a flannel suit and a tired-looking young woman with ink-stained fingers. Without an audience to simper or growl at, Grace just looked tired and a bit sad. Against my better judgment, I found myself wishing I hadn't made that promise to Nora.

By the time we got off the second tram we were all too hot and tired to say very much as we trudged along Drumcondra Road. When we reached the corner where our routes separated, I decided that it wouldn't count as an overture of friendship if I just asked Grace when she was going to the club on Tuesday.

'In the afternoon,' she said. She was clearly too exhausted to say anything snooty.

'Oh,' I said. 'Well, good luck. Will I see you on Tuesday, Nora?'

For a moment I thought Nora was going to tell me not to, but she just said, 'All right.' But she said it in such a flat way I felt rotten. Nora and I hardly ever fall out. But she was clearly still annoyed with me for suggesting a truce.

'Bye then,' I said.

'Bye,' said Nora. And she and Grace headed off in the direction of her house. I looked after them for a moment and slowly made my way down the road that leads to my road. I hadn't gone more than ten yards when I heard rushing footsteps behind me. It was Nora, and as soon as I turned around she flung herself into my arms.

'Steady!' I cried.

'I'm sorry!' said Nora, breathlessly. 'I've been a beast ever since we left the tearoom. Can you forgive me?'

'Of course I can,' I said. 'I blame the heat.'

'Call around on Tuesday morning as early as you can,' said Nora. 'Hopefully I will have survived our family outing tomorrow.'

'Good luck,' I said.

'I'll need it,' said Nora, but she did look happier now we had made peace. 'Now I'd better get back to Grace.'

I waved her farewell, feeling a lot more cheerful. Tomorrow is another day! And maybe I can use it to persuade Nora that we'll be better off if we try to get along with Grace. Wish me luck …

Best love and votes for women,
Mollie

Tuesday, 9th July, 1912.

Dear Frances,

I am looking at my itinerary and I realise you must definitely be in Boston now. I hope you manage to get to a bookshop in the city so you can investigate all the American (and Canadian) books. Imagine if you are reading *Anne of Green Gables* too! I have nearly finished it and I will be so sad when it's over. I do hope Mabel meant it when she said she would lend me the sequel.

But I have plenty of other things to think about, for today was an excellent day for many reasons. Number one, of course, was the fact that we were rid of Grace, so the question of being friendly with her or not didn't arise. And the second reason was that, for once, I myself was totally free. Not only had my mother not devised any terrible plans to keep me busy doing household chores, but she wasn't even at home to watch over me. In fact, I had the whole house to myself! Mother and Julia went out shortly after breakfast to visit Aunt Josephine, who has a bad cold and has taken to her bed. Everyone seems to be getting sick this summer. I hope I'm not stricken down by any fiendish germs before Mr. Asquith's visit (or after it, for that matter, seeing as we're meant to be going on holiday then).

I knew that Mother didn't particularly want to visit Aunt Josephine. (I'm pretty sure she doesn't like her any more than I do.) But Aunt Josephine had sent her a plaintive note asking if she could return a book of religious essays that Aunt Josephine had lent (unasked for) to Mother a few weeks ago and which, unbeknownst to Aunt Josephine, has been sitting untouched on top of the piano ever since. Apparently Aunt Josephine is now in need of divine solace and wants the book back straight away.

And Mother clearly felt so guilty about not reading the book (which looked very boring; I don't blame her for not going near it), and also about the idea of Aunt Josephine languishing on her sickbed looking for help from Our Lord, that she couldn't say no. She decided to take Julia with her because Aunt Josephine loves Julia and perhaps seeing her would cheer her up.

'And seeing the rest of us wouldn't?' I said, when Mother announced her plans over breakfast. I don't even know why I was saying it really, it's not as if I wanted to go. Quite the opposite in fact. But it's rather insulting to know someone doesn't want to see you, even if you don't want to see them.

'I'm afraid not,' said Mother. She turned to Julia, who

was looking particularly angelic this morning, even with a mouthful of toast and poached egg. 'You don't mind, do you, dear?'

Julia swallowed her egg and said, 'Of course not.' She is the only one of us who can stomach Aunt Josephine, and that's only because Aunt Josephine fusses over her and buys her lots of holy pictures and cards and things for her vast collection. Aunt Josephine has clearly given up the rest of us as a lost cause, but she thinks there's still hope for Julia.

Anyway, that took care of two members of the household. And then Phyllis was on an outing to Howth with Kathleen and Mabel, probably plotting secret suffragette business. (I didn't get a chance to ask her for details because she announced her plan shortly before breakfast and then left before I could talk to her on her own.) Harry was off in the Phoenix Park with Frank, playing cricket with some boys from school – apparently this cricket-playing has become a regular thing.

And Father was at work, of course, where I hoped he would find some time to write more of Peter Fitzgerald's adventures. Things have been very busy in the Department recently, so he hasn't had the leisure hours to devote himself to his fictional pursuits. In fact, we haven't had a new installment for a few days now, but he assures me there will be more of the story when things calm down at work. Last night I asked him what he is going to do when

Peter's adventures finally come to an end.

'You know, Mollie, I haven't really thought of that.' He looked quite surprised.

'You could always send the story to a publisher,' I suggested. I don't tell Father this very often, but really Peter Fitzgerald's adventures are terribly exciting and I bet other people would be as entertained by them as we all are. Father smiled.

'That's what I thought I'd do when I started writing it,' he said. 'But the story's rather run away from me, don't you think? I mean, if it were a book it would be hundreds and hundreds of pages long at this stage. I don't think anyone would be able to pick it up in order to read it.'

I suppose he really has been writing it for a long time.

'You could divide it into two separate books,' I said. 'Or three, even.'

I didn't think Father would take my suggestion seriously (he never usually does), but he actually looked quite thoughtful for a moment. Then he said briskly, 'Maybe I will. But I don't know when I'll have time to do any editing, not with all the work I have to do at the office.'

Anyway, sorry as I am that Father can't devote himself entirely to his literary endeavours, I knew that I would be alone in the house all morning, apart from Maggie and Mrs. Carr who had come in, as she does regularly, to scrub down the range and other heavy work. And I knew they wouldn't interfere with me as long as I didn't do anything dangerous or startlingly noisy. So it was with a light heart that I ran (well, walked quickly) round to Nora's house. I was going to tell Nora about my free house as soon as she came to the door, but I didn't get a chance straight away.

'She's gone!' Nora hissed in a noisy whisper, and without another word she grabbed my arm and whisked me up to her room. It turned out that Grace had set off for the tennis club straight after breakfast. Mrs. Cantwell seemed to have got over her disappointment that Nora had no desire to go there with her.

'I think she knew that expecting me and Grace to spend all our time together without killing each other was rather a stupid idea,' Nora said. 'I nearly burst with the effort of not fighting with her on the trip to Bray yesterday.'

'Was it really that bad?' I was impressed that Nora had managed to restrain herself.

'Just her usual self,' said Nora. 'But I think mother noticed the strain I was under. So for the moment she thinks anything that keeps Grace busy and away from me is A Good Thing.'

'Is she at the tennis club all day today?' I asked.

Nora nodded. 'And I jolly well hope she likes it because if she doesn't we'll be back where we started.'

'Well, even if she does hate it,' I said, 'we're free for today.' And I told her about my free house. She agreed that we should make our way there without delay, in case her mother had a change of heart and tried to force us to join Grace on the tennis court. As it turned out, Mrs. Cantwell seemed quite happy to see us go, though she did ask if we were sure we didn't want to go to the club. She really does want Nora and Grace to be friends.

'I'm sure you'd enjoy it,' she said (rather plaintively, I thought).

'We don't want to get in Grace's way.' Nora's expression was utterly innocent. 'We want to give her a chance to shine among her new club-mates.'

Which was very clever of her, I thought, and clearly impressed Mrs. Cantwell, who said, 'Well, it's nice of you to think of that.'

Ten minutes later we were back in my house, which is much nicer when my family aren't in it. We didn't even have to hide away in my room or in a corner of the garden, as we usually do when I have visitors. We could loll around in the drawing room without anyone coming in and telling me to do some boring chore (Mother) or demanding that we give up the good seats (Harry) or making us listen to their piano practice (Julia). It was very restful. And it meant that we could make suffragette plans without worrying about anyone overhearing.

'So,' I said, when we were both ensconced in the most comfortable chairs in the drawing room, the ones usually baggsed by Father, Mother and Phyllis. 'What are we going to do for Mr. Asquith's visit, now that Mabel has nixed the boat plan? He'll be here for a few days, after all.'

I have to admit that I'm very relieved Mabel advised us against taking out a boat. And it's not because I'm worried about my seasickness, which is a mere trifle. It's more that I don't actually know how to row. And neither does Nora. I'm not sure how we could manage to get out into the bay AND hold up a banner. We'd be more likely to be swept out to sea, and though I am willing to do a lot for the cause (like put myself through the horrors of seasickness and then spend a day wobbling about on land because my legs have gone funny), I am not exactly willing to meet a watery grave. And Nora feels much the same way. We both trust Mabel's wisdom so we don't feel too guilty for abandoning the idea.

I have also abandoned my plan of sneaking onto the stage at the Theatre Royal. I read something about Asquith's visit in the paper and it turns out that he is not going to a show in the Theatre Royal, he is just having some sort of meeting there. And women can only go if they are vouched for by a man, and even then they can only sit in the dress circle, so we certainly won't get in. But of course we are resourceful girls, and we came up with some other ideas. After all, he will be parading through the streets after he arrives at Kingstown so we'll have a chance to attract his attention.

'We should make our own unique posters,' suggested Nora. 'Not just the usual VOTES FOR IRISH WOMEN business. Something that shows Mr. Asquith that the young people of Ireland are pro-suffrage. You know, so he knows the problem isn't going to go away once all the older ladies get too feeble to protest.'

I thought this was an excellent idea.

'Votes for Irish Girls!' I cried.

'That's not bad, but we should also write "When We Grow Up",' said Nora. 'We don't expect the vote right now. It's not as if Irish boys have the vote either.'

'True,' I said. 'But maybe people would assume the "when we grow up" part. I mean, they couldn't think we believe we should have the vote straight away.'

'Those horrible Ancient Hooligans would believe anything of us,' said Nora. 'And they'd use it to make us look stupid.' Which was a very good point.

'Anyway, we can do more than wave posters,' I said. 'We could march along behind his carriage and sing our song.' In case you've forgotten, this is the song we wrote to the tune of the Kerry Dances. It's jolly good even if I say so myself. I'd rather hoped it would become a suffrage anthem, but we haven't really had a chance to share it with the rest of the movement yet. Apart from Phyllis, of course, and she seemed amused by it rather than impressed. But that's just because she thinks of me as her little sister and doesn't take my work seriously.

'Maybe we should write some new lyrics,' suggested Nora. 'You know, aimed directly at the Prime Minister.'

Well, I thought that this was a wonderful idea so I got a notebook and pencil and we set to work. But it turned out to be even more difficult than the last time. Of course, it would help if the Prime Minister had a surname that rhymed with more things. Nothing really rhymes with Asquith. Apart from 'ask with' of course, but Nora said that isn't really a rhyme because it's essentially the exact same sound.

I had suggested:

Come and listen Mr Asquith
To the cries of the Irish young
There is not much we can ask with-
out going on too long.

But even I had to admit it didn't sound very catchy. Or even make much sense. Or scan very well. Anyway, we've got over a week to think about it. In the meantime, we have decided to leave his name out of it altogether.

'How about this?' said Nora.

When you promise Home Rule to us
Some will scream and shout with joy
But we want it for the ladies
And not just for the men and boys.

'But you just pointed out that boys won't get it any more than we will,' I said.

'So I did.' Nora sighed and rubbed her eyes. 'I think my brain is getting addled from all this song writing. Will we see if Maggie has any lemonade?'

Unfortunately, Maggie didn't. She was too busy chopping up green things for a large salad that was going to be part of lunch.

'But you can have an apple each,' she said, pointing with her knife at the bowl on the dresser.

'Maggie,' I said, through a mouthful of apple. 'If we put "Votes for Irish Girls" on our posters for Mr. Asquith's visit, do you think people would know we meant we wanted the vote when we grow up and not now?'

Maggie put down the knife and turned to look at me and Nora. Her expression was so serious I swallowed quite a large chunk of apple in one go.

'Mollie.' Her voice was heavy. 'How many times do I need to tell you? Don't talk to me about any suffrage business. If your parents found out I was talking about these things with you, they'd think I was filling your head with notions, and that would be the end of me here.'

I felt ashamed of myself. She had pointed this out to me before, and I'd forgotten all about it. I do wonder sometimes if I'm a terribly selfish person.

'Sorry, Maggie,' I said humbly. 'I won't do it again.'

Maggie started chopping lettuce again. 'It's all right,' she said, without looking up at me. 'Now, off you go, the pair of you. I want to get this salad ready nice and early before your ma gets home.'

We went. I was just closing the door behind me when Maggie said quietly, almost as if she didn't want me to hear her, 'I don't think everyone would know you meant when you grow up. Try and think of something else.'

I didn't say anything. I just closed the door very gently and followed Nora into the drawing room. We were both unusually quiet for a moment. Then I told Nora what Maggie had said.

Nora sighed. 'Writing things for a cause is jolly difficult,' she said. Then I think she must have remembered our brave leaders in their prison cells, because she said, 'But I suppose it's nothing in comparison to what some people do.'

By the way, I now imagine the prison being like the Bastille in *A Tale of Two Cities*, which was absolutely ghastly and where you could languish for years while everyone forgot about you and you went mad with loneliness and misery. Phyllis told me that it's not quite that bad in Mountjoy. Apparently the suffragette prisoners are allowed to have meals sent in from the Farm Produce Restaurant – which I'm sure you remember is the place Phyllis and Mabel took us for buns last month – and people have been sending them books and flowers so they are in no danger of being neglected or forgotten. And they can wear their own clothes, not horrible grubby prison garb. But it must be pretty rotten all the same. For ages they were only allowed one visitor per fortnight and one letter per fortnight, which is hardly anything at all. And they weren't allowed to talk to each other when they were taking their daily exercise, which is so unfair.

They wanted the same rights as other political prisoners, which would allow them two visitors a day and an unlimited number of letters. Even the papers who are anti-suff said it wasn't fair that they weren't treated the same way as other political prisoners, so eventually the Lord Lieutenant agreed that they could have the same rights to visitors and letters. But they still aren't allowed to talk to each other in the prison yard. I keep imagining what it would have been like if Nora and I had both been sent to jail and then weren't allowed to exchange a single word. Nora says that we should come up with a way of sending messages through blinking or making shapes with our hands in case we ever do end up in Mountjoy, but I hope that won't come to pass. We should probably bear it in mind though.

Right now we were trying to come up with a poster, not a secret language. So I suggested that we just stick with something simple, rather than trying to do something clever.

'After all, we just painted "Votes for Irish Women" on the postbox, and that got into the police reports,' I pointed out.

'True,' said Nora. 'But this time we really need to catch Mr. Asquith's eye. After all, there are going to be crowds there.'

'Maybe we could do something different,' I said. 'Not a poster, I mean.' A thought struck me. 'Gosh, Nora, we could actually chain ourselves to some railings like the London suffragettes!'

But Nora didn't think this was practical.

'The only railings I can think of on his route through town are the Trinity College ones,' she said. 'And most of them are on top of a big wall. We'd never be able to chain ourselves up there.' This was true. And even if it weren't – or if we managed to fasten ourselves to the lower railings – there would definitely be plenty of crowds in front of us so the Prime Minister probably wouldn't see us. We needed to do something that allowed us to move around.

'I suppose posters will have to do instead,' I said. But by

the time Nora went home we still hadn't thought of the perfect slogan. I suppose we still have some time to do that.

~

I have some other news: Frank is arriving in our house on Friday. Nora of course is very amused by this prospect, but I just ignore her foolish remarks.

'You must admit it will be nice having him in the house,' she said.

'Only because he's generally a good influence on Harry,' I replied. 'Otherwise I really couldn't care less.'

Nora made a noise that sounded like a snort, but she refrained from making any more unamusing jests. Anyway, I was telling the truth. Well, I was telling the truth about Frank being a civilising influence on Harry. I suppose that's not the only reason it will be nice having him here. It'll be good to have someone in the house who doesn't talk down to me (Phyllis), insult me (Harry) or pray at me (Julia).

And that is the only reason I am looking forward to his visit.

Best love and votes for women,
Mollie

Wednesday, 10th July, 1912.

Dear Frances,

You must be in Boston by now, and I hope you are having a lovely time. For some reason I keep imagining that it is snowing there. I suppose it's because *Little Women* starts at Christmas. Though I know that in reality it must be jolly hot, even hotter than here, which is saying something. When Nora called over this morning she was bright red in the face. She was also on her own.

'Where's Grace?' I said.

'I don't know,' said Nora. 'Thank goodness. Gosh, it's hot.'

I was confused. 'Didn't she like the tennis club yesterday?'

'Oh, she loved it,' said Nora. 'But she's not playing there until this afternoon.'

'So where is she then?' Nora can be very annoying sometimes.

'She's gone to visit the Menace,' said Nora. 'And I hope they'll make each other very happy.'

'Was she actually serious about that?' I asked. 'I knew she liked him, but I thought she was just, you know, being Grace.'

'Apparently she was,' said Nora. 'She's going to take him for a walk. Though I'm sure she's regretting it now. He's probably dragging her down the middle of Dorset Street even as we speak.'

I remembered my last attempt to take the Menace for a walk, and shuddered.

'Let's go to the Botanic Gardens then,' I said. 'I brought a notebook. We can climb a tree and finalise our song lyrics.'

'Excellent scheme,' said Nora, and off we went. But we hadn't got far when we had an unexpected encounter.

'Good heavens,' said Nora. 'Look!'

I looked. An incredible sight met my eyes. Grace was striding along the pavement, looking as happy as I'd ever seen her. She was holding a leather lead, and on the end of it, strapped firmly into his harness, was the Menace. And the astonishing thing was, he was not behaving in his usual menacing fashion. Whenever I tried to take him for a walk ('tried' being the operative word), he strained and strained at his lead the whole time, as if eager to get away. He does this when Mrs. Sheffield takes him for a walk too, by the way, so it's not just me. But today he was very different. Today he was ... prancing.

Yes. Prancing. Barnaby the Menace, the most badly behaved dog in the world, was bouncing along the pavement on his fluffy little legs, looking as innocent as if he'd never run away from an unfortunate girl who was meant to be looking after him, or never jumped up on the same unfortunate girl's skirt and ruined it. (The stains still haven't come off. There must have been more than dust on his horrible paws.) Even his button eyes looked less malevolent and more benign than usual as he approached us.

'Hello, girls,' said Grace. 'Sit, Barnaby.'

AND HE SAT.

I was so astonished I couldn't say a word. For a long moment Nora and I stared at the incredible sight, until finally I regained the power of speech and said, 'How did you get him to do that?'

Grace tossed her curls.

'You just have to treat him with respect,' she said. 'He's a lovely dog.'

I have to admit I was genuinely impressed. I don't think even Mrs. Sheffield has managed to get him to sit on command before.

'Bravo.' I meant it, too. 'Honestly, Grace, he really is a Menace, I couldn't possibly manage him. You must be awfully good with him.'

I don't know who was more astonished by the fact that these words had come from my lips – me, Nora, or Grace, who was so surprised to hear praise from me she forgot to toss her hair or simper or look superior and just said, 'Oh, thank you.'

'Where are you taking him?' I asked, hoping it wasn't the Botanic Gardens. After Monday, I couldn't bear another silent trudge. Besides, I really wanted to work on the song lyrics with Nora.

'Down to the river,' said Grace. 'Mrs. Sheffield says he likes looking at the ducks.'

I could well believe that, though of course if Barnaby was looking at ducks, it was only because he was dreaming of chasing them. I wondered if he could swim. I bet he could, if only to unsettle people. The thought of him moving silently through the water, like the pike I once saw in the river when we visited Uncle Piers in Louth, was a very unnerving one.

'Well, I hope it's fun,' said Nora.

Grace looked at her suspiciously. She clearly thought Nora was being very sarcastic. But I knew Nora was making a supreme effort to be polite, and I was awfully proud of her.

'How was your first day at the club?' I asked. I knew Nora had said she loved it, but that could have been wishful thinking.

'Marvellous.' Grace's face lit up. 'Miss Casey – she's the lady we met on Saturday, you know – she really wants more girls to join the club. She thinks there should be just as many girls as boys. She's very keen on fair play, you see.'

'Goodness.' I couldn't help thinking of what Grace had

said in the past about women who wanted fair play for girls, but I thought it was better to say nothing. 'Well, we're going to the Botanic Gardens.'

I was quite relieved that they don't allow dogs there because it meant I couldn't possibly ask Grace and the Menace to join us, even if I'd madly wanted to. The Menace looked up at Grace and gave a gentle tug at his lead. If he'd been with me, he'd have undoubtedly yanked it right out of my hand.

'I'd better take him to see those ducks,' said Grace, sounding almost normal.

We bade her goodbye extremely politely and watched as she and Barnaby, who was, miraculously, continuing to behave himself, trotted down the street in the direction of the river.

'Maybe that Miss Casey is a good influence on her,' I said. 'She sounds very unlike herself today.'

Nora snorted. 'I think she's beyond good influences. Come on, let's go to the Gardens.'

We didn't get much further in our song-writing in the gardens. Or in our plans to join the protest. In fact, we got quite distracted because we bumped into Mary Cummins from school, who was there with her sister. Mary is awfully nice – you might remember that she was not unsympathetic to the cause when she found out we supported it. And she was horrified now when

Nora told her about Grace.

'In your room?' Her face was a picture. 'For a whole fortnight?'

Nora nodded. 'But she's joined the tennis club. So that's been keeping her busy.'

'Still …' Mary shuddered. And maybe it's because of my determination to be civilised, but I found myself feeling weirdly uncomfortable. It was one thing for me and Nora to give out about Grace, but talking about her behind her back with other people felt strangely catty. So I changed the subject and asked Mary how her holidays were going. Her family were going to Bray in a few weeks, but we arranged to meet when she was back and my family had returned from Skerries.

'I think,' I said to Nora, after we'd bidden Mary and her sister goodbye, 'that Mary is a possible convert to the cause.'

'I think you might be right,' Nora agreed. 'Though we won't convert anyone if we can't even come up with a song.'

'We can do that now,' I said. 'Come on, let's find somewhere nice to sit and we can write some new lyrics.'

But somehow we ended up sitting down by the river for the entire afternoon, talking about books. I finished *Anne of Green Gables* this morning and I have lent it to Nora. She already likes the sound of it, not least because, like Anne, she has reddish hair.

I feel a little guilty that we didn't come up with a perfect song or banner, but we have an entire week to do it. And besides, even the most doughty campaigners need a rest sometimes, don't they?

Best love and votes for women,
Mollie

Friday, 12ᵗʰ July, 1912.

Dear Frances,

Right now — at least, if you're sticking to the schedule you sent in your letter — you must be in New York City. When you come home I hope you can tell me what the tallest building in the world is like. Frank told me that it is in the centre of New York and is called The Metropolitan Life Insurance Building, which is a rather boring name for a giant tower. It has about fifty floors which I can't even imagine; I think a building with three floors is pretty big. I would love to know if you have seen it (I can hardly see how you'll be able to miss it) and whether it really does have fifty floors. That sounds like an exaggeration to me.

Anyway, as I mentioned Frank a few sentences ago you might be wondering if he has finally arrived in our house. And he has. In fact, he arrived this morning, just as we were finishing breakfast.

'That must be Nugent,' said Harry, pushing back his chair and jumping to his feet. 'At last, I won't be alone in this house of females.'

'Ahem,' said Father mildly.

'Sorry, Father,' said Harry, shoving his way past my

chair and practically knocking me into the leftover toast.
'I'll get it Maggie!' he yelled from the hall, and a moment
later the front door was opened and Frank, looking
uncharacteristically awkward, came into the dining room.

'Sorry Mr. Carberry, Mrs. Carberry,' he said. 'I didn't
mean to disturb your breakfast.'

'We're just finished, dear,' said Mother, and Father stood
up and shook Frank's hand.

'You're more than welcome, my dear young fellow,' he
said. 'Now, I think there might be some toast left if you'd
like some.'

But Frank shook his head.

'They gave me a huge breakfast at home,' he said.
'Not that they think you won't feed me properly here, of
course,' he added quickly, looking a little flustered.

'Come on, Nugent,' said Harry, slapping Frank on the
back in a ridiculously hearty fashion. He never normally
does things like that, and Frank was clearly taken by
surprise. 'Let's get your bags up to my room and leave this
lot to their toast.'

'See you all later,' said Frank, and followed Harry out of
the room.

'What a nice young fellow he is,' said Mother. She
looked at me and Julia. 'I hope you two won't be pestering
and annoying him. He's our guest after all.'

The cheek of her, lumping me in with Julia and

thinking I would – I can hardly bear to write it –
PESTER AND ANNOY Frank!

'Of course I won't,' I said. 'In fact, I'm going to stay out
of his and Harry's way. May I please be excused and go to
Nora's house?'

Mother nodded and, without another word, I got up
and stalked out of the room. At least I tried to stalk. Harry
hadn't put his chair back in under the table and I banged
into the corner of it, which really, really hurt, but I ignored
the agony and kept on walking. It is very difficult to retain
my dignity in this house. I could hear Frank and Harry
chatting away upstairs. Ever since Harry's voice started to
change he has sounded very grumbly. Frank's voice has
changed too, but he sounds like a normal person. I was
looking for my outdoor shoes when he came down the
stairs.

'Hello!' he said. 'Where are you off to?'

'Just Nora's house,' I said. There was a pause, but not an
especially awkward one. 'I hope it's not going to be too
boring for you staying here. When your parents are off on
holiday, I mean.'

'Well, it's not exactly a holiday.' Frank's smile was wry.

'My friend Frances is in New York,' I said. 'I wish I
could go there. It sounds so exciting.'

And that's when he told me about the tall building.
But before we could talk about it anymore, Harry came

thundering down the stairs saying, 'Come on, Nugent. Let's get some lemonade in the kitchen.' So I left them to it.

When I got to Nora's she was sitting in the garden reading *Anne of Green Gables*, while George hit a tennis ball against the wall.

'That's a strangely soothing sound,' I said, sitting down beside her.

'I've barely noticed it.' Nora's eyes were bright. 'Goodness, Mollie, this book is wonderful.'

It's always a nice feeling when you give someone a book you love and they like it as much as you do. We talked about it for a bit, and I almost gave away some bits of the plot that Nora hasn't reached yet, but I stopped myself in time. After a while, having made sure that George was out of earshot, I said, 'I've had an idea.'

Because I had. It had struck me on my way over to Nora's house.

'Really?' Nora looked insultingly surprised.

'We should go to the meeting tomorrow,' I said. 'You know, the weekly IWFL one in the Phoenix Park.'

'What good will that do?' said Nora.

'Well,' I said, 'Phyllis won't tell us anything about their plans. We don't even know for definite if they're going to go out in the boat. Maybe they'll announce their intentions at the meeting, and we can see if we can join in.'

'I suppose it couldn't hurt.' Nora was thoughtful.

'Well, we haven't come up with anything else,' I said.

Nora's face brightened. 'Actually, I have. A new verse for our song.'

'Go on then,' I said.

Nora took a deep breath and then, singing softly so as not to be overheard, she sang:

We will never cease our shouting
'til you heed our Irish call
Votes for men and votes for women
Votes for us and votes for all!

I stared at her in admiration. 'Goodness, Nora, that's not bad. And,' I added, 'Maggie's sister Jenny would approve of the votes for all. She thinks it's disgraceful that working men don't get the vote and men like our fathers do.'

'Well, that's just not fair play,' said Nora. 'As Grace would say.'

'Where is she, anyway?' I said.

'At the club, of course.' Nora yawned and stretched back in her chair. 'And long may she stay there.'

'You must admit,' I said, 'that the club seems to be doing her some good.'

'Maybe,' said Nora. 'But not at night. She told Mother she thought the camp bed was bad for her back and that meant she couldn't play tennis properly. So I've got to sleep in it all week!'

Maybe Grace hadn't reformed so much after all. But luckily she's playing at some beginners' tournament in the club tomorrow so we won't have to try and get rid of her before we go to the meeting in the park. We arranged to meet at our usual corner, and it wasn't until Nora had walked me out to the front door that she remembered something.

'Hang on!' she said, when I was already walking down the short tiled path that leads from her front door to the pavement. 'Didn't a certain SOMEONE arrive at your house today?'

'I'm so sorry, I don't know what you mean!' I said. And then I ran down the road before she could ask any more annoying questions. Besides, I was already late for tea. I was quite looking forward to talking to Frank over the cake and buns, but when I got home he and Harry were nowhere to be seen.

'Oh,' said Mother, when I asked – very casually, and as if I had no real interest in the answer – where they were. 'I believe they've gone out with Frank's uncle. There's no room in his house for Frank to stay, but he's taking both the boys out to the theatre to make up for Frank missing his holiday.'

And now I'm going to bed and they're still not back.

Not that I really care, of course. But it would be nice to have the opportunity to be polite to our guest.

Best love and votes for women,
Mollie

P.S.

I forgot to say that Mabel, that wondrous girl, gave Phyllis a copy of another book about *Anne of Green Gables* to give to me. It is called *Anne of Avonlea*, and I have just started it, but it looks just as good as the first one. I don't know if it's been published here yet but it is out in America — she got it from her cousins — so I do hope you get hold of a copy of it!

Sunday, 14th July, 1912.

Dear Frances,

I have been thinking about the suffrage movement in America. I wonder if it is popular. I realise that I don't really know anything about it at all. If I could afford to send you a telegram, I would ask you to get me an American suffrage magazine. I wonder what their meetings are like, because Nora and I went to the Phoenix Park Meeting yesterday and unfortunately it didn't go that well. For us, anyway.

I had thought it was better not to give Phyllis any hint that we were going to the meeting, but I didn't see much of her anyway because she left the house soon after breakfast. She said she was going to help Mabel try on her wedding dress so of course I knew she was off on suffrage business. I do think this fictional cover story about Mabel getting married has become very impractical. What is Phyllis going to do in a few months? Tell my Mother about an imaginary wedding? Start referring to Mabel as Mrs. Pretend-Surname? It's quite ridiculous. Though really, I'm hardly one to talk, given all the lies I've told over the past few months.

It was strange having Frank at the breakfast table. He seemed to find it a little strange too and was a bit quiet at first, though of course Harry made enough noise for the pair of them. But Mother and Father talked to him very nicely and soon he was laughing with the rest of us over a funny story about Father's office.

'I hope you'll be joining us to hear the next installment of my novel,' said Father. 'The Adventures of Peter Fitzgerald.'

Harry looked a bit embarrassed and said, 'Frank's too old for storytelling.' But Father said, 'Nonsense! Even Phyllis likes to listen to Peter's adventures.' And Phyllis laughed and said, 'I certainly do.'

'I look forward to it,' said Frank, who really is a very decent guest. But I didn't speak much to him after breakfast, because he and Harry were going off to the house of one of their many friends who don't seem to have first names – at least, they never refer to them by their first names. It's always Harrington and Sheridan and Murphy. Today it was Harrington and, as they were going, Frank grinned at me and said, 'See you later, Mollie.'

I felt strangely cheerful as I bounced down the road to meet Nora. I had told Mother we had met Mary Cummins in the Gardens the day before (which was true) and were going to her house for tea (which of course was not, but I thanked heaven that we had bumped into Mary because it gave me the idea for a fresh excuse. Although I am not sure I should be thanking heaven for something that inspired me to tell a lie). I had had to raid my money-box to get enough money for the tram fare to the park. I only just had enough; we wouldn't be getting any buns in the tea-room that afternoon.

'Being a campaigner is jolly expensive,' said Nora, as we paid our fare on the second tram.

'If only we had bicycles,' I said, 'we could just pedal there and back.'

I longed for bicycles even more as we trudged through the heat to the site of the meetings. I wish it were nearer the gates. The park was full of people and when we arrived at the spot where the usual platform was arranged, there was quite a large crowd. My heart sank as I realised that a few of them were already yelling insults. But there were a fair few people, men and women, who were clearly there to listen. I caught sight of Mabel, Kathleen and Phyllis standing near the platform with their bags of *Irish Citizens* and pulled the brim of my hat down over my eyes. A woman mounted the platform to the applause and jeers of the crowd.

'Now,' said Nora, 'let's hope they tell us what they're planning for Thursday.'

But alas the speakers didn't reveal any such thing. The speeches were jolly good, and very inspiring (even though sometimes the speakers' words were drowned out by the vulgar insults of the rowdies, in which the words 'You belong in Mountjoy!' featured prominently), but we didn't learn anything about Asquith's visit that we hadn't known already.

When the speeches were over, Nora sighed. 'Well, it was worth a try,' she said. 'What will we do now?'

I looked towards the platform, where Phyllis, Kathleen and Mabel were deep in conversation.

'Go home before they see us,' I said. But alas, just at that moment Phyllis glanced up and I knew from the expression on her face that she had spotted us. Before we could make a run for it (which we wouldn't have done anyway, it would be far too undignified), she strode across the grass to us, followed by Mabel and Kathleen. There was no escape.

'Hello, Phyllis,' I said, as brightly as I could.

'Oh for goodness' sake.' Phyllis's face was grim. 'What are you two doing here?'

'We're attending a public meeting,' I said. 'As we have every right to do.'

'You really should stay out of this.' Kathleen could barely conceal her contempt. 'It's not suitable for kids.'

I don't know why Kathleen has to be so superior all the time. She's even worse than Phyllis. Thank heaven for Mabel, who actually remembers what it was like to be young (you'd think the other two were a hundred years old, the way they carry on).

'Come on, Kathleen,' Mabel said. 'They're not doing any harm. I think it's rather impressive, how committed they are to the cause.'

'Mabel!' said Kathleen. 'Don't encourage them!'

'We can't afford to turn away any supporters,' argued Mabel.

'Kids don't count,' said Kathleen, brushing back a feather which had fallen over her face. I may be a kid in your eyes, I thought, but at least I'm not wearing a hat that looks like a bomb went off in a hen house. I didn't say that out loud, though.

'We want to protest the Prime Minister's visit,' I said.

'Out of the question.' Phyllis was firm.

'I don't see why they shouldn't do something,' said Mabel.

'They're too young!' cried Phyllis. 'And you're just giving them ideas.'

'I just think that if they want to join us in the Nassau Street house after the poster parade,' Mabel began, but Phyllis cut her off with a furious whisper.

'Shut up!' she hissed, just as I said, 'What Nassau Street house?'

'Don't tell her,' said Phyllis, but Mabel ignored her.

'Some people in the IWFL have rented an upstairs

room in a house on Nassau Street,' said Mabel. 'And a group of us are going to go there and hang flags and things out of the window as Mr. Asquith goes by.'

What a wonderful idea! And it would solve all my and Nora's problems about being too short to be seen by the Prime Minister.

'Oh Phyllis!' I cried. 'We have to go.'

'No, you don't.' Phyllis glared at Mabel. 'And you shouldn't have mentioned it to them. Now they won't give me any peace.'

'Well, I'm sorry about that,' said Mabel. 'But really, it shouldn't be a secret. It's not like the window smashing. We're not doing anything wrong or dangerous. Anyone can rent some rooms and wave some posters and flags and things. And it's even safer than the poster parade because we won't be out in the street.'

'We don't want children getting in the way,' said Kathleen, in her superior tone. I felt like knocking her stupid feathery hat right off her head.

'We wouldn't get in the way!' I cried.

'We're quite small,' Nora pointed out. 'We wouldn't even take up much room.'

'That's enough!' Phyllis snapped. 'We are not discussing this, and certainly not here. Go home, the pair of you. '

'But Phyllis …' I began.

'Go home!' Phyllis looked really angry now. Maybe we

finally had pushed her to her limits.

'All right then.' I sounded as dignified as I possibly could. 'Come on, Nora.'

As soon as we were out of earshot Nora said, 'We're going to get to that house, aren't we?'

'Of course we are,' I said firmly. Though by the time we got home we hadn't thought of a way of doing so. And I still haven't. But we will definitely think of something. If Phyllis won't give way, maybe we should try getting Mabel to plead our case? Although if that ploy didn't work, it would only harden Phyllis's heart further against us.

Oh, it is all very complicated. And there are only a few days left to sort something out. It was quite a relief to spend most of today on a trip to the beach at Dollymount Strand. We went out on the tram after Mass and had a picnic lunch. Then we all ran around on the beach (even Phyllis) and played beach cricket. Frank and I were on the same side with Phyllis, playing against Father, Harry and Julia (Mother was looking after the picnic and watched the game from a rug) I wasn't very good, but it was so much fun I didn't really care, and Frank didn't seem to mind even when I failed to catch what Harry rudely told me was 'the sort of throw a baby could have caught'.

If Frank hadn't been there, I might have taken my shoes and stockings off, to make it easier to run around on the sand, but I felt a bit odd about doing that in front of him so I kept mine on. So did Phyllis and Mother, of course, though Julia took hers off to have a paddle.

I didn't bother mentioning any suffrage stuff to Phyllis while we were on the beach. And although she was a bit funny with me in the morning she seemed to thaw as the day progressed. So you never know; maybe she will give in.

Anyway, I am not going to think about it now. I am going to read *Anne of Avonlea* instead. Speaking of books, I had a very good chat about books on the beach with Frank this afternoon while we were eating the picnic. He told me he has been reading an exciting book by H. G. Wells called *War of the Worlds*, all about terrifying creatures from Mars who take over earth. It sounds very thrilling and he says he will lend it to me when he is finished, if I like. What a generous and sensible boy he is.

Best love and votes for women,
Mollie

Monday, 15th July, 1912.

Dear Frances,

Something very serious has happened. And (just in case
you are thinking along the same lines as Nora) it's
nothing to do with Frank staying in my house. No, this
is something much more serious than that. Phyllis knows
about me and Nora and the postbox. And it's all my fault.
If I hadn't got into a row with Phyllis it would never have
happened.

It happened just now. We were on our own in the
house: Father was at work, Harry and Frank had gone to
the park for yet another game of cricket, Julia was at her
friend's house, Mother was visiting Mrs. Sheffield, and
Maggie had gone to collect some shoes that had been left
into Mr. Kelly's shop for repair. Phyllis was in the garden,
sitting in the basket chair that's usually in her room (and
usually covered in clothes that she hasn't bothered to put
in the wardrobe), which she had dragged outside and put
under the crabapple tree. It was a jolly good idea because,
as she pointed out to me, it was a lot more comfortable
than sitting on a lumpy rug on the grass, which is all I had
to sit on.

Phyllis was reading a book called *Ann Veronica* by H. G. Wells (yes, the same author Frank has been reading, though apparently there are no strange creatures in this one). I had just finished writing a letter to Stella and had brought out *Anne of Avonlea*, which is just as good as *Anne of Green Gables* (hurrah for Mabel and her excellent taste in literature). For a while we were both absorbed in our books. It was a gorgeous day, nice and hot, but with a little bit of a breeze. In fact, it was the perfect weather for lolling about in the garden. But I couldn't get rid of the nagging feeling that time was running out and I had to say something to Phyllis about the Asquith protest, so after about twenty minutes I reluctantly put down *Anne* and said, 'Phyl?'

'Mmmm?' said Phyllis, not looking up from her book.

'About the Asquith protests. Can Nora and I come to the house in Nassau Street?'

Phyllis put down *Ann Veronica*.

'Oh for goodness sake, not all this again,' she said.

'We want to show Mr. Asquith that Irishwomen of all ages are against him,' I said.

'Irishwomen, you!' Phyllis scoffed. 'I don't think so.'

'Irish girls, then,' I said. 'Come on, Phyl, we'll be in a house. Those Ancient Hooligans can't get in. What can happen to us there?'

'Listen,' said Phyllis. 'I told you last month that I wasn't going to take you to any more suffrage things. And I meant it. You talked me round too many times before. That is, when you weren't trying to blackmail me.'

'But Phyl,' I protested. Phyllis stood up, placing the book on the chair.

'I'm going to get some water,' she said, and strode off towards the house. I followed her into the kitchen.

'And stop following me,' she said. 'Go back out to your rug.'

'Stop acting like a grown-up,' I said. 'You're only four years older than me.'

'Those four years make a lot of difference,' she said. 'I'm going to be starting university in a few months – unless Mother and Father change their mind.'

'Why on earth would they do that?' I said.

'Oh, I don't know,' said Phyllis, with crushing sarcasm. 'Maybe if they thought I was taking my little sister to dangerous political events where she could get herself killed.' She went to the dresser and took down a glass.

'I can look after myself,' I said. 'I'm not a baby.'

'Oh, aren't you?' said Phyllis, turning on the tap and filling the glass with water. 'Well, you sound like the worst sort of baby to me.' She put on a wheedling, whining voice. '"Take me to a meeting, Phyllis!"'

'Well, it worked before, didn't it?' I pointed out. 'And don't forget, we saved you from being discovered in the park that time.'

'Stop going on about that!' said Phyllis. 'You don't even know if Mrs. Sheffield would have seen me, even if you hadn't been crawling around on the grass. Anyway, it doesn't matter what happened in the past. I'm not taking you to Nassau Street and that's that.'

'It's not fair,' I said angrily. 'We're suffragettes too, we have a right to take part …'

Phyllis whirled round to face me with such ferocity that a lock of hair fell down into her eyes.

'For the love of God, Mollie, you're not suffragettes!' she yelled. 'Just because you've wandered into a few meetings and read a few magazines doesn't make you a suffragette.'

'We ARE suffragettes!' I yelled back. It was a good thing there was no one else at home to hear all this, not that I think Phyllis or I would have noticed if there had been. We were so worked up that our entire family could have walked in and we wouldn't have cared.

'You're just a couple of silly little girls,' snarled Phyllis. 'And I'm tired of having to look after you.' She started to walk towards the door but I grabbed her arm. The water splashed from its glass and went all over Phyllis's skirt.

'Look what you've done!' cried Phyllis, but I ignored her.

'Me and Nora don't need looking after,' I snapped back. 'We've risked more for the movement than you have.'

Phyllis gave one of those awful mocking laughs she does so well.

'Oh yes?' she said. 'What have you risked? Being sent to bed without supper for sneaking out to a meeting?'

'Going to prison!' I cried.

Later, Nora asked what on earth I was thinking, telling Phyllis like this. But the truth is I wasn't actually thinking at all. I was just so angry with Phyllis and her patronising, smug superiority. It was like a red mist had descended over my brain. As soon as I spoke, Phyllis looked at me with even more contempt.

'Prison!' she said. 'I can't believe you can joke about such a thing, with those poor ladies still in Mountjoy. You don't go to prison for going to a meeting in a public park. Otherwise Mrs. Sheffield and Barnaby would be behind bars for walking past one.'

'We haven't just gone to meetings,' I said. 'We broke the law. Which is more than you've ever done.'

I must have sounded sincere because Phyllis's disdainful expression started to fade.

'What on earth are you talking about?' she said.

'Do you remember the police court reports last month? When Mrs. Sheehy-Skeffington and the others were arrested?' I said.

'Of course I do,' said Phyllis. She tried to do another one of her mocking laughs, but it didn't really work this time. 'You're not going to pretend you were up in court too, are you?'

I ignored her.

'The police said someone had painted "Votes for Irish Women" on postboxes around town, but they couldn't find the culprits,' I said. 'Well, me and Nora did it. Not all the postboxes,' I added hastily. I didn't want to take credit for the brave actions of others. 'But one of them. On Eccles Street. I don't know who painted the other ones.'

Phyllis's jaw dropped open. I'd read about this happening in books, but I'd never seen it happen in real life.

'It's true,' I said. 'Honestly. We used leftover paint from Nora's house. We sneaked it out of her garden shed. And we got up early with Harry's alarm clock. No one saw us do it, if that's what you're worried about. And,' I said hurriedly, 'if someone else had been arrested for it, we'd have owned up.'

Phyllis stared at me for a long moment. Finally she spoke. 'But why?' she said.

Now it was my turn to stamp my foot in frustration.

'Because we're serious about the cause!' I said. 'We're not just silly girls playing games. We really care about it. And we did some chalking in town too. In College Green and Rutland Square. We chalked notices about the big meeting. We did it together once and then I went in and did it on my own.'

Phyllis sat down on Maggie's favourite kitchen chair with a bump. She still looked stunned.

'So you see,' I continued, 'we really are committed suffragettes. And it's not fair to say we can't protest against the Prime Minister, because we've already done more militant actions than most people have. Including you, if you don't mind me saying so. And we've got as much right to be at the protest as anyone else.'

'I don't believe it,' said Phyllis. She looked up at me. 'Does anyone else know about this?'

'Only our friend Stella,' I said. 'And she won't tell anyone. She's sworn to secrecy.' Phyllis didn't look very convinced – well, she still looked dazed more than anything else. 'And we would trust her with our lives,' I went on. Which looks very dramatic when I write it down, but felt quite normal when I was saying it. I suppose it was a dramatic sort of morning.

'So you actually … went out with a tin of paint?' said Phyllis.

'I told you we did,' I said impatiently. 'I'm not making it up. We chucked the tin in a hedge afterwards. It might still be there,' I added. We'd never actually gone back to check. 'You can go and have a look if you don't believe me. And even if it's gone, there's probably still some paint on the ground near it.'

'If Mother and Father ever found out …' Phyllis's voice trailed off.

'They won't,' I said. 'Why would they? I didn't even want to tell you about it. And I wouldn't have,' I added, 'if you hadn't been so annoying and unreasonable.'

'I need a cup of tea,' said Phyllis. She got up and filled the kettle in silence.

'Well?' I said, as she put the kettle on the hob. I was starting to feel a little nervous. I wasn't used to Phyllis being so quiet. 'What do you think?'

'I think …' said Phyllis. And then she looked me straight in the eye. 'I think you were very brave. Both of you.'

Now it was my turn to be surprised.

'Oh,' I said. 'Um. Thanks.'

'But please, PLEASE don't break the law again,' Phyllis said, and this time she sounded more earnest than hectoring. 'You really could get into terrible trouble.'

'I know,' I said.

'And if you did,' Phyllis went on, 'Mother and Father would definitely blame me.' I might have known she had a selfish motive, at least partly. But I suppose I couldn't blame her. She was right, after all. 'And that's not all. If you got arrested, they might not only change their minds about me going to college. They might not let you go either. And they might send both of us to one of the country aunts. Or send you to boarding school.'

I thought of leaving Dublin. Leaving Nora and Stella and everyone at school and Mother and Father and Maggie and even Julia and Harry. Even the thought of not seeing the Menace again felt like a wrench, strangely enough.

'I won't break the law again,' I promised. And I really did mean it.

'Good,' said Phyllis.

'So will you take us to Nassau Street?' I said hopefully. Phyllis sighed.

'I suppose so,' she said. 'I can't pretend you don't deserve it. You've certainly shown your commitment to the cause.'

I felt like jumping for joy but I didn't in case Phyllis thought I was being flighty and changed her mind.

'If anything bad does happen – which it won't,' I added hastily, 'I will tell Mother and Father that you had nothing to do with it. I'll tell them you didn't even know we were there.'

'I don't think they'll quite believe that,' said Phyllis. 'But it's worth a try.'

'Anyway, I'm sure it'll all go peacefully,' I said. 'After all, no one made a fuss at the ladies' trial.'

'True,' said Phyllis. 'But this is different. This is the Prime Minister. It mightn't just be us and the Antis who are out on the streets. There'll be huge crowds. Anything could happen.'

She made a good point. We're so wrapped up in suffrage

things that sometimes I forget about what Father calls the National Question. You know, Home Rule and full independence and all that sort of thing. I know Maggie's sister Jenny thinks Home Rule isn't enough. She said as much a few weeks ago, during her last visit to the kitchen.

'What's the point in just having a little playacting parliament when London will still make all the big decisions?' she said, taking a bite of one Maggie's delicious fairy cakes. Maggie snatched the cake out of her hands.

'No talk like that in front of the child,' she said, and there was real anger in her voice. I know Maggie supports the suffrage cause, and she might support the nationalist cause as well, but she's made it very clear that she won't talk about any of these things with me. Which is fair enough, but I still didn't like being called a child.

'I'm not a child,' I said. I'll be fifteen in a few months. You were working when you were my age.'

'Yes. I was. And the fact that you're sitting here eating a cake and not scrubbing a floor for a few pennies a week and half a bed in an attic,' said Maggie, quite sharply for her, 'is the reason why girls like you are still children.'

'Sorry, Maggie,' I said.

Maggie's face softened and she put her arm around my shoulders.

'You should enjoy it, love,' she said. 'Lord knows I didn't have much fun when I was your age.'

It does seem so unfair that Maggie and Jenny and girls like them should have to slave away, while girls like me and Nora and Grace are allowed play tennis and sit in the garden reading all day.

But back to me and Phyllis. She sent me to the cold press to get some milk while the kettle boiled, and then I sat at the kitchen table while she first swilled hot water around in Maggie's nice brown tea-pot, then poured it down the sink and put in several spoonfuls of tealeaves before filling the pot with freshly boiled water. Then she encased the pot in the tea cosy I knitted for Maggie as her Christmas present last year, sat down opposite me at the table, and sighed. I ignored the sigh and said, 'So what do you think me and Nora can do in the Nassau Street house?'

'Stand back and stay out of trouble,' said Phyllis.

'Can we wave a flag out of the window?' I said hopefully.

'Don't push your luck,' said Phyllis. 'Now make yourself useful and get us some cups.' There were some clean cups and saucers on the draining board. I brought some over to the table and Phyllis poured out the tea.

'I can't believe you painted a postbox,' she said, handing over my cup. And all of a sudden I felt myself smiling.

'Neither can I,' I said. 'I couldn't believe we were doing it while we were doing it. If you know what I mean.'

'Was it fun?' said Phyllis. Suddenly she didn't seem quite so annoyingly older-sister-ish. She was talking to me as if I was just another person. 'Or was it just frightening? You know, because of the fear of getting caught.'

I considered the question.

'It was jolly frightening,' I said. 'But … well, after we'd done it, we both had the most wonderful feeling, like soda water was bubbling up inside us. I know that probably sounds silly, but that's how we felt.'

And to my surprise, Phyllis nodded.

'That's just how I felt the first time I took part in a poster parade,' she said. 'I mean, I was quite all right when we were getting ready but then, when we set off down the street with our posters and banners and things, I couldn't quite believe I was doing it. Lots of people were staring at us and a few men shouted things at us and it all seemed like a strange dream – you know the sort, the ones where you find yourself having to give a lecture to all your old teachers or something and then you realise you're not wearing any shoes.'

I nodded. Just a few weeks ago I dreamed I was in school and then I looked down and I was only wearing my petticoat and a pair of Julia's old socks. It was horrible.

'And then of course those awful Ancient Hooligans threw things at us,' Phyllis went on. 'And it was quite frightening. But then afterwards, when it was all over and we were having tea in Mrs. Mulvany's house, I felt that sort of bubbly feeling, and I was so glad I'd done it, and I knew I'd do it again. Not,' she added quickly, 'that you should be considering doing any postbox painting again. I'm sure you can get the soda water feeling from being a silent supporter in the Nassau Street house. You won't even have to wave a banner.'

I wasn't so sure about that, but I didn't object. Besides, I bet when we're there, me and Nora can manage to wave a poster out of the window. We'll be smaller than all the grown-ups so we should be able to wriggle in front of them and get it out. I was wondering about that when Phyllis said, 'I'm proud of you.'

No one in my family had ever said that to me before. In fact, I don't think anybody has ever said it to me in all my life. I was so shocked I couldn't think of anything to say in reply. And before I could come up with something, Phyllis took her tea and went out in the back garden. I thought I should probably stay away from her in case she regretted being so unusually nice to me and changed her mind about taking us to Nassau Street, so I went upstairs and wrote this letter to you.

Actually, I think I heard Phyllis go out about half an hour ago so I hope she hasn't decided to report me to the IWFL for letting their movement take responsibility for my own criminal activities. I know she was full of praise a few hours ago but you never know, she can be quite capricious. And even if she tells them that she approves of my actions, the rest of them might not agree with her. I will try not to think about it now, anyway. Since I started writing this letter Mother, Julia and Maggie have all come home so I had better go down in case Mother starts suspecting I'm 'up to no good' which is her usual accusation when she hasn't been monitoring my activities for more than ten minutes.

Later

Well, Phyllis didn't report me – at least, not in a bad way. But she did tell someone about me and Nora. She stayed out for most of the day – she had told Mother she wouldn't be at home for dinner – and she didn't turn up until after Maggie had cleared away what was left of our cold ham and salad this evening. Mother was having a lie down (the heat was making her feel faint, as it generally does – I really don't know how she breathes when she's wearing her corsets laced so tightly) and Father, Harry, Frank, Julia and I were in the drawing room. Frank suggested a game of cards.

'How about a round of Beg O' My Neighbour?' he said, producing a pack from his pocket.

'I've never played it,' I said.

'It's easy,' said Harry. 'Well, it's easy for me, I don't know if your feeble brain will be able to comprehend all the rules.'

I tried my best to give him one of Phyllis's scornful looks.

'If you can play it I certainly can,' I said. 'What do you think, Julia?'

'I don't play cards,' said Julia in such a disapproving way that even Father laughed.

'I think we can allow a game of Beg O' My Neighbour,' he said. 'It's not gambling, Julia. It's more like Snap.'

Julia didn't look convinced but we all assured her that she wasn't committing any sins by playing so, after Frank explained the rules, the game began. It was jolly good fun and even Harry forgot to be his usual bossy self once we all got caught up in taking each other's cards. Julia (who had forgotten all her misgivings about playing cards about five seconds after the game began) was arguing over whether Father had the right to take her King of Diamonds or not when the door opened and Phyllis came in, followed by a familiar face.

'Hello, Mabel!' I said cheerfully. I was so engaged in my cards that I had briefly forgotten all about telling Phyllis the truth that morning. But when Mabel said, 'Could I have a word with you, Mollie? Just for a minute,' I remembered everything. I had a horrible conviction that

Mabel was going to tell me I'd damaged the movement with my rash behaviour and that from now on I would no longer be allowed attend meetings, let alone join in the protest in Nassau Street on Thursday.

'If you leave the game now, you can't get back in,' said Harry.

'That's not fair!' I said.

'It makes sense, Moll dear,' said Father, and Frank said, 'We can play again later.'

By now I was so convinced that Mabel was going to expel me from the movement forever that I didn't particularly want to go and talk to her, but I knew I had to. And so, leaving the others to the game (which seemed to get even more rowdy and full of amusement as soon as I left the drawing room) I followed Mabel out to the hall, where Phyllis was waiting for us.

'Come on,' said Phyllis, and I followed her up the stairs to her room, Mabel close at my heels.

'Mabel,' I began, once we were safely ensconced in Phyllis's room and the door had been firmly closed, but I didn't get any further than that because Mabel suddenly flung her arms around me.

'Mollie!' She stepped back and holding me at arm's length. 'Phyllis told me all!'

She certainly didn't look as though she were going to expel me from the movement, unless that was a sort of hug of betrayal like Judas kissing Jesus, but I couldn't be sure. Not that I am comparing myself to Jesus, of course.

'You're not angry with me?' I said.

'Angry?' said Mabel. 'Why on earth would I be angry?'

'Well, you know, me and Nora painted the post box and didn't own up and take credit for it,' I said awkwardly. 'I thought you might have decided to expel me from the movement.' Even as I was saying it, it sounded ridiculous. Mabel clearly agreed, because she stared at me as if she could barely believe her ears.

'Why on earth would I do that?' she said. 'Even if I wanted to, which I wouldn't, that's not how the movement works. And if it did, I certainly wouldn't have the power to expel you from anything. Besides, it's not as if anyone got blamed for what you did.'

'If they had, me and Nora would definitely have owned up,' I said. 'You must believe me.'

'Of course we do,' said Phyllis. She folded her arms and looked at me in her most superior way. 'Really, Mollie, I wouldn't have told Mabel at all if I knew you were going to be so melodramatic about it.'

'So … why did you want to talk to me?' I asked Mabel.

'Oh, just to congratulate you,' she said. 'And to tell you that I fully agree you deserve to be in Nassau Street on Thursday.'

I felt a warm glow go through me. It was a very strange thing, being praised by grown-ups (or almost-grown-ups) twice in one day.

'Thank you,' I said.

'The only thing is ...' Mabel glanced at Phyllis. 'I can't be absolutely positively sure that everyone will agree. They may not want anyone as young as you taking part.'

'Do you think we should tell them all what we did?' I said. 'Then they'd know how serious we are about women getting the vote.'

'Well ...' said Mabel. 'I don't think they'd all be pleased that girls your age were breaking the law in the name of the cause. I mean, maybe they would. But I just don't know. They might think you were risking the IWFL's good name. Imagine how awful it would have looked if you'd been caught. The Antis would have accused us of using children. They'd never believe you'd come up with the idea and done it all by yourself.'

'What do you mean?' I said. 'Do you think I should stay at home?'

It was a depressing thought, especially coming a moment after I'd been positively basking in Mabel's praise.

'In an ideal world, yes,' said Phyllis. 'But Mabel has another idea.'

Mabel nodded.

'If we put your hair up,' she said, 'And you both wear your biggest hats and we get you longer skirts, I think we might be able to get you in without anyone noticing quite how young you are. I heard of two young girls in England who got into lots of meetings that way.'

My spirits, so low a few moments earlier, soared again.

'You mean a *disguise*?' I asked, unable to keep the excitement from my voice. Phyllis obviously noticed it, because she quickly said, 'Don't start getting any notions, Moll. This isn't a Peter Fitzgerald story.

'Well, obviously not,' I said. 'It's not like I'm going to wear a false beard.'

Mabel laughed.

'Maybe you should,' she said. 'We could dress you up as a little Mr. Sheehy-Skeffington.'

'Mabel!' said Phyllis. But she laughed too.

There were plenty of other things I could wear besides a beard, I thought. Maybe I could borrow Mother's sealskin jacket? It would look very grown up. Though of course it was far too hot for July. Then there was the very elaborate hat she'd worn to the Horse Show last year …

'I bet no one would recognise me if I wore Mother's Horse Show hat,' I said. 'You can hardly see her face under that enormous brim.' But Phyllis wasn't impressed by my clever logic.

'You're going to wear the plainest, least conspicuous things we can find,' she said. 'Not Mother's best summer hat.'

'Could Kathleen make me a hat?' I asked. Kathleen, you must recall, is fond of trimming hats in extremely unusual and striking ways.

'Plainest means no Kathleen creations, I'm afraid,' said Mabel, in apologetic tones. I had a feeling she understood my desire for an interesting disguise. 'I can get things for both of you from my mother. She has more clothes than she can possibly wear, so she won't notice if I take a few things.'

'Can I wear a wig?' I said. 'One of the senior girls had a long one in the boarders' show last year and she looked years and years older. Or maybe I could borrow Father's reading spectacles ....'

Phyllis was starting to look annoyed.

'No wigs, no beards, no spectacles,' she said. 'And if you carry on like this we won't take you at all, so behave yourself.'

'Yes, Phyllis,' I said, as meekly as I could.

'Go easy on her, Phyl,' said Mabel. 'I don't blame her for getting excited. Now, my dear girl, if you can stay away from that gambling den downstairs for a few more minutes ...'

'We weren't gambling,' I said. 'Father would never allow it.'

Mabel laughed. 'I was only joking,' she said. 'If you can put up with our presence for a little while longer, I'm going to attempt to put your hair up. Though if it's anything like Phyl's, I'm not sure how long it will stay there.'

'Mabel!' said Phyllis, smacking Mabel's arm in a very un-grown-up fashion.

'All right,' I said. 'Let's give it a try.'

Mabel gathered together as many little combs and hairpins as she could find both in and around the tin on Phyllis's dressing table (she is jolly careless with them if you ask me) and Phyllis sat me down on the straw-seated chair, untied my hair ribbons and started brushing out my hair with the silver-backed brush she got as an eighteenth birthday present.

'Oh dear,' said Mabel. 'Your hair does look as unruly as Phyl's. Ow! Don't poke me, Phyllis. You can be very childish. Anyway, I'll do my best.'

I looked in the mirror as Mabel began her work, assisted by Phyllis, who passed her a series of pins and combs. Every so often a pin would be dropped just as it was being put into place and chunks of hair would fall down over my eyes, but I generally had a good view of proceedings. Have you ever put your hair up? I've tried, of course, just to see what it'll look like in a few years when I do it every day, but I've never quite figured out how to do it properly.

'I say, Mollie,' said Mabel, taking a pin out of her mouth and putting it in my hair. 'I meant to tell you. You're not the only person interested in boats.'

For a moment I couldn't think what she meant.

'Some ladies,' Mabel went on, 'are going out to Kingstown tomorrow to meet Mr. Asquith when his boat comes in. And by going out, I mean going out to sea.'

I started to turn around to face Mabel, but Phyllis said, 'Don't move!' so I just stared at Mabel's reflection in the looking glass instead.

'My boat scheme!' I cried. 'How marvellous. I'm glad someone is doing it.'

'What on earth are you two talking about?' said Phyllis. I'd forgotten I hadn't told her about my excellent idea.

'Oh, Mollie and Nora told me about an idea they'd had,' said Mabel.

'We were going to get a rowing boat and go out with a banner,' I told Phyllis.

'And I happened to mention it to Mrs. Mulvany,' said Mabel. 'And well, it might be a coincidence, but some of the ladies have hired a boat – not a little rowing boat, I might add, a small yacht. And they're going to have a megaphone so they can yell out a welcome greeting to the Prime Minister.'

'How wonderful,' I breathed. I thought Phyllis would be jolly impressed by my brilliance, but of course she wasn't.

'I hope you weren't seriously considering rowing out to sea,' she said sternly.

'We were, as it happens, but I don't see what's so silly about that,' I said. 'After all, if Mrs. Mulvany thinks it's a good idea …'

'There's a big difference between grown women organizing something properly in a yacht and two fourteen-year-old idiots messing about in a boat when they don't even know how to row,' said Phyllis, which was very unfair of her if you ask me. I should have known all that stuff about being proud of me this morning wouldn't last long. Things were certainly going back to normal now.

'Quiet, you two,' said Mabel. 'I need to concentrate on Mollie's peculiar hair. I can't understand why this comb won't stay in it.'

I felt more and more grown-up as Mabel fixed my hair into place. By the time she'd finished, I was quite awe-struck at how mature and sophisticated I looked. I didn't look like a school girl at all. I looked like a young lady.

'Hmmmm,' said Mabel, stepping back and looking at my newly grown-up head in the looking glass.

'She might pass if she wears a hat with a particularly wide brim,' said Phyllis. 'I suppose we can say she's a very young-looking eighteen. And if she stays in the background and keep her mouth shut, hopefully people won't ask her any questions.'

'I don't need a hat with a huge brim,' I said indignantly. I have no idea what she was talking about, because I really did look awfully grown up. But for some reason neither Mabel nor Phyllis agreed with me. I suppose they're so used to thinking of me as a mere child they weren't able to see me as I would undoubtedly appear to strangers. I told them this and they seemed more amused than convinced.

'Well,' I said, with what I thought was crushing sarcasm, 'I could always draw some lines on my face with the grey from my paint box. Maybe then I'll look old enough for you.'

'Don't you dare,' said Phyllis, who clearly doesn't understand sarcasm at all. 'With a decent long skirt you'll just about do, as long as you don't start messing about like you're on the stage.'

I wanted to tell her that there was no chance of any messing, but I knew that the two of them might easily change their minds about disguising me and Nora as grown-ups. (I know Phyllis and Mabel don't think of it as being in disguise but it obviously is.) So I just said, 'All right. Thanks for doing my hair,' and started to leave the room when Phyllis grabbed me.

'You can't go down like that!' she said. And I suppose she was right, but it really did seem a shame to take all the pins and combs out. And not just because it took absolutely ages – you have to take them out very carefully to avoid getting your hair into a massive tangle – but because if I say so myself, I looked jolly nice with my hair up like that. It suited me much better than my usual plaits.

'There is one thing.' Mabel's face was thoughtful. 'Where are you going to change? We can't put your hair up here, and you can't leave the house dressed up. Someone will see.'

'I hadn't thought of that.' Phyllis's face fell. 'Maybe this isn't going to work.'

Mabel glanced at me, and must have guessed how I was feeling because she said,

'Oh, we'll think of something. Now, Mollie, off you go and get your hair back to normal.'

By the time I'd finished brushing it out and tied it into two rather uneven plaits, it was practically time for bed – in fact, when I came downstairs Julia had already been sent up to our room. Mother and Father were in the drawing room and Harry and Frank had taken the deck of cards to the dining room. At this time of year it actually gets some light in the evenings so they hadn't had to put on the gas, even though it was well after eight.

'What on earth were you doing up there?' said Harry, rude as ever. If Frank hadn't been there I'd have told him it was none of his business and maybe even thrown a cushion at him. But I couldn't let the family down in front of our guest with a display of rudeness (Harry clearly never worries about that sort of thing) so I just said, 'I was discussing educational issues with Mabel and Phyllis.'

Harry made one of his irritating snorting noises. 'Educational? I hope they were educating you about doing your hair. You look like something out of a circus with those plaits.'

'No I don't,' I said.

'One's twice the size of the other,' said Harry. 'What

were they doing to you up there?'

To my immense annoyance I could feel my cheeks going red. And it wasn't because Frank was now looking at me as if he were trying to figure out just how lopsided my head now was. It was just because I didn't want Harry to start noticing that I have been experimenting with my appearance, with the help of Phyllis and Mabel. Not if I'm planning a big disguise in a few days.

'A spider fell on my hair and I had to brush it out to get rid of it,' I said. 'And I'm sorry if I didn't rearrange my *coiffure* to suit your high household standards.'

'*Coiffure*' is a jolly good word, isn't it? It's French and means how you arrange your hair, more or less.

'I don't care what you look like,' said Harry. He gave another snorting laugh. 'Though I'm not surprised to hear you've got spiders in your hair. There's probably a whole nest of them living in your mop.'

'Oh shut up, Carberry,' said Frank. His tone was good-natured, but there was a hint of steel in his voice. 'Leave her alone.'

'Thank you, Frank,' I said with dignity. 'I'm glad someone in this house has manners.'

It was Harry's turn to flush.

'Sorry, I suppose,' he said to me. And then, to my surprise, he said, 'We're going to have another game. Do you want to play?'

Frank's niceness and good manners might actually be rubbing off on him.

'All right,' I said cautiously. There was always a chance he was playing some sort of unfunny joke and was going to say 'Well, you can't, so ya boo sucks to you!' But he didn't. He just pulled back a chair at the table and said, 'I'm going to deal.'

I remembered what Frank said a while ago about Harry not being half as bad when he was at school. Maybe, under Frank's influence, he was finally showing his decent side in the comfort of his own home.

Anyway, we played the game and it was probably the most fun I've ever had with Harry. Which isn't saying much, but still. In fact, I didn't realise how long we'd been playing until the dining room door opened and Mother came in to tell me it was time for bed.

'But we're in the middle of a game!' I said. 'And besides, it's the summer holidays.'

But Mother said she didn't care.

'You'll be fit for nothing tomorrow if you don't get a decent night's sleep,' she said. And I didn't want to have a row with Frank there (it was bad enough being told to go to bed like a baby) so I said, 'All right.'

Harry sniggered (I might have known he couldn't behave decently for more than half an hour) and said, 'Off to the nursery, then!' But he didn't snigger for long because Mother said, 'And you'll be up to your room in half an hour,' which shut him up.

Anyway, they can send me to my room but they can't stop me writing this – it's still practically daylight outside and I'm sitting behind the curtains to get as much light as possible. I can't wait to tell Nora about the disguise idea!

Best love and votes for women,
Mollie

Later

Something awful has happened. No, no one has died or been arrested or anything. But I am burning with embarrassment about it and even though I tried to go to sleep afterwards I just lay there tossing and turning for hours and eventually I had to light a candle and start writing this to you (I knew Julia wouldn't wake up; she is snorting away like a grampus, as usual. I do wonder if Mother should take her to a doctor, it can't be normal for a small girl to snore so loudly).

After I finished writing earlier, I settled down to read *Anne of Avonlea*. Julia was almost asleep but, to her credit, she doesn't mind me reading late if I just light a candle rather than a lamp, so I kept going after she began snoring. And I shan't spoil anything for you, in case you haven't read the book by the time you read this letter, but I will tell you that something very, very sad happens in it and when I read that bit I started to cry. And not just a delicate little tear falling down my cheek like the heroine of a romantic serial. Proper, red-faced weeping. I was crying so much I had to hide under the covers to muffle my sobs in case Julia woke up.

Eventually, the fit of weeping passed (though it threatened to kick off again every time I thought of the very sad thing that had happened in the story – even now I feel a bit tearful when I think of it). I looked around for a handkerchief to dry my eyes (and, I'm ashamed to admit, my runny nose too). But even when I'd dried myself off I felt very hot and red and tear-stained, so I went off to the bathroom to splash some cold water on my features. And as I was going down the steps to the first landing where the bathroom is, the door of the bathroom opened and who should come out but Frank!

He was carrying a candle (I am used to finding my way around our house in the dark so I hadn't bothered bringing mine), but when he saw me looming over him on the steps he was so shocked he nearly dropped it.

'It's just me!' I whispered, but as I did so it struck me that I was talking to a boy who was just wearing his pyjamas. And I was wearing nothing but a very old nightgown that used to belong to Phyllis and is now growing far too short for me. And is getting rather worn out behind.

And as the horror of this wildly inappropriate situation hit me, I remembered that I had just been sobbing my heart out under a blanket, and that my face was undoubtedly bright red, my nose was shining, my eyes were definitely puffy, and my hair looked like Lord knows what (it had been bad enough even before I went to bed). I must have looked like a little gorgon. No wonder Frank looked so startled to see me. And lest we forget, I was wearing my nightie in front of a boy and you could see a lot of my bare legs.

'Sorry,' he whispered. 'I …' But I didn't hear what he said next, because I turned and ran back to my room (forgetful of the nightie's worn-out behind) and plunged beneath the covers again.

I feel slightly calmer now that I have written everything down but I am sure that the embarrassment of that moment will never leave me. I caught a glimpse of myself in the glass when I rushed back into the room and I really did look a dreadful fright. Why did it have to be Frank? I wouldn't have cared if Maggie or Mother or even Harry had seen me in such a state. How can I face Frank tomorrow, now that he has seen me looking all blotchy and puffed and wearing nothing but a too-small nightgown?! It was almost indecent. I wouldn't be surprised if he never talks to me again. I am going to try to sleep again now but I don't expect to sleep very well.

Tuesday, 16th July, 1912.

Dear Frances,

I wish I could tell you that I woke up this morning and was able to laugh off the incidents of last night, but unfortunately I wasn't. In fact, the thought of going down to breakfast and sitting opposite Frank filled me with dread. Why oh why did he ever come to stay here? Back when he just called in to visit from time to time, there was no chance of him ever seeing me in my nightie with a bright red blotchy face. I couldn't bear the thought of facing him so I lay in bed and stared at the ceiling as Julia got dressed.

'You'd better get up,' she said, as she left the room. 'Harry and Frank will eat all the toast if you're not down soon.'

I groaned as she closed the door behind her. I'd happily starve if it meant I could avoid seeing Frank. But I knew that if I didn't go down soon, Mother would come in and order me out of bed, so I reluctantly rolled out. I put on one of my best frocks, the blue one with the nice broderie anglaise collar, and made sure my stockings were firmly in place and unlikely to go baggy about the ankles. I brushed my hair as vigorously as I could and tied a ribbon around it so it wouldn't fall all over my face. I looked as unlike my midnight self as possible.

And yet I couldn't bring myself to leave the room until I'd heard Frank and Harry thunder down the stairs to the dining room. (Thank goodness they were up early, I was absolutely dying to go to the loo.) I waited a moment, then hurried down to the bathroom, where I washed and looked at myself critically in the glass. I was certainly less blotchy and red-nosed than I must have looked last night, but I can't pretend I was a raving beauty. Not that being a raving beauty is important, obviously, but Frances, you must realise quite how ridiculous and terrible I looked last night. I wished I could hide away in my room and never come out.

But then I heard Mother's voice cry, 'Mollie! Where are you?'

I took a deep breath and went downstairs. I tried to avoid Frank's gaze when I entered the dining room, but I couldn't help noticing that he looked a little flushed too. And just as I was wondering if everyone would notice the awkwardness, your postcard arrived! And very relieved I was too when Maggie brought it in to me, because it gave me something to talk about that had nothing to do with Frank. Or nightdresses. Or crying. What a lovely picture of Concord you sent, and how funny those wooden houses look. Now I know just how to imagine the March's house in *Little Women*. How wonderful that you were able to see Louisa May Alcott's house – I hope some day I'll be able to go to America and see it for myself. I have a feeling I'll have to wait until I'm much older, though, and can pay for it myself (how, I'm not yet sure) because there's no chance of my family ever going abroad for a holiday. Not even to England.

When I'd shown it to everyone, including Frank (they were all jolly impressed. Harry pretended not to be, but has he ever received a postcard from America? No, he has not), I asked Father if we could go somewhere more exciting than Skerries next year.

'More exciting than Skerries!' he said. 'I don't know what you mean. Don't you remember what happened to Peter Fitzgerald there?'

For of course when Peter Fitzgerald left Ireland to go on his adventures, he did so by swimming out into Skerries Harbour and climbing aboard a fishing boat. And he was nearly caught too, as some of his enemies pursued him in a rowing boat – but one of the seals that are always swimming in the harbour saved him by pulling him beneath the water with his jaws and dragging him to the other side of the fishing boat. This allowed him to climb aboard the boat unseen by his enemies, who all assumed he'd drowned. Harry pointed out that seals didn't normally save people's lives from robbers and policemen, and that they probably weren't strong enough to drag a grown man under the water in their jaws, but Father said that this was a minor quibble and that we shouldn't expect perfect realism in a work of fiction. Whatever that means.

Anyway, we are unlikely to have such exciting adventures in Skerries, as my father knows perfectly well, and I told him so.

'Could we go to France?' I said. 'It's not that far away, is it? And I'd like to see all the places in *A Tale of Two Cities*.'

But Father shook his head.

'I'm afraid that sort of travel is just too expensive,' he said. 'But we'll have a good time in Skerries all the same.'

I suppose we will, but I would love to see the world. It seems hard that I've never even left the country. I'm glad you can go all over the place and tell me about your travels. It's the next best thing to going to interesting places myself.

I almost forgot about my general embarrassment while we talked about travel plans, but when the discussion was over and I was just sitting there eating my boiled egg my discomfort returned. And it got even worse when Mother turned to Frank and Harry.

'What are you boys up to today?'

Harry shrugged his shoulders. 'Nothing, yet. We thought we might have a game of cricket in the park with some of the fellows from school.'

'Well, if that's all you've got planned, why don't you take Mollie and Julia to the Botanic Gardens? There's a concert taking place there at lunchtime.'

Julia clapped her hands.

'That sounds lovely!'

But it didn't sound lovely to me. I wanted to avoid Frank as much as possible until he had forgotten all about the hideous vision of the night. So I was just about to make an excuse for why I couldn't go (as you know, I am worryingly good at coming up with them), when Frank, his manner awkward, said, 'Actually, Harry, did you forget? We told Sheridan we'd go and see his new dog.'

I was sure he was lying, and my suspicion was confirmed when Harry said, 'Wasn't that tomorrow? Ow!' He rubbed his ankle. 'Sorry, Mother, he's right. Sheridan's got a puppy and we're going to try and come up with a name for him. And,' he added quickly, 'we told him we'd be there at twelve. And he lives in Phibsboro.'

Mother, who clearly hadn't noticed Frank kicking Harry under the table, said, 'Oh well, they'll have another concert soon.'

'I can't go today anyway,' I said. 'Nora and I have plans. Please may I be excused?'

'You haven't finished your toast,' said Mother.

'I'll eat it.' Harry didn't wait for permission. He just reached across and stuffed my leftover toast into his mouth.

He is as greedy as a gannet. But I didn't care, I just wanted to get away from Frank, who had made it very clear that he didn't want to spend time with me any more than I wanted to spend time with him. Which shouldn't have bothered me, I suppose, but somehow it did.

I went up to my room and lay on my bed again, staring up at the ceiling and trying not to think about the embarrassment of last night. Instead, I thought about what had happened yesterday and how Mabel and Phyllis were going to help us and, miraculously, thinking of all these exciting plans really did make me feel a lot better. I wasn't thinking of Frank at all when I heard a knock on the front door and, a moment later, Maggie's voice calling up the stairs.

'Mollie! Nora's here for you.'

I went down to meet her just as Phyllis was leaving the house. She was going to meet Kathleen and Mabel to discuss all the anti-Asquith plans. As she passed Nora in the hall she looked at Nora and said, 'Well done,' in a very quiet voice before hurrying out of the house.

'What did she mean by that?' said Nora.

'I'll tell you in a minute,' I said in a low voice. I showed her your postcard.

'How I wish I were over there with her,' Nora sighed. 'In fact, I have terrible news for you.'

My heart sank. 'What?' I said. I wasn't sure I could

bear any more awfulness.

'Grace is going to call in here on her way back from the club in a couple of hours,' said Nora. 'She can't stay there all day today because some grown-up ladies are using the courts and they take precedence over the junior members. And before you say anything, I didn't tell her to call in here. Mother said she should join me after I told her I was going to see you.'

'Oh well,' I said, trying to be cheerful. 'At least we've got a few hours before she gets here.'

'It gets worse,' said Nora. 'She's taking her kindred spirit, the Menace, for a walk on her way back from the club. You know she's been teaching him tricks? And she's going to take him here!'

But even the thought of the Menace in my very own house didn't seem too much after everything else that had been going on. In fact, now I had Nora in front of me and could tell her all, I felt genuinely excited.

'That doesn't matter,' I lowered my voice to a whisper, 'I've got much more thrilling news. Come up to my room.'

Once we were there and the door was firmly closed, I told her everything – all about Phyllis finding out the truth, and about Mabel's scheme for disguising us to make sure we got into the house on Nassau Street on Thursday. Unsurprisingly, she was thrilled.

'Disguises!' she said. 'Can I have a wig, do you think?'

I shook my head sadly.

'I asked about that and they said not,' I said. 'But Mabel put my hair up last night and it looked awfully grown-up.'

'Try doing mine,' suggested Nora. 'Just to see what it looks like.'

'I don't have enough pins and combs and things,' I said.

'Phyllis must,' said Nora. 'Could we …?'

She didn't finish the question, but I knew what she meant. I also knew Phyllis would kill me if she knew we'd been 'sneaking around' (as she would see it) in her room. But after all, she was going to be out all morning, and as long as we put all the combs and pins back in the tin, there's no way she'd know we'd been in there (especially given how untidy her dressing table generally is). We couldn't spend too long at it anyway, for we'd have to be finished before Grace arrived at the house.

'I'll check on what Mother is up to,' I said. I didn't want to risk her summoning us while we were in the middle of putting up Nora's red curls.

Mother, it turned out, was crouched on the floor in the dining room, cutting out a new frock.

'Careful!' she said, as soon as I came into the room. 'Don't step on that cotton, I don't want to have to get it cleaned again.'

'Who are you making the dress for?' I said. From the pattern pieces laid out on the fabric, it looked too big for me, though you never knew. Mother is always having my new clothes made a little too big, 'so there's plenty of room for you to grow into.' Not that I get too many new clothes, as you know. Practically everything I wear is a ragged old hand-me-down from Phyllis, though whenever I say this to Mother she tells me it's nonsense and reminds me of some piffling new thing – like a ribbon – she got for me months ago.

'It's for me,' said Mother. I bent over to have a closer look. 'Careful! I had it perfectly flat, don't touch it.'

'Are you going to send it out to Mrs. Dunne?' I said. She's the dressmaker Mother pays to make quite a lot of the family clothes, especially bigger, more complicated things like dresses. Phyllis had been to see her just a week or two ago. But Mother said she wasn't.

'I'm making this one myself,' she said. 'With Phyllis going to university in October, we're going to have to economise a little.'

I hadn't really considered the fact that Phyllis going to college rather than trying to get a job was going to be an extra expense for Father and Mother. I've always known we weren't rich – at least, not in comparison to some people, including a few girls in school who live in much bigger houses than we do and whose families have two or even four servants. But I've never thought that we had to worry about money. It was rather a disturbing thought, and it must have shown on my face (I don't think I could be a spy after all, everyone seems to always know what I'm thinking) because Mother said, 'Don't look so worried, Moll! I'm just trying to be sensible, we're not headed for the poorhouse yet.'

'Yet?' I said.

'Or ever,' said Mother. 'Now go along, do, and let me cut this dress out. I want to start making it this afternoon so I can wear it when we go to your Aunt Josephine's dinner on Thursday.'

'What dinner?' I asked. This was the first I'd heard of it.

'Oh, didn't I tell you?' she said. 'Your cousin Gerard is home on leave from the army so she's having some of the family over for dinner. I was sure we told you. I definitely told Phyllis.'

I had no idea Aunt Josephine's son was on leave. Nobody tells me anything in this family. But I didn't want to complain about it now because I was wasting valuable Nora-hair-dressing time. And besides, it struck me that if Mother and Father are at the dinner on Thursday, I won't have to make excuses for going out to the protest on Nassau Street. Aunt Josephine always dines early and makes her guests stay for hours and hours. So I left Mother wielding her enormous sewing scissors, the ones she still hasn't let me touch ever since I used them on some cardboard two years ago and blunted them so much she had to get them sharpened by the knife man the next time he called round. When I got back to Phyllis's room, I found that Nora had begun putting up her hair without me. Or at least she was trying to.

'Nora!' I exclaimed. 'You'll do yourself a mischief!'

Nora had a large comb clutched between her teeth and her arms were twisted behind her head in an attempt to fix some errant locks of red hair. I took the comb out of her mouth.

'I think we're going to have start all over again,' I said.

'Oh, all right,' said Nora. 'I don't know how older girls do this on their own, do you?'

I agreed that it was a mystery and started taking out the pins Nora had pushed into her hair, seemingly at random. I tried doing it properly, remembering what Mabel and Phyllis had done the previous evening, and eventually most of Nora's hair was on top of her head. Nora was quite impressed.

'I look at least seventeen,' she said.

'It looks a bit funny from the back,' I admitted.

'We'll be wearing hats,' said Nora, which was a good point. 'Maybe there's a quick way of doing it. What happens if we just pin up your plaits and you hold back the front of your hair?'

'Let's try it and see,' I said. Of course, I couldn't have gone out holding my hair back with my plaits pinned up.

But just having my hair pulled up rather than flowing down to my shoulders did, undeniably, make me look like a grown-up lady. Or almost a grown-up. Nora and I stared at our reflections in the dressing-table mirror for a moment. You couldn't see our short skirts so in our neat blouses we might as well have been wearing proper ladies' clothes.

'Gosh,' said Nora. She turned her head to get a better view. 'Is this what we'll look like when we go to college?'

'I hope we've learned to do our hair a bit more neatly by then,' I said. 'And we'll be wearing long skirts, of course.'

Nora glanced down at her stockinged legs below her shin-length blue skirt.

'It does seem a bit of a shame,' she said, 'that we'll be so weighed down when we're older. I mean with long skirts and corsets and things.'

'Maybe we won't be,' I said. 'You know there are quite a few ladies who don't believe in corsets.'

'What do they wear instead?' said Nora. 'Under their clothes, I mean.'

I had to admit I don't know. They must wear something to hold themselves up.

'Maybe they've invented some other sort of underwear?' I said. 'Phyllis told me there are some who think we should be allowed to wear trousers, too.'

'Trousers!' Nora was shocked.

'I know,' I said. 'But I suppose they would be jolly useful sometimes. If you wanted to run around or climb things.'

'Well, in comparison with long frocks, they would,' said Nora.

'If we had bicycles, trousers would definitely be easier,' I said. We were discussing the other advantages of trousers when there was a knock on the front door. And a moment later Maggie's voice called, 'Mollie! Your friend's here. And she's brought Mrs. Sheffield's little dog.'

Nora and I stared at each other.

'What's she doing here so early?' I whispered.

'I don't know!' Nora whispered back. 'Quick, you go down and distract her while I take all these pins out.'

'All right.' I pulled out the pins that held back my plaits. 'But be quick!'

I ran out to the landing and down the stairs to where Grace and Barnaby were standing with discontented looks on both their faces.

'Hello!' I said, in my most friendly voice. 'I thought you were going to be at the club all morning.'

'They'd made a mistake with the court booking,' said Grace. 'A ladies doubles match was playing in our court. So Miss Casey had to change it to tomorrow. '

'Oh dear,' I said. 'What a shame. But at least you got to take out the Men— I mean, Barnaby.'

I must have been over-egging the friendliness because Grace's expression became suspicious.

'Where's Nora?' she said.

'Upstairs,' I said. 'But you can't take Barnaby up there. Let's take him out to the garden.'

'What's Nora doing?' said Grace. My mind whirled. And I'm afraid I said the only thing I could think of.

'Um, she's in the lavatory,' I said. 'She's been there for a while. She's not feeling terribly well.' As soon as I said it I realised I could have just said she wasn't feeling well without bringing the lav into it, but it was too late now. And Grace looked so horrified I thought she was going to drop Barnaby's lead.

'Mollie, you *are* disgusting,' she said. 'Why on earth did you tell me that?'

'Well, you did ask,' I said. 'Come on, let's take Barnaby out to the back garden. Nora said you've been teaching him tricks.'

'I wouldn't call them tricks,' said Grace, following me down the hall and into the kitchen. Maggie raised her eyebrows as we passed through with the Menace, whom she knows to be my sworn enemy. 'That's beneath his dignity.'

I wouldn't have thought a dog who seemed to attract dust and dirt like a feather duster every time he left the house had much dignity, but Grace clearly disagreed. And

I had to admit that the Menace did seem much better behaved when he was in her company. We walked across the lawn, the Menace trotting serenely by Grace's side.

'Go on, then,' I said.

'Barnaby!' said Grace. 'Die for Parnell!'

And the Menace lay down on the ground and rolled over.

'Gosh, Grace, that's awfully good,' I said, and this time my warm tone was not feigned. 'What else can he do?'

'Barnaby, heel!' said Grace, and Barnaby leapt to his woolly feet and trotted over to her ankles. 'Sit!' said Grace, and down he sat. Then she said, 'Paw, please!' And Barnaby offered her a front paw, which looked cleaner than usual. It was miraculous. I've never seen him behave like this, even when he's in Mrs. Sheffield's company.

'Goodness, I think you've tamed him,' I said. 'Do you think he'd obey if I gave him the same commands?'

'You could try,' said Grace with surprising enthusiasm, and then she seemed to remember that she didn't like me. 'But he'll probably refuse. He only obeys me.'

Sadly this turned out to be true. First of all I tried standing at the other side of the garden and saying 'Barnaby, heel!' The Menace just looked at me with disdain. I tried it again but there was clearly no point, so I went back to see if he was more likely to obey commands at close range. But of course he wasn't. He did lie down after a while, but it was when I was asking him to give me his paw. And I think he only did it because he was getting bored and wanted a nap. Grace was clearly bored too.

'It's not going to work,' she said. 'Where's Nora? She can't still be in the …' Grace blushed, unable to finish such a shocking sentence. I wished, again, that I had thought of a different excuse.

'She really wasn't feeling very well,' I began, but before I was forced to go into more detail, Nora appeared at the back door, looking slightly out of breath and with her hair looking very peculiar indeed. She hadn't had time to untangle it properly and so it was sticking up at some very odd angles.

'How's your tummy?' I said loudly. Luckily Nora is always quick on the uptake.

'Oh, it's much better now,' she said. 'But Grace, I really was awfully sick.'

'I don't want to know any more,' said Grace. 'But you should tell Aunt Catherine about it when we go home. You might need a castor oil dose.'

'Oh, there's no need for that,' said Nora quickly. 'Anyway, what have you and your dumb chum been up to?'

Barnaby clearly didn't like being referred to in such a familiar manner. He looked up at Nora and gave a little sharp bark.

'I've been showing Mollie how well I've trained him,'

said Grace. She looked closely at her cousin. 'What on earth have you done to your hair?'

'It's the weather,' said Nora, who really has become an awfully good liar. 'It always makes my hair go a bit funny. How was the club?'

Of course, Grace can't resist the opportunity to talk about her beloved club.

'I beat Catherine O'Reilly,' she said.

'Well,' said Nora, 'I hope you didn't gloat too much.'

'I didn't gloat!' Grace really did look outraged at the thought. 'Gloating simply isn't fair play.'

I sent a silent prayer to Our Lord that Grace's precious Miss Casey is so fond of fair play. Grace certainly didn't have any qualms about gloating at school whenever she triumphed over another classmate. I could tell that Nora was thinking the very same thing and was on the verge of saying it out loud, so I quickly said, 'You do seem to be a merry band of brothers – I mean sisters – at the tennis club.'

'That's exactly what Miss Casey says.' Grace's tone was serious. 'She says we should celebrate each other's victories.'

'Heavens.' This was so far from Grace's usual attitude to other people's victories I could scarcely believe my ears.

'She's taking us to play against the club in Rathmines on Friday,' Grace went on. 'And then for a meal afterwards.'

Rathmines, of course, is Grace's home turf. 'Do you think you'll join that club after you go home?' I asked. It struck me that this was the longest, most civilised conversation I've ever had with Grace.

'Of course not!' Grace looked shocked at the very thought. She said she couldn't possibly 'desert' the Drumcondra club now. 'I told you, we're a band of sisters.'

Of course, all this politeness was too much for the Menace, who interrupted our surprisingly pleasant chat with a volley of barks.

'Barnaby!' said Grace. The Menace was straining on his harness. 'I'd better get him home. Are you coming, Nora? You know your mother's expecting us for tea.'

I knew Nora didn't particularly want to walk home with Grace – especially as the Menace would be accompanying them as far as his house – but she didn't want to make a fuss.

'All right.' She threw me an expressive look. 'I'll call over tomorrow afternoon. You'll be at the club, won't you, Grace?'

Grace nodded. 'I'm going over to Catherine's for lunch first.'

'Catherine O'Reilly?' I said. 'Your rival?'

'Don't look so surprised,' said Grace, as I walked her, Nora and Barnaby out to the front door. 'We're friends.'

I realised I wasn't used to Grace having actual friends.

Gertie at school was more of an acolyte or henchman. Maybe having friends – people who didn't just trail after her or make her look good to grown-ups – would be good for Grace.

Of course, having friends hasn't done much for Harry, who spent dinner going on about how some other chap from school's family have a boat out in Clontarf and how good he'd be at sailing himself if only he had a chance. Father told him we couldn't afford to keep a boat, and the entire meal was dominated by their debate on the subject. The only good thing about this was that I didn't have to try and make conversation with Frank, who silently chewed his dinner and looked away in embarrassment every time he caught my eye. As soon as I could get away, I went up here to my room and wrote this letter to you. I never thought I'd say this, but right now I can't wait for Frank to leave. Maybe after he does, he'll forget all about our dreadful nighttime encounter.

Best love and votes for women,
Mollie

Wednesday, 17th July, 1912.

Dear Frances,

I don't think I would ever tell her to her face, but Phyllis really is awfully clever. This morning as we were finishing breakfast, she said, in her lightest tone, 'I say, Mollie, I found an old blouse that would do very well for you. Do you remember the one with the embroidered bodice?'

I did remember the blouse — I'd always longed for one like it.

'Do you really think it'll fit her now?' said Mother. 'I'd have thought it would still be too big.'

'Well, she can try it on and see,' said Phyllis. 'Come on, Moll.'

'You know, I do think it's nice that you girls are getting on so well these days,' said Father.

'What's seldom is wonderful,' said Mother with a smile, which was jolly unfair because both Phyllis and I have been very civil to each other for ages now. Or at least a few days. 'Oh, don't look so outraged, Mollie, I was only teasing.'

I followed Phyllis up to her room.

'Did you really find that blouse?' I said, once we were

safe from prying ears.

'Don't be silly, it'd be yards too big for you,' said Phyllis. 'I just needed to get you here to tell you that I've thought of a perfect way for you and Nora to change into your disguises – I mean grown-up clothes.'

'I knew you thought they were disguises too!' I said, triumphantly.

'Shut up, Moll, smugness doesn't suit you,' said Phyllis. 'Anyway, don't you want to know my plan?'

'Sorry, Phyl,' I said, as humbly as I could. 'Go on.'

'I thought, how can we find a safe place for two girls to change their clothes in the centre of town?' said Phyllis. 'And then I thought of the lav list.'

The lav list, as you probably remember, is what Mabel and Phyllis call their list of all the shops and cafes in town that allow suffragettes to use their loos when they're out on suffrage business. I couldn't believe none of us had thought of it before.

'So where would be suitable?' I asked, very impressed by Phyllis's ingenuity.

'There's a hat shop off Grafton Street that I'm sure will let us use their back room,' said Phyllis. 'There's a decent looking glass and enough room for us to change and put up your hair. And the people who run the shop are sympathetic but not terribly close to the movement, so we don't have to worry about them casually telling anyone that Mabel and I were helping two girls disguise themselves.'

'Goodness, you really have thought of everything.' I was very impressed.

'I told Mabel to meet us there tomorrow,' Phyllis continued. 'And to be on the safe side, it'd help if you both shoved your hair under your hats after we leave here, so the difference won't be so obvious after we put your hair up properly. It might look odd if two girls with giant plaits went into a shop and two similarly sized ladies in big hats came out. We don't want to attract too much attention, do we?'

'It's all so complicated, being a secret agent,' I said.

Phyllis gave me a sharp look.

'Don't make me regret arranging all this,' she said. 'If you pair start getting notions about playing spies in disguise …'

'We're not playing,' I said. 'Honestly, Phyl, we won't let you down.'

'You'd better not,' said Phyllis. 'Now go on, let's go downstairs before Mother comes up to check how well that blouse fits.'

'You know, you could always give it to me and I could have it taken in,' I said hopefully.

'That'd wreck the embroidery,' said Phyllis. 'You can have it in a year or two. You might have grown by then. You're still pretty scrawny for your age right now.'

Scrawny! But I let the insult go. I can't wait until I'm older and don't have to rely on Phyllis's whims when I want to go to a suffrage meeting or protest. Though of course hopefully by the time I'm her age we'll actually have the vote.

I wanted to tell Nora about the plan straight away, but I had to wait until she called around late this afternoon. And when she did Grace was with her.

'Oh, hello Grace.' I tried to hide my disappointment when Maggie showed them both into the garden, where I had been lying on a rug eating apples. 'I didn't think you were calling today.'

'We just bumped into each other on the doorstep,' said Nora.

'Weren't you going for lunch with Catherine?' I asked Grace. 'And then the club?'

'I did,' said Grace. 'But the court was double booked so we had to cut our match short.'

I couldn't think of a polite why of asking her why on earth she had come to my house, but luckily I didn't have to, because Grace then announced that Mrs. Sheffield had given her a note for my mother. 'I left it on the hall table. I think it's about the tennis club fête.'

'The club fête?' This was the first I'd heard of such an event.

'It's next week I think,' said Grace. 'All rather last

minute, to raise money for new nets, so it's all hands on deck.' She looked her old smug self for a minute. 'I'm going to be helping, of course.'

'Of course.' There was a hint of sarcasm in Nora's voice, but Grace didn't seem to notice it.

'You two should help out too,' she said. 'They need all the assistance they can get.'

I had no desire to help out at a tennis club fête, and I knew Nora didn't either, but I didn't want to antagonise Grace when we seemed to be getting on reasonably well. Luckily, that was when Mabel arrived with the clothes and shoes belonging to her mother. She bounced into the garden swinging a large basket with a covered bundle inside it.

'Hello girls!' she said. 'Julia told me you were here. I've brought your …' She stopped mid-sentence when she saw Grace. 'Oh hello there. Grace, isn't it?'

'Hello, Miss Purcell,' said Grace. 'Have you been to the shops?'

'Sorry?' said Mabel.

'The basket,' said Grace.

'Oh, that!' said Mabel. 'No, it's just some old clothes belonging to my mother. I thought Maggie might like them.'

'Maggie?' said Grace.

'Our maid, you know,' I explained, impressed by Mabel's quick thinking.

'Yes,' said Mabel. 'Our Bridget is practically ten feet tall so none of our old clothes fit her, the poor thing.'

'I'll take you to Maggie,' I said, scrambling to my feet.

'Didn't you pass her on your way out here?' said Grace.

'Oh no, she must have been doing the grates or something,' said Mabel. 'Julia let me in. Come on, Moll.'

I threw Nora an apologetic glance and hurried into the house with Mabel.

'You do think quickly, Mabel,' I said. 'That was a very good excuse.'

'I've had lots of practice making up things to tell Mother,' said Mabel. 'And telling your mother all about my imaginary engagement. Now come on, let's hurry upstairs and you can try these on.'

We scurried through the kitchen – Maggie rolled her eyes as we passed – and up to my room. Luckily the drawing-room door was closed so Mother didn't see us. Once in my room I forgot all modesty and scrambled out of my skirt and petticoat.

'Here you go,' said Mabel, who looked unfazed by the sight of me in my undergarments and handed me the skirt. I put it on, hoping it would fit. It was a bit too big at the waist and a tiny bit too long but it looked jolly good.

'Perfect!' said Mabel, clapping her hands.

'I wish Nora could try hers while you're here,' I said.

'Well, she's about the same size as you, isn't she?' Mabel said.

'More or less,' I replied.

'Then it'll be fine,' said Mabel. 'What about her feet?'

'They're smaller than mine,' I said. 'She borrowed a pair of my shoes once and they were a bit too big,'

'Well, see how these fit,' said Mabel. 'Sorry they're in a bit of a state.'

The toes of the neat leather shoes were badly scuffed and water stained.

'Mother wore them on a country walk last year and the road turned out to be rockier and wetter than expected,' explained Mabel. 'She's never really worn them since then. But if you polish them dark brown they won't stand out too much.'

I put them on. They were a decent fit on me, which meant they wouldn't really fit Nora. But there was nothing to be done, because Phyllis's shoes would be too big as well. And it wasn't as if my feet were so much larger than Nora's. If we padded the toes with cotton wool they should be all right.

'This is wonderful,' I said. 'Thanks, Mabel.'

'Don't mention it,' she said, and grinned. 'I'd better go. I told your mother I was just popping in to lend you another book. Did you enjoy *Anne of Avonlea*, by the way?'

'I loved it,' I said, although just mentioning the book reminded me of my midnight embarrassment. 'But it made me cry.'

'Don't tell anyone,' said Mabel, 'but I cried too.'

And with that, she was gone. I changed back into my ordinary clothes and hid my skirts and shoes at the bottom of the chest of drawers, under the bag where I keep the clean cotton for my monthlies. Julia never looks in there so I knew they'd be safe from prying eyes. I bundled Nora's clothes in brown paper, planning to slip them to her after Grace had gone. Then I ran back down to the garden, hoping we could get rid of Grace for a minute so I could tell Nora all. I half expected to find the two of them at each other's throats – I knew how irritated Nora was by Grace, even if the latter had become more mellow in recent weeks, but they were actually sitting on the rug in what looked like a remarkably companionable silence, eating the rest of the apples.

'You were a long time,' Grace observed.

'I had to help Maggie go through the clothes.' Yet another lie. It really is worrying how easily they spring to my lips.

'Well, I have to go.' Grace stood up and brushed some grass from her skirt. 'I said I'd take Barnaby for a walk this afternoon. I'll see if your mother has an answer for Mrs. Sheffield. '

'Does Barnaby always behave himself for you?' I knew how badly the Menace carried on for Mrs. Sheffield and her family, which is why they were always so keen on getting other people to take him for walks. It seemed almost miraculous that he could be so consistently good with Grace.

'Of course he does.' Grace seemed genuinely baffled by the question. 'I don't know why everyone acts like he's some sort of monster. He's a lovely little dog.'

There was no point in arguing with her, so I didn't. I just bade her farewell with great politeness. And as soon as she left I told Nora all about Phyllis's plan and Mabel's clothes delivery. She hadn't brought hats but we decided we could borrow old ones belonging to our mothers.

'Do you think I could try on the clothes now?' Nora said.

'Let's see where Julia is,' I said. But when we went inside, she and her friend Christina were in my room, writing things down in a school exercise book.

'What are you two doing?' I demanded.

'Nothing!' Julia looked rather flushed. Surely someone so saintly wasn't up to no good?

'We're writing a story,' said Christina. She was rather a nice-looking kid, with very straight black hair and brown eyes, as different from Julia as could be.

'Christina!' Julia sounded furious. 'It's a secret.'

'Don't worry,' I said. 'I won't tell anyone.' And I left them to it. I certainly wasn't going to object if Julia had found a pastime that didn't involve praying all the time.

It might even distract her from her other pastime of lecturing me for not praying enough. In fact, the two of them were so devoted to their story that they didn't notice me taking out the bundle of clothes Mabel had brought for Nora and sneaking it out of the room. But it did mean that Nora couldn't try on her disguise before she went home. Still, it couldn't be helped.

'How will you get that into the house?' I said, pointing at the bundle as we said goodbye on my front step.

'I'll hide it in the hedge outside my house for now,' said Nora. 'And hope it doesn't rain before I can collect it.'

'I wish we could wear the scarves Stella made us,' I said. 'But it really is too hot.'

'Yes,' agreed Nora. 'And we'd look very conspicuous wearing woollen scarves at this time of year. Especially if anyone noticed the secret message.'

We agreed to meet at the corner of her road tomorrow.

'And you really can't be late,' I said, 'because Phyllis will insist on leaving without you.'

'Of course I won't be late!' Nora was indignant. 'I never am.' She sometimes is, though. But I am quite sure she will be on time tomorrow, because she is as excited as I am. This time tomorrow I will be waving a banner at the Prime Minister!

And it's a good thing that I have such exciting events to think about, because things between me and Frank are still rather awful. Tonight Father read to us all from Peter Fitzgerald, but I couldn't really concentrate even though Peter Fitzgerald was trapped on a beach at the foot of a sheer cliff face with the tide coming in fast. And I couldn't concentrate because when Frank and Harry joined the rest of us in the drawing room for the story reading, the only empty seat was beside me on the sofa, and Harry, being (for once) a good host, urged Frank to take it.

'I can bring a chair in from the dining room for myself,' he said. But Frank, looking rather red, said, 'No, no, I'll do that.'

'All right, if you insist.' And Harry laughed in an obnoxious fashion. 'I wouldn't want to sit next to Mollie either.'

And Frank didn't deny it! He just mumbled something inaudible and left to get a chair from the other room. You can see why I couldn't give much of my attention to Peter Fitzgerald after that. But at least writing this account of today's events has stopped me thinking about Frank. And now I will try to go to sleep by imagining what Mr. Asquith will look like tomorrow when he sees me and Nora brandishing a banner at him.

Best love and votes for women,
Mollie

Friday, 19th July, 1912.

Dear Frances,

I don't know where to start this letter. So much has
happened, and lots of it wasn't good at all. By the time you
read all my letters you might have already read about it
in the papers – but maybe you haven't. I don't know how
much they write about European news over there. Anyway,
whether you've read about it or not, I was actually there
for much of it, and it really was very dramatic and very
frightening.

But I'm getting ahead of myself. I can't remember
if I mentioned in my last letter that me and Nora had
managed (very cunningly, if you ask me) to convince our
parents to let Phyllis and Mabel take us to 'the theatre'
last night. They didn't suspect a thing. Actually, they were
almost too enthusiastic about the scheme.

'Harry, why don't you and Frank go with them?' said
Mother over lunch that afternoon. 'You can all make an
outing of it.'

My blood ran cold. Harry does like going to the theatre,
and he was generally quite willing to put up with his
supposedly annoying sisters if he got to see a play or a

musical show. In fact, he looked quite willing to put up with us now.

'What do you think, Nugent?' said Harry. 'Want to go to a play?'

'I don't know,' said Frank, glancing over at me. 'I don't suppose the girls would want us to tag along.'

I felt very odd inside. Of course I didn't want Frank and Harry to spoil our suffragette plans. But on the other hand, a part of me wished that Frank was more enthusiastic about going to the theatre with me. He clearly didn't want to go.

'Of course we don't mind,' I said, forcing a smile. 'Though I'm sure you'd be horribly bored.'

Then, to my enormous relief, Harry sighed.

'Oh blow, we can't go,' he said. 'It's Harrington's birthday tea thing, remember? We won't get back in time.'

Harrington (I can't remember his first name and they never call him by it) is a boy in their class who Harry always wants to impress because he's very good at rugby. Boys (or at least Harry) can be very silly sometimes. I didn't think boys his age had birthday teas anymore, but apparently Harrington is awfully rich – or at least his parents are – and to celebrate every birthday he's allowed take his pals to a hotel for a fancy feast. Which will be wasted on Harry because, if his behaviour in the family home is anything to go by, he will just gobble up whatever is in front of him, regardless of how delicious or beautifully prepared it is. A pile of old ham sandwiches would do for him. He is not what the French call a connoisseur (I am not sure if I have spelled that right but I can't be bothered looking for my French dictionary to check).

Anyway, I felt very grateful to Harrington (It sounds a bit rude to just refer to him by his surname, but I can't do anything about that), because thanks to him, Phyllis, Nora and I would be unobserved as we left the house carrying our disguises. I was also grateful that it's the summer holidays because otherwise my parents would definitely not let us go anywhere on a Thursday night, even with Phyllis and Mabel.

After breakfast, Phyllis went off to meet Mabel to discuss the evening's plans, and I sneaked off to my room and gathered together the elements of my disguise, which I put in a carpet bag that Harry had taken home from our Uncle Piers in Dundalk last month. I put the shoes at the bottom of the bag, then the skirt, and carefully placed Mother's old hat on top. I hoped it wouldn't get too squashed in the carpet bag, but it was a risk I had to take. Knowing my luck, if I went out wearing it I'd bump into Mrs. Sheffield or someone else who'd ask difficult questions about why I was wearing such a grown-up hat.

After I'd packed the disguise, the rest of day seemed to drag and drag. I wondered how the brave suffrage boatswomen had got on out in Kingstown. I hoped no one had been seasick or fallen in. They were, I had to admit, probably better organised than Nora and I would have been. A yacht sounded a lot more stable than a rowing boat. And a megaphone would be a lot more effective than a banner. After all, someone can look away from a banner or even just not notice it. But you simply can't ignore the sound of someone yelling at you through a megaphone.

I was lying on a rug in the back garden, where I'd been trying unsuccessfully to concentrate on my excellent book, wondering for the first time if it was illegal to yell at the Prime Minister, when suddenly Mother loomed up over me.

'There you are!' she said. 'Come and help Maggie in the kitchen. I just don't have time today.'

I didn't want to argue with her in case she told me I couldn't go out later, so I followed her back into the house, where Maggie was standing at the kitchen table with some freshly washed lettuce and tomatoes in front of her.

'I've found you a helper, Maggie,' said Mother. 'I'm not sure what good she'll be. Oh, don't look so outraged, Moll, I was only teasing. Now, I'm going to practise that Mozart piece so don't disturb me for the next half hour. I need to perfect it by tonight and that last movement still isn't quite right.'

'What's the hurry?' I asked. Mother looked like she was trying to control her irritation.

'Your aunt sent over a note this morning,' she said. 'She wants me to play for her guests.'

'Why can't you play something you know already?' I said.

'She heard me play the first movement the other week,' said Mother. 'So she wants to hear the rest of it now.'

'Well, I think you should refuse,' I said firmly. 'Why don't you tell her you don't know the whole thing properly yet? You're not her private musician!'

Mother laughed.

'I don't mind really,' she said. 'I've been getting rather lazy recently about tricky pieces. I probably needed something to force me to perfect this one.'

Which is fair enough, but I still don't think Aunt Josephine should be going around ordering my mother to play the piano for her. Mother pointed out that if she had actually fulfilled her youthful dream of becoming a concert pianist, she would have to play things on demand all the time, 'for much more annoying people than your aunt.' But I'm not sure such people exist. And even if they did, at least they'd be paying her. All she's going to get from Aunt Josephine is dinner and it probably won't be much good because her cook walked out last week and she hasn't found a new one yet, so the kitchen maid is doing all the cooking by herself. The cook had had enough of putting up with Aunt Josephine's domineering ways (and who can blame her?).

Anyway. Mother went off to play her Mozart (which actually sounded perfect to me, but clearly wasn't up to her own exacting standards), and I got a knife and helped Maggie chop up the salad ingredients. We chopped away in silence for a while, side by side, and then Maggie said, 'I suppose you might see the Prime Minister this evening. On your way to the theatre.'

She didn't look at me as she said it, and anyone who didn't know her well might not have noticed the tone of voice that suggested there was more to her remark than a simple observation.

'I suppose I might,' I said, chopping a tomato in half. 'Maybe on Nassau Street.'

'Well,' said Maggie. 'Be careful. It might get lively in town tonight.'

'I will,' I said, handing Maggie the last head of lettuce. 'Be careful, I mean.'

And Maggie put down her knife and gave me a hug.

'Good luck to you,' she said. She was looking right into my eyes now. 'Now go back out there with your book before I forget myself and start asking questions I shouldn't know the answer to.'

'All right,' I said. When I reached the kitchen door I

paused and looked back at the table where Maggie was chopping the last lettuce. 'I wish you could come with us.'

Maggie smiled at me.

'So do I,' she said.

The rest of the afternoon seemed to go by even more slowly. It was even worse than the day Nora and I had gone (or tried to go) to the meeting in the Antient Concert Rooms. Normally I should have been glad that Mother was leaving me to my own devices and that no one was making me look after Julia or darn some socks or something, but to be honest I'd have welcomed having something to do. I couldn't volunteer for any domestic work, though, or Mother would definitely have got suspicious. So I just stayed in the back garden, trying to read Phyllis's copy of *A Room with a View*. It's a jolly good book, all about a girl who goes to Italy, but you really do need to concentrate on it and I was finding concentrating on anything very difficult. I felt extremely fidgety and uncomfortable, and I was relieved when Phyllis arrived home and joined me in the garden. She was flushed with excitement and her eyes were sparkling.

'What's happened?' I whispered, as she flung herself down next to me on the rug.

'Was that supposed to be a whisper?' said Phyllis. 'Or have you got a cold?'

'Of course it was a whisper,' I said. 'I was trying to be discreet.'

'Well, it sounded just as loud as your normal voice,' said Phyllis. 'Anyway, no one can hear us out here.'

I ignored her jibe, something I am very practised at doing these days.

'So?' I said. 'Have you heard anything about the boat?'

'I certainly have,' said Phyllis. 'Kathleen went out to Kingstown to cheer them on. Mabel and I met her in town afterwards.'

'And what did she say?' I asked, trying to keep the impatience out of my voice.

'It all went wonderfully.' Phyllis beamed. 'They got quite near the steamer, and the megaphone worked perfectly.'

'Did the Prime Minister say anything back to them?' I said. I rather liked the idea of a conversation taking place between two boats.

'I don't think so,' said Phyllis. 'Apparently someone yelled something back from the ship, but they didn't have a megaphone so the IWFL ladies couldn't hear what they were saying.'

'Still,' I said. 'It must have jolly well made Mr. Asquith take notice.'

'Indeed it must!' said Phyllis. 'And he'll take even more notice later on, when we wave our flags out of those windows. By the way, I hope you got your things together, because we'll be leaving in about half an hour. Mother's already dressing for dinner.'

'Thank goodness Aunt Josephine is so demanding,' I said, for the first and probably the last time. An ordinary person wouldn't have insisted on their guests arriving so early, and if Mother and Father were still around when we left, it could have led to awkward questions about the carpet bag.

'Come on,' said Phyllis, standing up and pulling me to my feet. 'Let's go and see them off.'

It was clear that neither Mother or Father were looking forward to the evening – Mother looked more like someone being sent to the gallows than someone going to a party – but they managed to cheerfully urge us to have a good time at the theatre.

'Make a note of the music in the show,' said Mother, as she and Father left to get a cab. 'I always like hearing what songs they use.'

'I say, I hadn't thought of that,' I said to Phyllis after they'd gone and Maggie and Julia had gone to the kitchen, where Maggie was showing Julia how to make buns. 'What if they ask us lots of questions about the show?'

'I've thought of that,' said Phyllis, with a touch of smugness. 'Kathleen's mother went to the same play last night and Kathleen asked her lots of questions about it, so we'll know what to say if anyone asks us.'

'What if something unusual happens?' I said. 'I mean, what if someone falls off the stage or the theatre goes on fire or something and it's in all the papers?'

Phyllis looked a little worried but pulled herself together.

'We'll cross that bridge,' she said, 'when and if we come to it.'

Once Mother and Father had gone Phyllis and I hurried to get our things together. Phyllis threw a hairbrush and a tin of hairpins into the carpet bag, and carried it down to the hall. I stuck my head through the kitchen door.

'We're going now, Maggie,' I said. 'I know it's early, but Phyllis is going to take me and Nora for a meal beforehand.'

'Isn't that generous of her?' said Maggie. 'Good luck, Mollie.'

'Why are you wishing her good luck?' asked Julia, as I slipped away. I didn't hear Maggie's answer. I was too busy shoving my plaits under my hat. A few moments later Phyllis and I were striding down the road, the bag swinging from Phyllis' wrist. As we stood at the corner waiting for a lorry to pass we caught each other's eye. To my surprise, Phyllis grinned.

'It's awfully exciting, isn't it?' she said.

I grinned back. It's been ages and ages since Phyl and I felt like co-conspirators. Probably not since she was about twelve and I was about eight and she and Harry and Julia and I joined forces in order to smuggle a kitten into the house. We'd found it in a hedge at the bottom of our road, where its mother (who was nowhere to be found) must have left it. We all knew that we had to take it home and look after it – it's one of the very few times the four of us have ever been in total agreement. We smuggled it into Phyllis's bedroom and got it a cardboard box to use as a lavatory. And we managed to feed it on scraps and saucers of milk for a whole week until it made a mess on Phyllis's bed and we couldn't hide it from Mother and Maggie any longer. Kittens make mother sneeze, so sadly we couldn't keep Cyril (as we had called the kitten, after one of the children in *Five Children and It*), but he went to live with the Kellys who live down the road. He's huge now and whenever I see him I give him a little wave, but I don't suppose he remembers living with us now. Anyway, during the week Cyril lived with us, it really felt as though Phyllis and I were on the same secret team. And that's what it felt like as the two of us made our way to the corner where we'd arranged to meet Nora.

She was there before us, bouncing on the tips of her toes as if she were so excited she couldn't stand still. When she saw us she ran towards us, a suitcase swinging by her side.

'Thank goodness!' she gasped. 'Quick, we'd better go. My mother could be here any minute.'

'Your mother!' said Phyllis. 'Oh Nora, she hasn't found

out where we're going, has she?'

'No, no, it's nothing like that,' said Nora. 'Come on!'

And she practically ran down the road towards the tram stop. Phyllis and I hurried after her and caught up with her at the junction of Drumcondra Road. Once we'd turned the corner Nora paused to catch her breath.

'Sorry about that,' she said. 'Mother is going around to Mrs. Sheffield's house. She wanted to walk out with me and I had to tell her I was late to meet you and couldn't even wait for her to put her hat on. And then I ran all the way to the corner. I couldn't risk her seeing our bags. She'd be bound to ask some very nosy questions.'

'But surely she saw your bag if you were both getting ready to go at the same time?' said Phyllis.

'I hid it under the hedge last night,' said Nora, triumphantly. 'So I could just grab it on my way out without being seen.'

Phyllis looked impressed despite herself.

'Good thinking,' she said. 'Now come on, girls, let's get that tram.' And the three of us ran across the road to the tram stop.

It felt terribly exciting to be out during the week on suffragette business, and I couldn't help thinking of the last time Nora and I set out on a mission. Tonight's outing was a lot less nerve-wracking, however, especially as Phyllis was with us. And the whole thing wasn't as dangerous (or as illegal) as painting on a postbox. I said this to Nora and Phyllis said, 'Oh, do stop going on about that postbox,' which is a bit much considering she has never risked her liberty for the suffragette cause and we have. But then she paid for our tram fare so I forgave her.

'Now remember,' she said quietly, as we took our seats at the back of the tram., 'there might be serious trouble this evening. More than at any of the suffrage meetings. This is the Prime Minister, and he's going to attract a lot more people than even Mrs. Sheehy-Skeffington ever does – people who are for him AND against him. So if anything starts when we're out on the street, I want both of you to go into a shop and stay there until I come and find you. All right?'

We both nodded meekly and I gripped the handle of the carpet bag with both hands as the tram shot into town. Imagine if I left it behind me, like the time I lost my favourite gloves! Or what if someone stole it (a less likely prospect, I have to admit – I couldn't imagine anyone wanting to snatch a rather threadbare old carpet bag). Nora was clutching her suitcase with equal firmness.

'What did your mother want with Mrs. Sheffield, anyway?' I asked, as the tram headed down Dorset Street.

'You won't believe it,' said Nora with a sigh. 'She's going to collect Barnaby. He's coming to a late tea in my house.'

'He's what?' I cried.

'Ssh!' said Phyllis, who was sitting on my other side.

'Sorry,' I said, and turned back to Nora. 'Why on earth is he doing that?'

'It's a treat for Grace,' said Nora. 'You know, because she's going home on Monday.'

Imagine thinking the Menace visiting your house would be a treat. I hope Grace can exert her civilising influence on him. If he paid an official visit to our house he'd probably eat all my socks or get sick in my shoes or something. Anyway, at least Nora was missing his little tea party.

When we reached town there were quite a lot of people milling about, more than I've ever seen on a Thursday evening.

'Lots of people will be coming in to see Mr. Asquith,' said Phyllis. I wondered were there any Ancient Hooligans in the groups already gathering around the Pillar on Sackville Street. We got off the tram in College Green and followed Phyllis through the crowds who were waiting to see the Prime Minister. Some of them were already waving little union flags, while others had green flags and banners. We wriggled through them and walked towards Grafton Street (where a rude man barged past us and nearly knocked me off the pavement and under a delivery van). After making our way along the busy pavements we turned off Grafton Street onto a small lane where, opposite a church, there was a smart little hat shop that I'd never noticed before.

'Here we are,' said Phyllis, and she pushed open the door. A bell jangled and a slightly harassed-looking young woman emerged from a curtained door.

'Hello, Miss Murphy,' said Phyllis. 'Can I have a quiet word?'

'Of course,' said Miss Murphy. 'In here, please.'

Phyllis followed her through the curtained door. As she pulled back the curtain, she looked out and mouthed the words, 'Don't touch anything' at me and Nora. As if we were babies! Though I must admit that some of the hats on display did look very tempting. I wondered what I'd look like in a particularly charming straw one with a cherry-red ribbon and an arrangement of berries and cherry-blossom on one side. A moment later Phyllis stuck her head out from behind the curtain and said, 'Come on, then.'

Nora and I hurried through the curtain and into a small hall. There was a door to the left that opened onto what was clearly a dressing room, in which clients could try on hats in front of a full length mirror. Phyllis and Miss Murphy were waiting for us there.

'I'll leave you to it,' said Miss Murphy. She smiled at me and Nora, and the harassed expression lifted from her features. She looked much younger. 'You're a pair of young sports, that's what you are,' she said, and went back to the shop.

'All right,' said Phyllis. 'You start getting changed. Hopefully Mabel will have arrived by the time you get those skirts on and can help me do your hair.'

I hoped so too. I didn't really trust Phyllis to put up our hair properly. At least, put it up so that it stayed up. She's bad enough at doing her own. Nora and I took off our shoes, wriggled out of our skirts and petticoats and put on the skirts that Mabel had borrowed for us. Luckily, Nora's was a decent fit.

'Thank goodness,' she said.

'Mine is a bit long,' I said. I tucked my blouse under the waistband and tried to look tall.

'Don't forget they won't be too long once you've got your shoes on,' said Phyllis. 'Thank goodness waists have got higher, you can't tell you're not wearing corsets.'

Nora and I put our shoes on, Nora stuffing some cotton wool into the toes of hers. And thanks to her long skirts, you couldn't see the scuffs at all. Well, hardly at all. We walked around a bit in the shoes, trying to get used to the unfamiliar high heels.

'See?' said Phyllis. 'The skirts aren't too long at all now. Oh thank goodness!'

Mabel had arrived.

'Hello, all!' said Mabel. 'Goodness, girls, you do look

grown up – apart from the plaits. Right, Mollie first, I think. She needs the most work.'

I sat down and let Mabel work her magic. This time, probably because she'd had some practice, it didn't take her half as long to put up my mane and then move on to Nora. While she ran a brush through Nora's red curls, I got up and went to the full-length looking glass that stood in a corner of the room.

'Gosh,' I said softly.

I almost didn't recognise myself in the glass. I don't know if it was the hair or the long skirt or the shoes – which looked right with the long skirt, in a way they hadn't looked when I tried them at home with my stockinged legs sticking out of them. I didn't even feel like I was in disguise anymore. Or if I was, I was dressed as my future self.

'I suppose you'll do,' said Phyllis, slamming Mother's hat on my head and jamming in a hat pin to keep it in place. 'As long as you don't stand in direct sunlight.'

'I think I look jolly good!' I said indignantly. Mabel laughed and pinned a last lock of hair on top of Nora's head.

'You both look marvellous,' she said. 'Right, Nora, go and feast your eyes on your unnatural beauty.'

Nora's hair looked very nice – much better than when she'd tried to do it herself. But I realised that when she was walking towards the glass she did look a bit funny.

'I think you need more cotton in the shoes,' I said. 'You're almost slipping out of them.'

'I'll ask Miss Murphy,' said Phyllis, and she slipped back through the curtained entrance into the shop. She returned a moment later with some cotton wool.

'If this doesn't work, you may have to give up,' she said sternly, handing it over to Nora. 'We can't have you wobbling around drawing attention to us.'

Nora's face was grave as she prodded the cotton wool into place. She put the shoes back on and took a few tentative steps. This time, she looked much more at ease. Though I must say I don't understand why grown-ups wear high heels. They really aren't very practical at all.

'Good,' said Phyllis. 'Now come on, we'd better get down to Nassau Street.'

The pavements were even more crowded when we got back to Grafton Street. I felt terribly conspicuous in my new garb, but to my great relief no one seemed to notice anything strange about me or Nora. Maybe things would have been different if there hadn't been so many people around, but as it was we could just blend in with the crowd. The crowds, in fact, were so numerous at the Nassau Street end of Grafton Street that Mabel suggested taking a more circuitous route. So we went down Duke Street, where a man (who Nora said afterwards must have been intoxicated) emerged from Davy Byrne's pub and cried, 'Hello there, young misses!' after us as we passed. We turned onto Dawson Street, and I couldn't resist looking at the books displayed in the windows of Hodges Figgis.

'Don't dawdle,' said Phyllis tersely, pulling me away by the arm as if I were a kid and not the sophisticated young lady she wanted me to be.

'The crowds are too thick,' said Mabel. 'Let's go back around by Molesworth Street.' She strode off in that direction, the rest of us hurrying in her wake.

'Where's Kathleen?' Phyllis asked. 'Is she meeting us there?'

'She's going to protest in Sackville Street,' was Mabel's reply. 'She had to meet her mother for dinner in the Gresham so she wasn't sure if she'd get over here in time.'

'I can't walk fast in these shoes,' muttered Nora as we crossed the road, narrowly avoiding being hit by a 'bus.

'It can't be long now,' I reassured her. 'Can it?'

Luckily, it wasn't. We followed Mabel down Frederick Street and onto Nassau Street, where the crowds were already spilling out onto the pavement. Policemen were walking along the road, urging spectators to stand back.

'Come on,' said Mabel. 'It's down here, I believe.' She led us through the throng and towards a door situated next to a shopfront. She rang the bell, and a moment later a vaguely familiar woman (I later realised I'd seen her at one of the IWFL meetings) answered the door.

'Hello, Mamie,' said Mabel. 'We haven't missed him, have we?'

'No, of course not,' said Mamie. 'Quick, come in.' We all squeezed into a narrow hall. Mamie eyed me and Nora with faint suspicion. I pulled down my hat and tried to look tall and grown up.

'Who is this?' said Mamie.

'My cousins,' said Phyllis. 'This is Mollie Carberry, and this is Nora Cantwell.' Mamie relaxed a little and gave me her hand.

'Mamie Quigley.' Her handshake was firm. 'Call me Mamie. Sorry to be so suspicious, but you can't be too careful these days, now can you?'

'Where's our room?' asked Mabel.

'Upstairs,' said Mamie. 'Follow me.'

The room was quite big, but it was so full of people, nearly all of them women, that it felt almost cramped. Several large flags were folded on a sideboard at one end of the room, the fabric bunched and trailing onto the floor; it was impossible to see what they said. Large windows looked out onto Nassau Street and across to the playing fields of Trinity College, where I could see some young men in cricketing whites making their way back to the sports pavilion. Somehow I found myself thinking of Frank, and wondering what he would say if he could see us in our disguises, ready to protest. I'd like to think he'd be impressed – he was jolly supportive of the chalking, after all – but you never know.

'Look at the posters,' whispered Nora. Several posters with straps at the top of them were propped against the wall. One said 'HOME RULE FOR IRISH WOMEN AS WELL AS MEN'; another read 'WE DEMAND WOMAN SUFFRAGE AMMENDMENT TO THE HOME RULE BILL', as well as others with shorter slogans.

'Well, we needn't have worried about our poster slogan ideas being too long and complicated,' I whispered back.

'What are you two muttering about?' said Phyllis, in what I can only describe as a mutter. 'You'd better not be planning any silly stunt.'

Yet again, I was struck by how unfair Phyllis always is.

'We were just looking at the posters,' I said indignantly.

'Oh yes.' Phyllis didn't even have the grace to apologise for unfairly suspecting us. 'I'd forgotten about the poster parade.' She went over to Mamie Quigley, who was standing near one of the other windows, leaning against a small table and talking to Mabel with a serious expression on her face. Nora and I followed her.

'How did the parade go this afternoon?' Phyllis asked Mamie.

'Not bad, actually.' Mamie's face brightened. 'We sold quite a few *Citizens*.'

'Any trouble?' said Mabel.

Mamie shrugged.

'A few silly jokes,' she said. 'But nothing we haven't heard before. It was all quite good humoured, really.'

'There you go,' said Mabel, with customary cheerfulness. 'We get more of the public on our side every day.'

'Hopefully we'll have a few more by tomorrow,' said Mamie. 'Have you seen the confetti?'

'What confetti?' said Mabel and Phyllis at the same time.

Mamie grinned. 'This you must see,' she said. She picked up a small paper bag which was sitting on the table and gently shook some of the contents out onto the palm of her hand 'Look!'

The bag was full of small paper circles, but when you looked at them closely you could see the words VOTES FOR WOMEN printed on them in small but legible letters. Mabel laughed in delight.

'How absolutely wonderful!' she said.

'We're going to scatter it out of the windows,' said Mamie. 'There are another few bags of it over there. Maybe some Antis will carry our slogans around on their hats for the rest of the evening!'

That's when I was struck by an excellent idea. Phyllis had made us promise not to try to wave any flags. But she hadn't said anything about confetti.

'Could I please throw some confetti?' I asked Mamie.

'Mollie!' said Phyllis. But Mamie smiled.

'I don't see why not,' she said. 'Is this your first suffrage event?'

'Oh no,' I said. 'I've been to lots of meetings. So has Nora.' I wished I could tell her about the postboxes, but I knew that wouldn't be a good idea.

'Sorry,' said Mamie. 'It's just that you look so young.'

'Oh, we're both eighteen.' I hoped my cheeks wouldn't betray me by going bright red, as they so often do. But if I did blush, I hope my hat (which I was keeping firmly on my head, as Phyllis had instructed) covered enough of my features to make it unnoticeable.

'Here you go,' said Mamie. She handed me the bag of confetti and looked at her watch. 'Goodness, he'll be here soon. We'd better get the flags ready. They're terribly awkward in an enclosed space like this. I told Mrs. Mulvany we have to make sure we don't smash a window pane.'

'Let me help,' said Mabel. One of the flags was carefully attached to a long pole.

It took several people to manoeuvre the flags across the room without the poles hitting or breaking anything (or anyone).

'All right, everyone,' said a woman whom I recognised as Mrs. Mulvany, the woman I'd spotted giving leaflets to Phyllis in the street, what felt like years ago. 'The Prime

Minister should be passing soon. Mrs. Quigley and Miss Purcell, you take that flag, and Miss Carberry and Miss Clarke, you can take that one. Mrs. Byrne should be here soon with another flag pole, but, in the meantime, we can just hold the flags out of the window. Mr. Donnelly and Mrs. Murphy, please push up the windows as far as they will go. Careful now!' The windows were pushed up, but just as the flags were being placed into position, Mabel, who was leaning out of the window, said, 'I say, there are some policemen outside the door.'

'Well, there are bound to be lots of policemen, with crowds like this,' said Mrs. Mulvany. 'Come on, everyone, get the flags out.'

Just then, however, there was a loud banging on the front door. The flag bearers exchanged worried glances.

'Carry on, everyone,' said Mrs. Mulvany. 'I'll go down and see what they want.'

I squeezed through the group and found a position at the window that wasn't being used for a flag. Quite a crowd of policemen seemed to be gathered outside the building we were in. They couldn't all be here because of us, could they?

But then I heard Mrs. Mulvany cry out, and a moment later a crowd of police officers burst into the room. They were followed by several men without uniforms who turned out to be plain-clothes policemen.

'Oh my God,' said Phyllis. She looked at me and Nora and then stared wildly around the room. There was no way any of us could get past the policemen now. 'Get behind me.'

'But why are they here?' I said. 'No one's doing anything wrong.'

'All right, ladies,' said a large police officer in booming tones. 'I'm Inspector Campbell and I must order you to take down that flag.'

An old woman in spectacles stepped forward.

'What's going on?' she demanded. 'We've rented this room perfectly legally. We're not breaking any laws. How dare you barge in like this?'

'We have it on good authority,' said Inspector Campbell, 'that this room is being used to launch an attack on the Prime Minister.'

Everyone started talking at once. I could hear Mrs. Mulvany shout, 'That's an outrageous lie!'

'Quiet, please!' boomed Inspector Campbell. A young policeman rushed into the room carrying a large flag pole.

'I got this at the door, sir,' he said. 'Some old biddy …'

'Ahem!' said Inspector Campbell. 'Some respect, please, Constable Brosnan.'

'Sorry, sir,' said the abashed Constable Brosnan. 'A woman, sir, was coming in with this big old stick. A dangerous weapon, sir.'

'It's a flag pole, you great fool,' said Mrs. Mulvany contemptuously.

'Flag pole it may be,' said Inspector Campbell. 'But it's also a dangerous weapon. What would happen if you hurled something like this from the window in the direction of the Prime Minister's carriage?'

'I wouldn't be able to do any such thing,' said Mrs. Mulvany. 'It's far too heavy. We just want to attach a flag to it and wave it out the window.'

'A likely story,' muttered Constable Brosnan.

'All right, Brosnan, that'll do,' said Inspector Campbell. 'But really, Miss …

'*Mrs.* Mulvany,' said Mrs. Mulvany.

'Mrs. Mulvany, then,' said Inspector Campbell. 'This visit is a very serious occasion. We can't have dangerous radicals waving giant sticks at the Prime Minister.'

'What of the crowds below?' said Mrs. Mulvany.

'What about them?' said Inspector Campbell, who was starting to look impatient.

'Well, some of them are waving paper flags,' said Mrs. Mulvany. 'Perhaps one of them could be thrown at Mr. Asquith and poke his eye out.'

'This isn't a laughing matter Mrs. …' Inspector Campbell's face reddened as he tried to remember her name. 'Mrs. Mulvany. We take the security of the prime minister very seriously. Brosnan and Donnelly, stay here with me. The rest of you, go outside and keep an eye on the street. Don't let anyone else in here.'

'We've rented this room perfectly legally!' protested Mamie Quigley.

'That's as may be, Miss,' said Inspector Campbell.

'Mrs. Quigley,' said Mamie, primly.

Inspector Campbell sighed.

'Mrs. Quigley, then,' he said. 'As I told your friend here, we have a right to search the premises. And that's what we're going to do.'

There was a burst of protest from the assembled suffragettes and their supporters, and then another police inspector strode into the room. He wasn't as burly as Inspector Campbell.

'I've checked the roof, Campbell,' he said. 'Nothing up there.'

'Of course there's not!' cried Mabel. 'Really, this is outrageous.'

Both inspectors ignored her.

'Thank you, Inspector Cummins,' said Inspector Campbell. 'Search the room, boys!'

Constable Brosnan and his colleague Constable Donnelly started poking through all the poster boards and opening the various drawers, under the watchful eyes of the two inspectors. They shook out the flags before dumping them on the floor by the suffragettes' feet and even went through the pockets of the coats that were hanging on a hatstand in the corner, despite the protests of their owners.

'What do they think they'll find?' I whispered to Phyllis.

'Shut up,' Phyllis hissed back. Her face was very white. 'Don't bring any attention to yourself.'

Then Mabel, who had been glowering out of the window, unable to bring herself to look at the policemen, let out a cry.

'He's coming! He's coming!'

I whirled round and, looking out onto Nassau Street, saw a large and impressive carriage making its way down the street from the direction of Westland Row. The crowd started to cheer and lots of people waved their little flags. Everyone in the room, apart from the policemen, crowded around the windows.

'Stand back there, ladies!' called Inspector Cummins, but we all ignored him.

'Quickly,' said Mabel. 'Roll out the flags!' And several suffragettes grabbed the flags and rolled them out of the window, clutching the edges tightly to stop them falling down onto the crowds and policemen gathered below. One said, 'HOME RULE FOR IRISH WOMEN' and the other just said, 'VOTES FOR WOMEN'.

'Stop that at once!' said Inspector Campbell, but it was too late. Mr. Asquith's carriage was practically upon us, and now I could actually see his face, so familiar from pictures in Father's newspaper. Mr. Redmond, whose features were equally familiar, sat next to him in the carriage.

'VOTES FOR WOMEN!' roared Mabel, and everyone else took up the cry. I knew I should have been trying to fade into the background, but I couldn't resist. I roared 'Votes for Women!' along with the rest of them, and so did Nora. And, even though she was so worried about me and Nora getting arrested (and, more importantly as far as she was concerned, getting her into trouble), so did Phyllis. As the Prime Minister went past us, he turned his head towards the sound of the roars, and I'm not going to say he acknowledged our shouts, but he definitely heard them and he couldn't possibly have missed the enormous flags.

'Mollie!' cried Nora. 'The confetti!'

And I pushed under Phyllis's arms, leaned as far out of the window as I could, and shook the paper bag with all my might. The little circles of paper floated down onto the crowd, and several people looked around to see where the mysterious confetti was coming from.

'Votes for women!' I cried, and 'Votes for women!' yelled Nora, and then Phyllis yanked me back so hard I nearly fell onto the floor which, as I pointed out later, would really have made the policemen notice me, so she should have just left me alone. Not that she was thinking of that.

'Stop fooling about!' she snarled. 'Good lord, why did I take you here?'

But before I could answer her, the two constables were in our midst and were pulling the flags out of the hands of those who had been waving them out of the window.

'All right, all right, you've had your fun,' said Inspector Cummins. 'Now, why don't you go home to your husbands and stop this play-acting?'

'You'd be better off occupying yourselves down there,' said a stout woman in a dark purple coat, pointing down to the street below, where two drunken men had pushed their way through the crowds and were now following the procession with many roars and rude chants.

'And that pair probably have the vote,' muttered Mamie.

'Come on, lads,' said Inspector Campbell. 'We've done all we can do here.' He raised his hat at the suffragettes still gathered by the window. 'Ladies.' And with that, he strode out of the room, followed by his colleagues. Mrs. Mulvany went over and shut the door, then turned to face the rest of us.

'Well!' she said. And she sat down very suddenly in the nearest chair. 'Good lord, I feel quite faint.'

'I've got some salts,' said Mamie, rushing to the hat stand and picking up a small velvet bag, from which she produced a bottle whose strong-smelling contents soon restored Mrs. Mulvany. I have never been revived by smelling salts but they smell jolly strong so I am not surprised that just having them wafted under your nose would restore you.'

'Thank you, Mrs. Quigley,' said Mrs. Mulvany. 'I don't know what came over me.'

'It sometimes happens after great exertion,' said Mabel. 'My father's a doctor and he says that when one's been very brave, one sometimes collapses once it's all over. As if one's run out of oil.'

'What could have led them to raid us?' said a young man with curly hair, who was folding up one of the flags.

'Ignorant trouble-making,' said Mrs. Mulvany.

'They can't have thought we were really going to do something to the Prime Minister,' said Phyllis. She looked nervously around the room. 'Can they?'

'You've read how we're described in the papers,' said Mamie Quigley. 'They'd believe us capable of anything.'

'Apart from voting,' said another suffragette dryly, and everyone laughed.

'Well, ladies,' said Mrs. Mulvany, sounding much restored. 'We may have been rudely interrupted, but we managed to get our point across nevertheless.'

'Three cheers for the I.W.F.L!' cried the irrepressible Mabel. 'Hip, hip, hooray!'

And everyone joined in. Then they all started gathering their coats and bags and discussing what to do next.

'Are there more protests happening this evening?' asked Nora.

'If there are, you won't be anywhere near them,' said Phyllis firmly. 'I'm going to get you two home before anything else dangerous happens. If the hat shop's still open, you can change there. And if it's not, we'll go to the Farm Produce.'

There was no point in arguing with her. We followed her down the stairs, with Mabel bringing up the rear.

'I was thinking of trying to get in to the Theatre Royal meeting tomorrow,' Mabel said. 'You know, where Mr. Asquith and Mr. Redmond will be speaking.'

'There's no point,' said Phyllis. 'You know they're only letting women in if they can be vouched for by a man. And they've already been refunding tickets to any men they've discovered are sympathetic to the cause.'

'Such babies!' said Mabel in disgust. 'Call themselves politicians, and then they can't even bear to answer a few simple questions.'

'I heard Mr. Sheehy-Skeffington is going to try to get in anyway.' Phyllis had reached the street door when suddenly she paused. A familiar figure was pushing her way through the crowd towards us. 'Kathleen! I didn't think you were coming.'

'I had to warn you ...' gasped Kathleen. She looked as if she had just run a mile. Her cheeks were flushed, and her hat, a typically flamboyant affair the shape of an upside down pie dish, with a large cream satin rose that looked more like a cabbage to me, was askew over her dark curly hair.

'Come in here and sit down.' Mabel took charge. She led Kathleen back into the building and sat her down on a small hard chair near the door. 'What's happened?'

'It was on Sackville Street,' said Kathleen, whose breathing was returning to normal. 'Just at the bridge. Someone threw a hatchet at the Prime Minister.'

There was a shocked silence for a moment. When Phyllis broke it, her voice was shaking.

'You're joking.'

'I wish I was,' said Kathleen.

Nora's face was very pale. 'Is he … dead?' she asked.

I felt my stomach lurch. The Prime Minister was my enemy, being opposed to the cause. But I certainly didn't think he should be murdered.

Kathleen, however, shook her head. 'It didn't hit him. It got Mr. Redmond, but he wasn't badly hurt.'

'But who could have done something like that?' said Phyllis. 'Was it a Nationalist? Or someone against Home Rule?'

'No,' said Kathleen. 'It was a suffragette!'

We stared at her, too stunned to speak.

'I was shocked too,' said Kathleen. 'But there's no doubt.

Mrs. Joyce saw it happen.'

'But that wasn't one of our plans,' said Mabel. 'I know we don't get told everything, but there's no way any of the leaders would agree to something like that. Not here. Not now.'

'She was from a group of Englishwomen,' said Kathleen. 'At least, that's what Mrs. Joyce told me. She was next to them in the crowd and she heard them talking – I was a little further back. They threw a hatchet with a message tied to the handle. She couldn't make out what it said.'

'What were they thinking?' cried Phyllis. 'If they wanted to throw hatchets at him – not that I think they should – why couldn't they do it in England? Why did they have to come over here where we'll all get the blame?'

'I think we should all get home straight away,' said Kathleen. 'The crowds were getting very angry. I only came over here to warn you.'

I know she's always been rather snobbish and patronising towards me and Nora, but braving the crowds in order to warn her friends was jolly decent.

'If we go around by Westland Row and then across the bridge to Beresford Place we can go down Gardiner Street,' said Phyllis. 'At least that way we'll avoid Sackville Street.'

That was when Kathleen seemed to notice me and Nora for the first time.

'What on earth are those two doing here?' she demanded. 'And why are they dressed up like that?'

I stopped feeling sympathetic.

'They've earned the right to be here,' said Mabel firmly. 'Now come on, let's get going.'

She, Kathleen and Phyllis led the way, with me and Nora trailing behind. It wasn't easy to walk quickly in high-heeled shoes. There were still a lot of people milling around Nassau Street, though the policemen were nowhere to be seen. I pointed this out to Nora.

'They're probably down in Sackville Street arresting the English suffragettes,' she said.

'Come on, you two,' said Phyllis, grabbing my arm and yanking me along like a baby. 'I'm not going to risk losing you in this morass.'

'You don't have to pull me,' I grumbled.

'I shouldn't let you out of my sight.' Phyllis looked genuinely worried, not just annoyed (her usual expression when dealing with me). 'We could all have been arrested!'

'It was terribly bad luck,' said Nora. 'I mean, we were in a nice, safe private room. You couldn't have known we'd be raided by the police.'

'It was quite exciting, though,' I said. 'Come on, Phyl, you must admit it was. After all, nothing bad really happened.'

Phyllis wasn't going to admit any such thing.

'It wouldn't have been exciting if you'd been carted off

to jail for throwing that stupid bloody confetti.'

I have never heard her swear before. And calling the confetti stupid as well! Nora and I gaped at her in horror.

'Phyllis!' I said.

She had the grace to blush.

'Sorry,' she said. 'I shouldn't have said that in front of you.'

'Or at all,' I said severely. 'Anyway, we weren't carted anywhere. We're all perfectly safe. And now we have a jolly good story to tell.'

'You'd better not tell it to anyone,' said Phyllis.

'I meant when we're old and grey,' I said. 'We can tell our great-grandchildren.'

'I doubt they'd be interested,' said Phyllis. 'Oh, blast it all, these crowds!' We had reached Great Brunswick Street, where just a few weeks ago we had tried to attend the giant suffrage meeting. We had no choice but to walk down to Tara Street, where we could cross the river.

'I think we should try and get a cab,' said Mabel in a low voice. 'The crowds could turn on us if they realise we're suffragettes.'

'But weren't the jarveys protesting today?' said Phyllis. 'I read in the paper they're objecting to motor cabs.' You may have forgotten, but 'jarvey' is our Dublin word for cab driver.

'They're still operating their cabs, though,' said Mabel. 'I saw a few on my way here. It's worth a try.'

Phyllis nodded. There was a jarveys' rest near the train

station, so we went back to Westland Row and luckily managed to get one straight away.

'I'll be happy to take you ladies home,' said the jarvey. 'Town's not safe this evening, with those suffragettes roaming the streets.'

None of our group trusted themselves to say anything, but the jarvey didn't seem to care.

'Did you hear about the hatchet? Bleeding disgrace – pardon my language, ladies.'

'It's quite all right,' said Mabel, faintly. With a subtle movement, she adjusted the lapel of her coat so that her I. W. F. L. Votes for Women badge could not be seen. 'Can you take us to Drumcondra, please?'

'Just climb aboard,' said the jarvey.

As the cab clattered along the street and over Butt Bridge, I saw that the crowds were still fairly thick. There were quite a large number of angry-looking men, and I was very glad Phyllis had thought of getting a cab. The crowds had thinned out by the time we reached Gardiner Street, and it wasn't until we were rattling down Drumcondra Road that something very important struck me.

'Phyllis,' I said. 'Our clothes!' In all the fuss and excitement, we'd forgotten to change back into our own things. As soon as she realised this Phyllis looked as if she were going to cry. But once more, Mabel took charge.

'Kathleen, block out that window. I'll get in front of this

one. Right, girls, get changed. And do it quickly.'

We were so squashed that it was difficult to move at all, let alone unbutton and wriggle out of the borrowed long skirts. We barely had room to open the bag and get out our ordinary clothes. There was a terrible moment when we thought one of Nora's own shoes had been left behind in the hat shop, but it was found wrapped up in her skirt. As the cab turned off Drumcondra Road and towards the corner where we'd asked to be let out, I managed to squash the borrowed hats, skirts and shoes back in the carpet bag. There was no time to take down our hair but as Mabel said, 'It can't be helped. Besides, you can brush that off as a joke. Just say you were trying to look sophisticated for the theatre. It's harder to explain why you were parading around the streets in long skirts and my mother's shoes.'

The cab clattered to a halt and we tumbled out (almost literally in the case of me and Nora). Mabel paid the jarvey, who looked at us curiously as he drove away, probably wondering why two sophisticated young ladies who had got into his cab half an hour earlier had been transformed into slightly grubby schoolgirls. Our appearance wasn't improved by the fact that, when they were all squashed into the bag, our shoes had managed to transfer a surprising amount of dust onto our skirts.

'It'll brush off,' said Nora optimistically, and turned to Phyllis. 'Thanks awfully for taking us today, Phyllis. I know you didn't particularly want to …'

'I didn't,' said Phyllis.

'But we really do appreciate it. Don't we, Mollie?'

I nodded. 'And thank you too, Mabel.'

'It's the least we can do, after all you've done for the cause,' said Mabel. 'I hardly dare imagine what you'll do next.' Her tone was solemn, but there was a twinkle in her eye.

'You keep going on about all they've done for the cause,' said Kathleen peevishly, 'but as far as I can see, all they've done is cause a lot of trouble and worry.'

'Oh, they've played their parts,' said Mabel. 'We'll tell you all about it another time.

'Why don't you all come back to our house?' said Phyllis. 'Mother and Father won't be back for ages yet.'

But Kathleen's mother was expecting her so she couldn't go. I can't pretend I was disappointed as she said goodbye and headed off towards her own house.

'What about you, Nora?' said Mabel. 'After all, your parents won't be expecting you home yet. We can all have a nice cup of tea. And maybe some cake, if Maggie's made one'

'All right,' said Nora, to my delight. It was nice for us both to be treated as equals by Mabel and Phyllis – well, Mabel, anyway, but Phyllis didn't object. I remembered how we'd been invited to a suffragette tea after the Brunswick Street meeting but we couldn't go. Now we were going to have a suffragette tea of our own (well, sort of). As we made our way to our house, I suddenly felt utterly exhausted. It must have been what Mabel had been talking about earlier – as if I were an engine and all my oil had suddenly run out. By the time we got home, I was starting to yawn.

Nora nudged me.

'Stop yawning,' she hissed. 'If they think you're tired they'll probably send me home and send you to bed.'

'What are you two muttering about?' called Phyllis, who had walked a few yards ahead of us with Mabel.

'Nothing,' I said. 'Do you have a key?'

But Phyllis had forgotten her latch key (I, of course, am not trusted to have one of my own) so she knocked on the door. And who should answer it but Frank!

I don't know why, but I had totally forgotten that Frank and Harry might be at home. I think Phyllis had too, because she looked quite surprised to see him.

'I thought you and Harry were at a party,' she said, in an almost accusatory tone.

'It was afternoon tea. We've been back for a while.' Frank sounded apologetic as he answered. Then he caught sight of me and Nora and his eyes widened as he took in our unusual hair arrangements. 'Oh, hello, Mollie. And Nora.' He glanced at Mabel. 'I'm terribly sorry, but I can't remember your name, Miss …'

'It's Mabel Purcell,' said Mabel. 'But you can call me

Mabel. Now, has Maggie made any cake?'

And she strode past a slightly flummoxed-looking Frank, followed by Phyllis. Nora and I went after them. I still felt very awkward in Frank's presence, but this was a time to rise above such petty feelings. As we passed him I whispered, 'Don't tell Harry about our hair. Please, Frank.'

'I won't, if you don't want me to,' he whispered back. 'But he's in the dining room. He could be out here any minute.'

I turned to Nora.

'Come on!'

And taking her hand, I ran upstairs and into my room.

'These stupid pins!' said Nora, pulling them out as quickly as she could.

'Careful!' I cried. 'You'll be a tangled mess if you don't watch out.'

It took simply ages to get our hair down; I hoped Mabel and Phyllis would realise what we were doing and wouldn't send Harry up for us. When we were both brushed and plaited we raced down to the kitchen, where Mabel and Phyllis were sitting at the table with Maggie, drinking tea. Phyllis looked relieved to see us with our usual boring schoolgirl hair and even poured out two cups of tea without being asked.

'Here you go,' she said. 'And there's cake too.'

'Lemon drizzle,' said Maggie. She got up and closed the door to the hall.

'We were just telling Maggie about the policemen,' said Mabel, her mouth full of cake.

'Mabel, you have the manners of a bear,' said Phyllis.

'Bears don't eat cake,' retorted Mabel. 'Or use napkins.' She picked up hers and wiped away a few crumbs.

'I'd rather not talk about any policemen now the girls are here,' said Maggie firmly, handing me a slice of lemon drizzle cake.

'Just this once won't hurt, Maggie,' said Mabel. 'After all, if by any chance Mr. and Mrs. Carberry walk in and hear what we're talking about, you can say you were cleaning up and couldn't hear us. No one could accuse you of being involved.'

Maggie didn't look convinced, but she went to the sink and started filling it with hot water.

'So what are we going to do tomorrow?' Nora's eyes were bright.

'*You* are not going to do anything,' said Phyllis. 'Mabel and I are going to go to the Beresford Place meeting and sell some *Citizens*.'

'I don't see why we can't go too,' I retorted. 'I could tell Mother and Father I'm going to Nora's house. I've done it plenty of times before.'

'I can't hear anything,' said Maggie in a loud voice.

'And I can say I'm coming here,' said Nora. 'Grace is going to some special fête, or match, or something, in

Rathmines with the junior members of the tennis club and they're being fed afterwards in someone's house, so my mother won't expect me to stay in and look after her.'

'No,' said Phyllis firmly.

Nora and I exchanged glances as if to say, 'we've got around her before'. But Phyllis clearly suspected what we were thinking, because she said, 'I really mean it, Moll. I know you've shown your commitment to the cause, but something very bad could have happened this evening. And don't even think of blackmailing me again because I know you wouldn't dare.'

She was right. I tried doing it before, if you recall, and I felt far too guilty to go through with it. I looked to Mabel for support, but she shook her head.

'I agree with Phyllis,' she said. 'After that hatchet business ...'

Maggie turned quickly around.

'What hatchet business?'

'Some English girl threw a hatchet at Mr. Asquith. He wasn't hurt,' Mabel added quickly. 'But it means that the police will be even more determined to stop any activity. And not just the police. Imagine what the Ancient Hooligans and their chums will be like now.'

'Then it's not safe for you to be in town either,' Nora pointed out.

'We're old enough to make that decision for ourselves,' said Mabel. 'And you two are not.'

I was just about to answer her when the kitchen door opened and Frank and Harry came in.

'Oh, there you are,' said Harry. 'What are you skulking down here for? Poor Maggie is trying to work.'

'We were trying to hide from you,' I said, in my most cutting voice.

Harry looked affronted.

'Well, I was going to see if you wanted to play cards with us,' he said. 'But I wish I hadn't bothered now.'

Frank gave Harry a friendly punch in the arm. 'Ignore him.'

'I usually do,' I muttered.

'So, do you and Nora want to play cards?' Frank asked. He was clearly making an effort to be friendly today. He was obviously trying to forget about the embarrassing nightgown/pyjamas/red-faced incident. And I wanted to show him that I was keen to forget about it too, and let things go back to normal. But I couldn't leave Mabel and Phyllis now, not when we had so much to discuss. So I just said, 'We're fine here, thank you, Frank.'

'All right,' said Frank. 'I'll leave you to it.'

'Come on, Nugent.' Harry had already left the kitchen. Frank, looking a little flustered, followed him, closing the door behind him.

But even though I had just spurned Frank's olive branch of friendship, I still wasn't able to successfully plead my case. Even though we begged and begged, Nora and I simply couldn't persuade Mabel and Phyllis to take us.

'And if you think of sneaking along anyway,' said Phyllis in her most threatening voice, 'I'll find that Inspector Campbell and have you both arrested.'

Mabel stifled a laugh, but I had a horrible feeling Phyllis meant every word. And then I had an idea.

'Come on, then, Nora,' I said. 'If they don't want our support …'

'Oh, don't be like that,' said Mabel, but I wanted to talk to Nora alone.

'Thanks awfully, both of you,' said Nora, getting up and brushing away the cake crumbs. 'It's been a wonderful day. Even with the police and everything.'

Mabel grinned back at her. 'It has, hasn't it?'

'Apart from someone throwing a hatchet at Mr. Asquith,' said Phyllis, taking a moody bite of lemon drizzle.

Harry and Frank were still in the dining room, and I knew Julia was in our room, so we went into the dining room and closed the door behind us.

'We are going to go along tomorrow, aren't we?' Nora's voice was low. 'There's no way I'm missing any more excitement.'

'Of course we are,' I said. 'And I've thought of a good way of doing it.' I paused for dramatic effect, but Nora doesn't seem to understand such things because she said,

'Well, go on then, don't make me wait all night.'

'Disguises!' I said.

'But Phyllis has seen our disguises,' said Nora. She really can be obtuse sometimes.

'We don't have to wear the same ones,' I pointed out. 'If we borrowed some things from your mother, they'll be things she's never even seen before.'

'And hats are rather low-brimmed this year.' Nora was clearly warming to the idea. 'If we pulled them quite low over our faces and put our hair up under them, Phyllis would never notice us in a crowd.'

'Exactly!' I said. 'Do you think you can get hold of some things?'

Nora pondered the question. 'If I get some winter coats down from the attic Mother wouldn't notice they were gone. We'll be awfully hot, though.'

'And we'd look very conspicuous, wearing woolly coats in the middle of summer,' I said. 'Even worse than if we'd worn Stella's scarves.'

Then Nora's face brightened.

'I know! There was a problem with our laundry this week, and the clothes couldn't be sent out. They're still in a bundle in the kitchen, waiting for Monday. And I know for a fact that Mother's linen jacket and last year's summer coat are in there. They might be a bit stained, though ...'

'That doesn't matter,' I said. 'And we can wear the same

skirts as last time, Phyllis won't really notice them in a crowd. What about the hats?'

'Father is always telling Mother she has far too many,' said Nora. 'She definitely won't notice if two more are missing. I'll hide them in the shed tonight so I can get them tomorrow without anyone seeing.'

'What about the laundry clothes?' I asked. 'Do you think you can sneak them out easily?'

'I'll do it tonight,' said Nora. 'I'll sneak down after everyone's gone to bed.'

I wasn't sure I trusted Nora's ability to stay awake that late, but she insisted she could do it.

'And even if something happens to stop me, I can keep a careful eye on Agnes and sneak in there whenever she goes out. Mother's going to Belfast tomorrow morning on the train and Grace is going to be at her tennis thing in Rathmines all day so I don't have to worry about her.'

Then she glanced at the clock on the mantelpiece and jumped to her feet.

'Heavens, I'd better go,' she said. 'They'll wonder why I'm so late. Unless of course Barnaby's done something really dreadful to distract them.'

We arranged that she would call over here late this afternoon to give us plenty of time to get to the meeting. It wasn't until after she'd gone that I realised we didn't have anywhere to change our clothes. In fact, we still don't. But we'll think of something. Where there's a will, there's a way!

And now I must finally stop this account of our dramatic time yesterday. I've been writing it all day – I just took a break for lunch – and my hand feels like it's about to fall right off. But I did want to write everything down before I forgot it. I hope you're doing the same with your American adventures! I haven't really seen Frank all day because he and Harry have been out, but it's probably for the best. Knowing my luck, my stockings would probably fall down, or the Menace would jump on top of me, or something as soon as I saw him.

Best love and votes for women,
Mollie

Saturday, 20th July, 1912.

Dear Frances,

I don't know where to begin. I thought Thursday was a dramatic day, but I've never been so scared in my life as I was last night. I really thought someone was going to die. It wasn't exciting, like the police raid, and it didn't feel like fun afterwards. It was just very, very frightening. In fact, just thinking about it makes my hand go a bit shaky, so I apologise if my writing is less legible than usual.

Just after I finished my last letter yesterday afternoon, Phyllis came into my room brandishing a newspaper. Of course, she hadn't knocked.

'Have you seen the *Evening Telegraph*?' she said.

'And hello to you too,' I said. 'No, I haven't.'

Phyllis thrust the paper into my hands. The headline read 'LADIES WHO HAVE NO RELIGION – ONLY VOTES FOR WOMEN.'

'And this is typical,' she said. '*The Irish Independent* called what happened a "Reign of Terror". People are out for our blood. Turn to the *Telegraph* letters page.'

I flipped through the pages until I found it. Phyllis pointed to one letter.

'That's why I don't want you going out tonight,' she said.

I quickly read the letter. The writer, whoever he was, declared that suffragettes deserved to be thrown in the Liffey and said that he hoped someone would do just that. It was very strong stuff but ...

'But it's just a silly letter,' I pointed out. 'No one will take it seriously.'

'I wouldn't be so sure.' Phyllis's face was grave. 'The hatchet wasn't the only thing that happened last night. Some English suffragettes set fire to a box in the Theatre Royal. And there was an explosion there too.'

'Was anyone hurt?' I said.

'No, thank heaven,' said Phyllis. 'I suppose they did it because the Prime Minister is speaking there tonight. But I want you to swear that you won't go to Beresford Place. On Mother and Father's lives. And your honour as a suffragette.'

Telling a measly little lie to Phyllis was one thing, but I simply couldn't break such a solemn vow.

'You're being ridiculous,' I blustered.

'Am I?' said Phyllis. 'I know you. Go on, swear you won't try and go to the meeting.'

'I already told you I wouldn't,' I said, but I suspected she wouldn't be satisfied with this. And I was right.

'That's not the same as swearing a sacred oath,' Phyllis insisted.

I couldn't think of what to say to that. But by a great stroke of luck, I didn't have to say anything, because the door flung open and Julia rushed into the room.

'Have you seen Mignon?' she said. 'I can't find her anywhere.' Mignon is a doll that Mother's aunt who is a nun brought Julia from France a few years ago. She is large and has a china face and hands and the most astonishing clothes, including a beautiful little corset that is just like a grown-up one.

'Aren't you a bit old to be playing with dolls?' said Phyllis, which was jolly rude of her if you ask me. Julia drew herself up to her full height and gave Phyllis a disdainful look. (If she could have raised an eyebrow like Phyllis herself, I bet she would have.)

'I don't want to play with her,' she said. 'Christina is coming and we're going to make Mignon some new clothes. Mother said we could use her sewing machine.'

'She's on the chest of drawers.' I pointed at Mignon, who was wearing a very impressive plumed hat. 'Maggie put her there yesterday when she was cleaning the room.'

'Thank you.' Julia grabbed the doll. I must say that she's definitely the most polite member of my family, even if her praying and virtuous expressions can be a little annoying. Maybe all the praying has actually been good for her character? 'I'm going to make her a frock out of Mother's old lace nightgown. Do you want to see it?'

'All right,' I said, and followed her out of the room.

'I meant it, Moll,' said Phyllis in a fierce whisper as I passed her. 'Don't come tonight.'

'I already told you a million times that I wouldn't,' I hissed back. And then I ran down the stairs after Julia.

Phyllis didn't have a chance to harangue me again because by the time I emerged from the dining room, where Christina and Julia were cutting out pieces of a pattern that Mother had helped them to copy from a grown-up dress pattern, she had left for Mabel's house, where she was going to have tea before heading in to the meeting.

I went back to my room for some peaceful thinking about how we could change into our disguises. I lay down on my bed and stared at the ceiling in the hope of divine inspiration (well, praying clearly works for Julia), and just as I was starting to fall asleep I was struck by a brilliant idea. I was so excited about my brainwave that, when I bounced down the stairs and almost crashed into Frank, who had just arrived home with Harry, I forgot to feel self-conscious or embarrassed.

'What are you doing galumphing about like an elephant?' Harry was his usual charming self. I gave him my best Phyllis-ish look.

'I'm not galumphing anywhere,' I said. 'I'm just full of energy.' And I strode past him and into the drawing room, where Mother was lying on the sofa with a handkerchief over her eyes.

'Are you all right?' I said. I hoped she wasn't coming down with scarlet fever or whatever Grace's family have. The last thing I want is for us all to be quarantined.

Mother removed the handkerchief, and I got a whiff of Eau de Cologne.

'It's just a headache,' she said. She does get them sometimes. 'Draw the curtains, there's a good girl.'

I obeyed. I wasn't sure if this was a good time to ask her if I could go over to Nora's house, but I didn't really have a choice. Luckily, if slightly offensively, she seemed happy to be rid of me.

'Julia's invited Christina over for tea,' she said. 'So that'll save Maggie some trouble. She's been run off her feet with an extra person in the house all week.'

I had to admit that I had never thought about the fact that Frank being here meant more work for Maggie. I thanked Mother and went down to the kitchen to tell Maggie that I wasn't going to be home for tea.

'I hope you're not thinking of going into town.' Maggie's face was stern as she turned from the sink, where she was busy washing the dishes.

'Phyllis won't take us,' I said, which wasn't a lie.

Maggie turned back to the dishes.

'That hasn't stopped you before,' she said.

I was glad she couldn't see my face because I'm quite sure I was blushing.

'I'm just going to meet Nora,' I said. 'I'll see you later.'

But when I reached the hall, the door to the dining room opened and Harry appeared.

'Where are you going?' he demanded, with typical lack of manners.

'I'm going to see Nora, if you must know,' I said, in my haughtiest tone.

'Well, me and Frank and Father are just about to start a game of Consequences. You can play if you like. Father told me to ask you.' This, by the way, is about as close as Harry ever gets to a polite invitation.

As you may recall, I love playing Consequences. It's the funniest paper game. (You know, it's the one where you write down different things and fold over the paper and the next player continues the story without reading the first part.) It did sound like a jolly evening. And maybe even a chance to make things go back to normal with Frank, but then I heard the clock in the drawing room strike the hour. I had more important things to do than play Consequences with a very nice boy (and my stupid brother and quite nice father).

'Sorry,' I said. And I really was. 'But duty calls. I mean, Nora calls. I'm going to her house.'

'Oh well,' said Harry. 'I don't care if you play or not.'

And he went back into the dining room. He really does have the manners of a pig.

I had arranged to meet Nora at the corner near her house. I have to admit I was relieved when I saw her trotting around the corner with a large bag in her hand and two large but simple straw hats tucked under one arm, stacked on top of each other. I hadn't had total faith in her ability to sneak into the kitchen and get the clothes out of the bundle in the manner of one of Peter Fitzgerald's skillful jewel thieves.

'Well done!' I said.

'I told you I could do it.' Nora seemed affronted by my lack of faith. 'But where are we going to change into them? We were idiots not to think of that last night.'

'I've thought of something,' I said. 'But it's rather … well, daring.'

I told her my idea.

'The church?' she said. 'But Mollie, we can't!'

'There won't be anyone there at this time of day!' I said. 'We could just hide in the pews if we hear someone come in.'

'We can't take our clothes off in a church!' Nora was still appalled.

'We won't really be taking them off,' I argued. 'Well, I mean, we sort of will, but only our skirts and we could put the long skirts over them first so we won't be standing there in our petticoats. And then it's only a matter of changing coats, and that's hardly indecent.'

'I suppose so,' said Nora, but she didn't look absolutely comfortable with the idea.

And to tell you the truth, as we slipped through the side door of the church and cautiously looked around, I felt quite uncomfortable myself. There was no one around, and we made our way to a dark corner where Nora took the skirts and coats out of the bag. It did seem wrong to take off anything. But desperate times call for desperate measures. We put the long skirts over our usual ones (and very difficult that was too) and then stepped out of our own skirts. Once we had changed into Mrs. Cantwell's coats (there was an unfortunate stain where, Nora said, Barnaby had once jumped up on her mother at the tennis club after rolling in something unspeakably horrid) and tucked our hair up under the hats (there was no time to do it properly so we just pinned our plaits on top of our heads, puffed the front of our hair out a bit, and hoped our hat pins would keep it all in place), we looked quite grown up. Or at least grown-up enough not to earn a second glance in a crowded street.

'After all,' said Nora, 'it's not like yesterday, when we had to fool a room full of grown-up suffragettes at close quarters. We just have to make sure Phyllis and Co. don't notice us from a distance. In a crowd.'

We had to walk into town – the bag wasn't very heavy

with just our skirts in it, and we wanted to save our money for the tram fare home – and I was pleased to see that apart from some ragged children playing near the canal, no one seemed to notice anything strange about our appearance. We hadn't bothered with the grown up shoes – I hadn't taken Phyllis's warnings very seriously, but just in case there actually was any trouble in town I wanted to make sure we were wearing shoes we could run in. And after all, no one was going to be looking at our feet in a crowd. My skirt was still a little bit too long, but I folded over the waistband which pulled it up a bit, and I could walk easily in it without any danger of treading on the hem. But, even with our comfortable shoes, it was quite late by the time we reached Gardiner Street and made our way down towards Beresford Place (we had decided to avoid Sackville Street in case we bumped into Mabel or Phyllis, who usually took that route).

In fact, by the time we reached the Custom House, we could see that a huge and restless crowd had already gathered at the corner of Beresford Place, where the suffrage meeting was due to take place. For the first time I felt a genuine twinge of nervousness. Nora was clearly feeling the same way.

'They don't look very friendly, do they?' she said. And I had to agree.

The people gathered there were nearly all men and the

atmosphere was riotous. I couldn't be sure that some of them were Ancient Hooligans, but it seemed likely. There were a few women there, but they didn't look particularly friendly either. One of them was staggering around and laughing in a way that, like the man outside David Byrne's yesterday, made me think she might be intoxicated. (I have never knowingly met an intoxicated person but I have read about them in books.)

There were so many people that at first I could barely see the lorry from which the speakers would give their speeches, and I could see no sign of Phyllis and Mabel at all as we made our way closer to the lorry platform. But I was very glad we were wearing disguises that (hopefully) meant we wouldn't stand out too much in the crowd. I didn't like the idea of attracting any of these people's attention. All of sudden there was a mixture of raucous cheers and boos and hooting, and a woman whom I recognised as Mrs. Cousins mounted the lorry to address the audience.

'Thank you for coming, everyone,' she said, as the hooting continued. 'My fellow campaigners are here this evening because we love liberty as much as, I am sure, you do.'

'What about the hatchet?' roared a red-faced man not far away from me and Nora.

'What about the hatchet?' cried someone else in the crowd. And although Mrs. Cousins tried to continue her opening remarks, soon what felt like the entire crowd was roaring 'What about the hatchet? What about the hatchet?'

'I will explain our views on that matter,' cried Mrs. Cousins, but to no avail. The crowd continued their chanting. Now they were yelling, 'Down with the suffragettes!' They all seemed to be enjoying themselves tremendously, which I suppose was a good thing for me and Nora, because they were too busy yelling to pay much attention to a pair of small ladies with their hats pulled over their eyes. Because of their roars we could barely make out a word of Mrs. Cousins's speech, and when it was over she left the makeshift stage, and two other ladies took her place.

'Down with the suffragettes!' came a cry, and 'We will never forget the hatchet!' If there had been any good humour in the hooting at the start of the meeting, there certainly wasn't any now. Some of the drunken women were now very near the stage, and they started shouting at the speakers, saying that *they* didn't want the vote. One drunk woman screamed that she didn't want to listen to these old – and then she said a word which is used to describe dogs, but which I know should never be used to describe a lady. For the first time I definitely wished we hadn't come. But we were hemmed in by the crowd now, and I feared that if we started to push our way through, we would attract attention from the rowdies.

The woman on the stage (whose name, we just about managed to hear, was Mrs. Chambers) was trying to speak. But every time she opened her mouth, the boos and roars were so loud that not a word could be heard by the audience. The speaker cried out as some of the drunken women, who had apparently crept up behind the lorry, seized her from behind and tried to pull her off the stage. She broke free, but they just laughed and reached out to seize her again. Suddenly she stumbled, and I realised that some of the mob were trying to push over the lorry. I looked around and saw that the crowd had now grown so much it stretched right back to Abbey Street in one direction and the quays in another. No traffic could pass that way now. And, unless we pushed our way through with more force than either of us possess, neither could we. I hoped Phyllis and Mabel were all right, wherever they were.

Mrs. Chambers stopped speaking, and another woman took her place. By this time, Nora and I had been pushed forward by the crowd and were now so close to the lorry that, under normal circumstances, we would have been easily able to hear the speech. But as soon as she began to talk, someone in the crowd started singing 'A Nation Once Again' and soon what felt like the entire mass of people was singing along, drowning out the suffragette's words. The men shook their fists, and the drunk women waved their hat pins in the air. Then the woman on the platform stumbled and I realised another attempt had been made to push over the lorry.

'Stop that, you bowsies!' bellowed a strangely familiar voice nearby, and I looked around to see Inspector Campbell and some of his men approaching the speakers. They quickly dealt with the rowdies and stood guard in front of the lorry, but the crowd was becoming even more threatening. I grabbed Nora's hand and she squeezed mine tightly.

'Do you think we could get away?' she whispered, her voice shaking.

'I don't think so,' I said. 'We'll just have to wait until it's over. Oh!' Someone in the crowd had thrown a stone at the speaker, narrowly missing her face. Another missile soon followed. Inspector Campbell turned to her.

'I think you'd better stop the meeting now, madam,' he said in his booming voice.

The woman on the stage nodded, her face pale. Inspector Campbell and his men helped her off the lorry and formed a ring around her and the other speakers. As the crowd surged towards them, Nora and I were almost lifted off our feet. I clung on to Nora's hand as hard as I could as we stumbled with the mob towards the lorry. I thought I saw Mabel on the other side of the vehicle and then a section of the crowd surged towards the ring of policemen, briefly leaving a gap.

'Come on!' I cried, and dragged Nora through the gap and underneath the lorry. We huddled together, watching the stamping boots of the mob as they continued to hurl abuse at the brave women and their protective policeman guards. I remembered Phyllis saying that the Dublin policemen behaved in a much more gentlemanly manner to the Irish suffragettes than their brutal English equivalents. We couldn't see Inspector Campbell and his men, but from the noises made by the crowd it sounded like the protective circle was moving away, followed by their harrassers. I heard a woman scream and I clung to Nora's hand even more tightly.

'What should we do?' Nora's eyes were wide in the darkness beneath the lorry. 'Will we wait here until it's over?'

'I think so,' I said, but just then the lorry shuddered above us as some of the men barged into it. 'Oh dear, oh dear. This doesn't sound safe.'

'We should go,' said Nora. 'Now. This way.' She led the way and we crawled out from under the lorry, emerging on the far side where the mob had thinned out a little. Mabel was nowhere to be seen, if she'd ever been there at all, and luckily the drunk women had gone. We crept to the end of the lorry, climbing up on one of the wheels of the vehicle to get a better view, without being seen by the mob.

In the distance, the policemen and their charges were heading towards Abbey Street. There was a shriek and some raucous laughter, and I realised that the mob had torn the hats from the heads of two of the ladies. Inspector Campbell and his men drew their batons and roared at the crowd to stand back, which they briefly did, but as the suffragettes and their protectors moved towards Abbey Street, the mob continued their assault.

'Mollie!' cried Nora, forgetting to whisper. 'Look!'

One of the women had been dragged away from her friends. We watched in shock as she was roughly shoved to the ground.

'We have to do something!' I said. But what could we do against the mob? The woman screamed in pain and fear as a laughing man gave her a sickening kick in the stomach. Some of the policemen realised what was going on and tried to reach the fallen suffragette, but the crowd was jostling around them and they could only move towards her with what felt like agonizing slowness. I almost closed my eyes in horror – I knew we couldn't help her, but it felt so awful to just watch. Then, thank heaven, some other men shoved away her attackers and helped the woman to her feet. The policemen finally broke through the crowd and formed a sort of shield around her, leading her towards Butt Bridge. They passed a few yards away from our vantage point, and as they drew near I could see that the woman's face was cut and she held one of her arms with the other hand, as if in great pain.

'They're probably taking her to the police station,' said Nora, her voice shaking. 'Oh Mollie, I wish we hadn't come.'

'Most of the crowd seem to have moved down to Abbey Street.' I tried and failed to keep my own voice steady as I thought of all those horrible men pursuing the suffragettes and their policeman guards. 'Maybe if we get a tram on Westmoreland Street we'll avoid them.'

'I wish we weren't wearing these stupid clothes.' Nora sounded as if she might burst into tears at any moment. 'If we were wearing our ordinary clothes they'd leave us alone. But they have no qualms about attacking ladies.'

'If we hadn't been wearing our disguises Phyllis might have …' I stopped mid-sentence. 'Where is she? You haven't seen her, have you?'

'No,' said Nora. 'Or Mabel.'

'They weren't with the women who went with the policemen,' I said. 'Maybe they got away through the quays? We might bump into them if we go that way.'

'That's a risk we'll have to take,' said Nora. In the distance we could hear what sounded like glass being broken, followed by raucous cheers. 'I want to go home right now.'

We climbed down from the wheel of the lorry. Keeping

as close to the grounds of the Custom House as possible rather than striking out across Beresford Place, where I feared we might attract more attention, we made our way towards the bridge.

'Look straight ahead,' whispered Nora. 'We mustn't catch anyone's eye.' The crowd had thinned out, as most of the mob had either followed the suffragettes and their escorts or given up and gone home. We had just reached the corner opposite Liberty Hall, that new union building I passed on my way to my very first suffrage meeting, when I heard a scream from the corner of Eden Quay.

I couldn't help looking around, and to my great horror I saw that a group of men were gathered around someone – a young woman, judging by the scream. The policemen who had been standing guard over the meeting seemed to have vanished – most of them had left with the speakers, while the others had gone with the woman who had been kicked to the ground. There was no one left to intervene now.

'Look!' I clutched Nora's hand.

'What will we do?' Nora looked as distressed as I felt. 'We can't just leave her to her fate!'

'We'll have to try to find a policeman.' We began to cross Beresford Place, but there wasn't a policeman to be seen. I looked wildly around me. 'There must be someone!'

There was another scream from the corner of the quay,

and the gang began to chant.

'Throw her in the Liffey! Throw her in the Liffey!'

'Oh, where are the policemen?' wailed Nora as we hurried towards the rowdy crowd.

Suddenly, from the middle of the mob, a struggling, shouting young woman was lifted into the air by a group of laughing men. Her hat had fallen off but there was something familiar about her coat, and her hair …

'Phyllis!' I cried, and ran through the crowd as fast as I could in that stupid skirt. I pulled it up over my knees and kept going, Nora racing at my heels. The mob were carrying Phyllis toward the wall that bordered the river, and although she was struggling to get free with all her might, they held her fast.

'I'm going to find a policeman,' yelled Nora. 'We've got to stop this.'

'I can't leave her,' I yelled back.

'I know.' Nora nodded. 'I'll be back as soon as I can.' She ran around the crowd and down the quays in the direction of Sackville Street. And I pushed my way through the jostling men. (This is where it is an advantage to be quite short, it is much easier to wriggle through a crowd than it would be for elegant tall people.) If I'd thought about it, I would have realised just how dangerous it was, that there was nothing to stop the men seizing me and tossing me into the air too. But I didn't think. I just knew I had to try and save Phyllis from being thrown in the river. That was all.

Now I could see that someone else was trying to save her. Mabel, her face desperate, her hat long gone, had grabbed onto Phyllis's thrashing foot, and was trying to pull her from the men's grasp.

'Let go of her, you beasts!' Mabel's voice was hoarse from shouting.

I seized hold of Phyllis's skirt, which was when Mabel noticed my presence.

'Pull!' she cried. 'We can't let them …'

But whatever she had planned to say was left unfinished, as one of the men gave her a fierce shove from behind. She lost her grasp of Phyllis as she fell forward, crashing into me. The men raised Phyllis right over the parapet.

'Phyllis!' I screamed.

'Throw her in, boys!' yelled a raucous voice. 'With a one …'

Phyllis was swung towards the crowd and back again, as the men roared their approval of this hideous game.

'And a two!' yelled the voice. Again they swung the wriggling Phyllis back and forth. Her hair was over her face, and she was making an awful whimpering sound that was worse than the screams.

'And a three!'

And just as I thought Phyllis was going to be swung right over the parapet and into the water, there was a piercing whistle, so loud it seemed to stop the mob in their vile tracks. For a second, everyone seemed to freeze. Suddenly several policemen, batons drawn, barged their way through the crowd. Nora was right behind them, clutching the bag to her chest and red in the face from the exertion of running.

'Release that young lady!' roared a red-faced constable. Nothing happened. The constable seemed to get even redder as he waved his baton. 'Right now!'

The men who had been abusing Phyllis dropped her roughly on the pavement next to the parapet. Nora, Mabel and I rushed to her aid as the policemen, batons drawn, shoved her attackers away. Phyllis looked as if she were on the verge of fainting. Her lace blouse front was torn, and there were several large rips in her jacket.

'Oh Phyllis,' I said, and as I spoke I realised I was crying.

'Are you all right?' said Mabel. 'I thought they might have broken your wrist …'

'They didn't.' Phyllis's voice was barely a croak. She tried to get to her feet, but when she stood up her legs seemed to give way and she clutched the parapet for support. 'No, no, I'm all right …'

'Lean against the wall for a moment,' said Mabel. 'The policemen are still here. We're safe for now.'

'I'll see if I can spot your lost hat,' said Nora, looking down Eden Quay towards Sackville Street.

'Long gone,' said Phyllis faintly. She seemed to be in a sort of daze. 'One of those hooligans' wives will probably be wearing it tomorrow.'

I looked around in the other direction to make sure there were no more rowdies attempting mischief. And that was when I saw the group of well-dressed young girls in white, standing with their strangely familiar chaperone at the corner of Butt Bridge. They seemed to be frozen in fear, and had clearly witnessed Phyllis's terrifyingly narrow escape. And standing right at the front of the group, staring straight at me, was none other than Grace.

For a long moment we held each other's gaze. Then the chaperone seemed to unfreeze herself, and said something to her charges, leading them back across the bridge towards Tara Street. I realised why she looked so familiar. She was Grace's beloved Miss Casey. She must have been taking the group of girls back from that tennis club outing to Rathmines.

I looked around for Nora. She'd been facing the opposite direction, and I don't think Grace had even noticed her, especially as she was still wearing her mother's hat and the long skirt. But I couldn't pretend that Grace hadn't recognised me. I felt panic bubble up inside me. Grace had clearly witnessed the violence. This wasn't the same as her knowing we supported the cause or had even done a bit of chalking. She now knew that I had been at a suffrage meeting where a mob had attacked the speakers and where my sister had almost been killed. What would we do if she told Nora's mother? I was distracted from my panicked thoughts by Mabel.

'Mollie? Are you listening? I said we'll have to try and get a cab.' Her voice was strained. 'I'm not going to risk meeting another mob. Asquith must be in the Theatre Royal by now, and that might give them another excuse to cause trouble.'

In case you've forgotten, the Theatre Royal is just on the other side of the Liffey, almost opposite to where we were standing. It seemed all too likely that trouble could break out nearby. Luckily, at this stage the crowd at Beresford Place had almost entirely dispersed, and traffic was making its way through again. But still, it took us a while to hail a cab. If the jarvey had any opinions on our generally peculiar appearance – Nora's plaits had descended from beneath her hat, I had trodden on the hem on my skirt, and Phyllis and Mabel were not only hatless, but their clothes looked, as Mabel said ruefully when we were all inside the cab, as if they'd been dragged through a thorn bush backwards – he kept them to himself as we climbed aboard.

'I'm going to have some hideous bruises tomorrow,' Mabel said as we settled into our seats, trying and almost succeeding in keeping up her usual cheery tone. 'What about you, Phyl?'

And Phyllis, without warning, suddenly burst into tears.

'I'm sorry!' she sobbed, as Mabel and I tried to comfort her. When I put my arm around her, I realised she was shaking. 'I thought I was all right. But it's as if …' She couldn't finish the sentence. 'They were going to throw me in the river! And they kept grabbing me and crushing me …'

I wasn't used to seeing Phyllis like this. She was usually strong and bossy and even though it was very annoying sometimes, it always seemed like the correct way for a big sister to behave. It was horrible seeing her so upset. It was all wrong.

'Sssh, you're all right.' Mabel's voice was soothing as we waited for Phyllis's sobs to subside. 'You're safe now.'

After a while, Phyllis dug around in the pocket of her coat for a handkerchief, which luckily hadn't been lost in the assault. She wiped her eyes and blew her nose loudly.

'Oh goodness,' she said. She looked down at her clothes and rolled up her sleeves. Bruises were already starting to form, and you could almost see the imprints of the strong hands that had grabbed and dragged her. 'Oh Lord. What am I going to tell Mother and Father? That mob is going to be in the paper tomorrow. They'll guess I was there.'

'I've been thinking about that,' said Mabel. 'And I had an idea. We can tell our parents we were knocked over by a cab on Rutland Square. Nice and far away from the riot.'

'A cab?' Phyllis stared at her.

'Well, don't you remember the cab protests? The jarveys are in turmoil. We can tell your parents that one of them was distracted by a motor car or something.' She looked guiltily in the direction of the driver, whose profession she was maligning (albeit for a good cause). 'It's not as though we're going to blame an individual jarvey.'

'All right.' Phyllis was clearly too weary to argue. And then it was as if she noticed me and Nora for the first time. 'What are you two doing here?' She didn't even sound angry. I think she was too overwhelmed by the terrible events of the evening.

'We went to the meeting,' I said. 'I'm sorry, Phyl. You were right, it was too dangerous.'

'It certainly was,' said Mabel, in unusually stern tones. 'You girls could have been badly hurt. It's a miracle you weren't.'

'I know,' said Nora. 'We hid under the lorry.'

'Very ingenious of you,' said Mabel dryly. 'But you shouldn't have been there at all.'

'It was Nora who got the policemen,' I said. 'So if we hadn't been there …'

'Did you really?' said Mabel. Nora nodded.

'Thank you, Nora,' said Phyllis. 'If they hadn't come when they did …' Her voice cracked, and I thought she might burst into tears again. But she didn't.

'At least you can swim,' said Mabel. 'Imagine if it had been Kathleen. She nearly drowned in a foot of water in Skerries last year.'

'She'd have been more worried about her hat,' said Phyllis, and gave a laugh that almost turned into a sob.

Mabel turned a discerning gaze on me and Nora.

'Obviously I'm glad you were the means of saving Phyllis from a watery, smelly grave,' she said. 'Or at least a watery smelly bath. But where exactly do your mothers think you are?'

We explained about our usual method of deceiving our parents.

'You're not going to be able to get away with that forever,' said Mabel.

And that's when I remembered what I'd seen on the bridge. My stomach sank.

'Oh no,' I said.

'What's wrong?' Nora's brow furrowed. 'You look a bit green. You're not going to get sick, are you? Should we stop the cab?'

'I saw something.' I took a deep breath. 'On Butt Bridge. Grace. She was on the corner. With her tennis club friends.'

'Oh dear,' said Nora, turning as pale as I felt. Phyllis and Mabel exchanged worried glances.

'Do you think she saw what happened?' said Mabel.

I nodded miserably. 'I'm almost certain she did. Her group must have been crossing the bridge while those awful men were trying to chuck you in, Phyl. They couldn't have missed it. And she definitely recognised me.'

'Which means,' said Mabel, her face grim, 'that she probably recognised me and Phyllis too.'

'She can't tell anyone,' said Phyllis. 'You've got to make sure of that.'

'I'll try,' said Nora miserably. 'But she really can be very difficult.'

'I don't care!' said Phyllis. 'If she tells your mother what she saw this evening, I'm sure she would be straight round to our house to tell ours.'

I was quite sure this was true. And if she did, everything would come out – not just Phyllis being a suffragette. Not just the fact that she had put her life in danger (at least, this is how our parents would see it – of course it was only in danger because that mob of hooligans were causing trouble, but I knew our parents would blame her for being anywhere near them). Not just the fact that me and Nora had been there in disguise – I know Grace didn't actually see Nora's face, but I wouldn't be able to persuade her that I'd been there on my own, especially when she knew Nora had planned to spend the evening with me.

All of that was bad enough for one evening. But of course, it wouldn't just be about one evening. If Nora's mother and my mother actually met and had a proper conversation about our activities, they would doubtless realise that over the last few months, Nora and I had told each of our parents that we were going to the other one's house, when really we had been roaming the streets chalking and going to meetings and getting dressed up in (I felt sick at the thought of what she'd say when she found this out) Mrs. Cantwell's very own clothes. They would realise that we had been lying to them for ages and ages. I couldn't even imagine how they would respond to this. We'd never be let out of the house again. Or worse, they might decide to send us away to boarding school – different ones, obviously – where we would be supervised at all times.

And now it's the next day and I still don't know what they're going to do. Because I haven't seen or heard from Nora since the cab dropped us off. (We had managed to change back into our skirts while squashed onto the floor of the cab.) The jarvey was taking Mabel on to her house in Clontarf, and she leaned out the window as he drove her away.

'*Courage, mes amies!*' she cried. 'Talk to your cousin, Nora!'

'I'd better run,' said Nora. She looked quite neat now she'd taken off her mother's clothes. Well, she didn't look as if she'd just been in a riot, anyway. I hoped I looked the same. 'Maybe I'll get home before her.'

'Call around tomorrow,' said Phyllis. 'Tell us what happened.'

Nora nodded and sped away, and Phyllis and I turned and headed for home. She was walking slowly.

'Are you sure you're all right to walk?' I said. 'I could run ahead and ask Maggie to come and help support you …'

'I'm fine,' said Phyllis. 'Just sore. Mabel's right, I'll be a mass of bruises tomorrow. Anyway, it's not fair to Maggie to get her involved.' We walked the rest of the way home in silence.

I had forgotten that Phyllis is a jolly good actress. I remembered that she was pretty decent when the senior girls put on that play when I was a junior baby, but she was quite extraordinary last night, especially when you consider what she'd been through that evening. Mother and Father completely believed her tale of being hit by a cab on Rutland Square, and then bumping into me around the corner from our house as she staggered home from the tram.

'Those blasted jarveys!' said Father, and I knew he was very upset because he'd never have said that word in front of us otherwise. I felt a bit guilty about the poor jarveys being maligned in this fashion, especially when they are worried about being taken over by motor cabs, but it couldn't be helped.

'I'll call Doctor Butler tomorrow,' said Mother from the sofa, where she was bathing Phyllis's pale brow. Phyllis raised herself from the cushions on which she was lying.

'There's no need,' she said. 'There are no bones broken. After all, I was just a little bumped by the wheel. It's not as though I were literally run over.'

'Still, maybe you should let him have a look ...' I said. But Phyllis threw me an angry look, and I remembered the marks on her arm. If a doctor saw them, he would know she had been attacked by a person and not hit by a cab.

'No, you're right,' I said quickly. 'I'm sure you're fine.'

'The police should have arrested the jarvey,' said Father.

'Well, they were busy,' said Phyllis. 'I heard some suffragettes were attacked by a mob somewhere near the Theatre Royal. The police must have been gathered down there.'

'Attacked by a mob!' said Mother. 'How dreadful.'

'What on earth were they doing, attracting a mob?' Father seemed less sympathetic. 'They must have been breaking windows again.'

'They weren't,' said Phyllis. 'I mean, as far as I know. I was told they were just trying to give speeches, and some roughs started throwing stones and grabbing them.'

'What is this city coming to?' said Mother. 'Girls being run over by cabs – well, almost run over, Phyllis – and women being attacked by mobs.' And she blew her nose very loudly, just as Harry and Frank walked into the room. Of course, Harry wanted to know why Phyllis was lying on the sofa 'looking like a dying duck' and when he was told that she'd been hit by a cab he went quite pale and said, 'She's all right, isn't she?'

'I'm fine,' said Phyllis. 'Just bruised.'

'Well, I hope you're going to throw those grubby rags you're wearing in the rubbish bin,' said Harry, sounding like his usual rude self again. But I could see that for a second he had been genuinely worried about Phyllis.

'Are you all right?' Frank asked me. 'Did you get knocked down too?'

'Me?' Surely I didn't look like a dying duck too? 'No, I just met Phyllis on my way home. Why do you ask?'

'Sorry, I just thought ...' Frank looked embarrassed. 'The collar of your blouse ...' I glanced at my reflection in the glass over the mantelpiece and realised the collar was torn. I hadn't noticed it before, but it must have happened when that man who was attacking Phyllis crashed into me.

'Oh, she always looks like that,' said Harry. 'Haven't you noticed?'

I could feel my cheeks flushing. Ever since Frank came to stay in our house, it seems to have been one embarrassing incident after another. And suddenly I felt exhausted by it all.

'I'm going to bed,' I said. And I left them all to discuss my scruffiness, and Phyllis's ailments, and the state of Dublin, and whatever else they wanted to talk about. I didn't think I'd sleep at all when I went to bed, especially as Julia was already snoring, but I fell asleep straight away, even though it wasn't very late. Which is probably why I woke up at five o'clock this morning. But at least that has given me time to write this very long account of our adventures to you. I still haven't heard from Nora so I have no idea if Grace has told Mrs. Cantwell what she saw this evening. I only hope that I will be able to write again and that I won't be immediately sent off to one of the aunts in the country once Nora's mother tells my mother all. If I was posting off this letter now, I would ask you to say a prayer for me. As it is, I will have to pray for myself and hope that God doesn't mind that it is a prayer asking Him to help us keep a secret from our parents. But before I pray, I will go and ask Maggie for some toast because I really am awfully hungry …

Best love and votes for women,
Mollie

Later

Well! I don't know where to begin. This has been one of the most extraordinary weeks of my entire life. Since Monday, I have become a master of disguise. I have been caught up in a police raid. I have been in a riot and almost saw my poor sister tossed into a river by a vicious mob. But nothing has shocked me as much as what happened this afternoon.

After I had written my last letter, I went down to get some toast. The door of Phyllis's room was closed and although I desperately wanted to talk to her about what we should do if Grace told tales to Mrs. Cantwell, it didn't seem right to disturb her. I could only imagine how horrid it must have been to be seized by those terrible men, and how scared she must have been of what they would do to her. And I could only imagine how bruised and sore she must be today. So if she was still asleep – or at least resting – I knew I should leave her in peace.

When I reached the hall I could hear voices from the dining room. Father must have already gone to work, but Harry, Frank and Mother seemed to be having a lively discussion. I paused for a moment outside the door, and my heart sank right down to my toes as I heard Harry say the words, 'silly suffragettes.' A horrible thought struck me. I had been holed up in my room for a long time, and I had been concentrating so hard on my letter that I doubt I'd have noticed if anyone had knocked on the door. What if Mrs. Cantwell had already been around to tell Mother about me and Phyllis, and Harry and Frank were now talking about our supposed misdeeds?

For a second I felt like running down to the kitchen and avoiding all of them for as long as possible. But I knew I had to face the truth, whatever it might be. So I took a deep breath and opened the door. Mrs. Cantwell wasn't there, but Harry was still in full flow as I walked in. He had a newspaper in one hand and a cup of tea in the other.

'The police had to escort them to the tram,' he said, through a mouthful of toast. He really has no table manners. 'And then the crowd smashed the tram windows!'

'That's hardly the suffragettes' fault,' said Mother mildly. 'Oh, there you are, Moll. What on earth have you been doing up in your room all morning?'

'Writing to Frances,' I said.

'It's their fault for making shows of themselves in public,' said Harry, ignoring me.

'That's a bit much,' said Frank firmly. 'They had every right to have their meeting in peace.'

'They shouldn't have had a meeting at all,' retorted Harry. 'They should have known there'd be trouble, after that hatchet business.' He looked at Frank suspiciously.

'Anyway, why are you defending them? You're not becoming one of those feeble men who go on about women being equal, are you? Apparently one of them sneaked in to Mr. Asquith's meeting last night. Such fools.'

'As a matter of fact, I agree with them,' said Frank. 'And I don't think they're fools. Or feeble. Quite the opposite, really. I think they're jolly brave, standing up for women.'

'You can't really believe that rot!' Harry's face was a picture.

'Now, now,' said Mother. 'No fighting at the breakfast table. Especially in the holidays.' She turned to me. 'There's some toast left, if you want it.'

'No there isn't,' said Harry, grabbing the last slice from the rack and slathering some butter on it before shoving half of it into his gaping maw. He really is revolting. And he was clearly spoiling for a fight. But I refused to rise to his bait.

'I'll ask Maggie to make me some,' I said. 'How's Phyllis?'

'She says she's fine.' But Mother didn't look totally convinced. 'Maggie brought her toast and tea in bed.'

'I'll go and get some breakfast for myself,' I said, pointedly turning my back on Harry, who was finishing the toast with exaggerated expressions of pleasure. When I reached the kitchen Maggie was sitting at the table, a cup of tea in her hand and a weary expression on her face.

'I've just come to get some bread and butter,' I said. 'If there's any bread left.'

'And have you ever known this kitchen to run out of bread?' Maggie may have looked tired, but there was humour in her voice. 'I'll slice it for you.'

'You sit there,' I said, as firmly as I could. 'I'll do it.'

Maggie didn't argue as I unwrapped the loaf from its paper covering and got out the breadknife.

'Did Phyllis tell you what happened last night?' I cut myself two sturdy doorsteps of bread.'

'She did,' said Maggie. 'And she told me you were there too. After everyone telling you not to go.'

'I'm sorry.' I couldn't help blushing, this time out of guilt. 'But I didn't lie to you. I just told you I was meeting Nora.'

'That's lying by omission, which is a sin as you know very well.'

I couldn't meet Maggie's stern gaze as I buttered the bread.

'I'm sorry,' I said. And I was. I didn't really feel guilty about going out on Friday, but I felt guilty about lying to Maggie. I told myself that she hadn't wanted to know about my suffrage activities, so it was lie told in good faith. But I still felt a bit queasy.

And then there was a knock on the door, and I felt even queasier. If it was Nora – and I had a feeling it was – soon

I would know my fate.

'I'll get it!' I cried, and ran into the hall, a slice of bread and butter in one hand. I flung open the door and there indeed was Nora, looking as if she'd run all the way to my house which, as it turned out, she had.

'Did she tell?' My voice was a desperate whisper. Nora shook her head. I felt my shoulders sag with relief.

'Thank heaven!' I said. 'Do you think she will?'

'I don't know,' said Nora, regaining her breath. 'Can we go upstairs?'

I nodded and Nora followed me up to my room.

'So?' I said, when the door was safely closed and I'd put the bolster against the bottom of it to make sure no sound drifted out. 'What did she say? When you talked to her, I mean.'

'That's the thing,' said Nora. 'I haven't talked to her!'

I stared at her in disbelief. 'But how?'

'She was already home when I got there,' said Nora. 'That tennis-club lady must have got them a fleet of cabs, for I can't imagine how Grace managed it so quickly otherwise. And when I went up to bed she was pretending to be asleep.'

'Did you try and get her up?' I asked.

'Of course I did!' said Nora. 'But she pretended she couldn't hear me.'

My stomach churned at Nora's words. This didn't

sound good. A Grace pretending to be asleep to avoid Nora sounded like a Grace who was preparing to reveal a terrible secret about her cousin and couldn't bring herself to face her future victim.

'What about this morning?' I said.

And now it was Nora's turn to blush.

'She left before I got up,' she said.

'I thought she always made lots of noise in the mornings!' I said.

'She does, usually! But she can be sneaky when she wants to be. And,' Nora added honestly, 'I probably wouldn't have woken up even if she had been stamping around the place as usual. I really was exhausted.'

I couldn't blame Nora for not waking up and intercepting Grace. I had slept like a log as well.

'Where is she now?' I asked.

'At the tennis club,' said Nora. 'But she's due home for lunch. So I thought we could intercept her en route. We could wait at the corner – you know, near the bridge. And we should probably go there now, just in case she leaves early.'

'All right,' I said. 'Let's go.'

I was worried that Mother might object to me going off with Nora again – the very idea might make her realise just how late I'd come home last night – but when I stuck my head into the dining room Harry was telling her a long and boring-sounding story about yesterday's cricket match so she barely noticed me telling her I was off to the Botanic Gardens (not entirely a lie, if we took Grace there to have a stern talk with her). I quickly made my escape and a few minutes later Nora and I were trotting down the road in the direction of the tennis club. We hadn't gone far before we spotted a familiar figure coming towards us.

'Hello girls!' Mrs. Sheffield was cheerful. Possibly because she wasn't accompanied by Barnaby, who as I know from experience is not an easy walking companion. 'I've just come from the tennis club and I was wondering ...' But before she could get any further, I interrupted her.

'I'm most awfully sorry, Mrs. Sheffield, but we really have to go,' I said. 'Mrs. Cantwell is expecting us and we're already frightfully late.'

'We really are,' said Nora helpfully.

And without waiting for Mrs. Sheffield to reply, we hurried on down the road.

'We weren't too rude, were we?' I said, as we turned the corner.

'I don't think so,' said Nora. 'We said we were late for my mother. That's a decent excuse.' A thought struck her. 'Oh Lord, you don't suppose Grace told her about yesterday, do you? She knows Mrs. Sheffield is a friend of your mother.'

'Surely not!' My stomach lurched. 'No, she can't have. I

don't think Mrs. Sheffield would have been so jolly if she was on her way to tell my mother I'd been in a riot.'

'You're probably right.' Nora sounded calmer. 'We'll just have to persuade Grace to stay quiet.'

'You never know, she might not take too much persuading,' I said hopefully. 'She hasn't been too hateful to us recently.'

'I think you're giving her far too much credit,' said Nora. 'You know what she thinks of the movement. She's going to think that we're all a lot of street brawlers and that she's doing the right thing by stopping us.'

I thought of what Harry said when he was stealing my toast.

'I'm afraid you're right,' I said. 'And the last time she threatened to tell on us, Stella stopped her by threatening to throw her notebook down the lav. But we have nothing to bargain with now.' We had almost reached our destination. 'Oh Nora, what will we do if she reveals all?'

'We'll have to face our punishment like Mrs. Sheehy-Skeffington and the others,' said Nora in a brave voice. But her voice wobbled a bit as she added, 'I hope we don't have to.'

The corner where we planned to pounce on Grace was occupied by a house with a low wall running around its garden.

'At least we have somewhere to sit while we await

our fate,' said Nora.

'Until the owners chase us away for vagrancy,' I said. But we sat down anyway. Neither of us said anything for a while as we peered anxiously down the road in the direction of the tennis club.

'I wouldn't mind us being punished,' I said suddenly, 'if it felt like it was for the sake of the cause. You know, like the leaders going to prison. They made a dramatic statement and everyone knows about it. But if we get sent off to boarding school just for being at a meeting, we haven't really done anything for the cause. We haven't left anything behind. And no one in the world will know why we're being punished besides our families. It won't be in the papers. It won't actually do anything. If you know what I mean.'

'I was just thinking the same thing,' said Nora gloomily. 'I mean, I don't mind making a sacrifice for the cause. But it doesn't do the cause much good if no one knows about it.'

'Maybe we could alert the newspapers,' I said. 'I mean, if they're going to send us off to boarding school anyway, what have we got to lose?'

But Nora didn't answer. She was jumping to her feet.

'There she is!' She sheltered her eyes from the sun and peered down the road. 'And she's not alone!'

She certainly wasn't. As Grace drew closer, I could see

that one of her hands held her tennis racket, while the other held a lead. And on the end of the lead was a sturdy harness, and in that harness, prancing along gleefully, was the Menace.

'What on earth is he doing with her?' I wondered.

'Maybe he's joined the tennis club,' said Nora impatiently. 'It doesn't matter. What matters is that we talk her out of saying anything about us.'

But that task looked like it would be easier said than done when Grace caught sight of us. She froze for a moment. (The Menace was pulled short on his harness, and barked his disapproval.) She glanced at the road, and if she could have run across it she would, but luckily there were several delivery vans making their way down the street so she was stuck on the same side of the road as us. Nora and I hurried towards her.

'Grace!' Nora was trying to keep her voice calm, but you could tell how worried she was. 'We need to talk to you.'

'No, you don't,' said Grace, hurrying past us, the Menace trotting along as fast as his twinkling little legs could carry him.

'Please, Grace,' I begged, walking fast to catch up with them. 'It's about last night.'

'I don't want to talk about last night.' Grace's voice was tight. 'Leave me alone.'

'But Grace …' began Nora.

Grace stopped walking and whirled round to face us.

'Can't you do *anything* you're told to do?' she cried. 'Go away!'

And Barnaby, as if sensing his heroine's mood and wishing to defend her from danger, made a growling noise that stopped me in my tracks. I had heard him bark before (many, many times, as you know) but I'd never heard him growl.

'Don't follow me!' said Grace, and Barnaby gave another growl, his woolly white ears sticking up on each side of his head. I had never seen him look so enraged. I suppose it was quite impressive that the thing that had spurred him to such dramatic action was a desire to protect a human being. Even if that human being was Grace.

'All right,' I said meekly. 'Sorry.'

Because really, what else could we do? We weren't going to persuade her to keep our secret by chasing her when she was in a mood like this. Especially with the Menace turning into the Hound of the Baskervilles (which is one of my favourite Sherlock Holmes stories, but a savage hound is not as entertaining when it's actually menacing you in real life). We stood on the path for a few minutes, watching Grace hurry away. Every so often Barnaby turned his head and glowered at us with his button eyes until they were out of sight.

'Do you think she's going to tell on us?' I said.

'I have a horrible feeling she is,' said Nora. 'It would explain why she doesn't want to talk to us. She can't face us knowing that she's going to send us to the scaffold.'

This was a bit of an exaggeration, because even if our parents were very angry they weren't going to have us executed, but I knew what she meant. We might as well be dead if we were sent off to separate boarding schools in the middle of nowhere. The sky, which had been clear and blue when we left my house, had begun to cloud over, and a sharp and strongly scented breeze blew in from the canal.

'We could always run away,' I suggested.

'I thought of that when Grace first came to stay, remember?' said Nora. 'And you pointed out how impractical it was.'

I sighed. I knew she was right. And as if in sympathy with my mood, the clouds suddenly burst and large rain drops began to fall. In the distance there was a rumble of thunder.

'Let's go back to my house,' I said. 'Even if Grace has told all, your mother probably hasn't gone round there yet.'

'I suppose so,' said Nora, whose skirt was already half-soaked with rain. 'Let's go.'

We ran as fast as we could but we were still utterly soaked AND I had a terrible stitch by the time we reached the corner of my road.

'Bless us and save us,' said Maggie when she opened the door to find two sodden figures on the doorstep. 'Where have you two been?'

'We just went for a walk,' I said. We were so wet that our clothes were dripping all over the hall tiles.

'Well, go up and change into dry clothes before you catch your deaths,' said Maggie. 'You must have something Nora can borrow, Mollie.' She smiled at Nora. 'Then you can have tea with your cousin in the drawing room. I've made biscuits.'

'My cousin?' Nora froze with one foot on the bottom stair.

Maggie nodded. 'She's in with Mrs. Carberry and Mrs. Sheffield — she's got Mrs. Sheffield's little dog with her again.'

'What are they doing there?' I tried to keep my voice steady. It somehow hadn't crossed my mind that Grace might avoid Nora's mother and go straight to mine.

'You'll have to ask her that,' said Maggie. 'Now, go and get changed while I boil the kettle.'

Nora and I exchanged anguished looks and hurried up to my room.

'So this is it,' I said, struggling to unbutton my sopping wet blouse.

'It's all over.' Nora looked as if she were about to burst into tears as she pulled off her cotton skirt.

I couldn't bear the thought of going into that drawing room and seeing Grace's face (and Barnaby's for that matter) as we heard our fate.

'Let's wait until she's gone,' I said, handing her an old blue dress that luckily happened to be clean. 'I can bear it – I can almost bear it – if she's not there.'

'All right,' Nora said. She fastened the buttons on the blue dress, which was a little too short for her. 'I feel like Mary Queen of Scots on my way to have my head chopped off.'

'We should be wearing black velvet,' I said miserably. I had changed into a linen blouse with embroidery on the collar that looked far too cheerful for such a mournful day. I was wondering if I should change into something more sombre when my mother's voice came ringing up the stairs.

'Mollie! Can you come to the drawing room, please?'

I stared at Nora, my eyes wide. She grabbed my hand and squeezed it.

'If they send you away right now and we're not allowed see each other again,' I said, 'I want you to know that I'm sorry for getting you mixed up in all of this.'

Nora let go of my hand and elbowed me sharply in the ribs.

'Don't talk rot.' Her voice was a little shaky. 'I knew exactly what I was doing. And I'd do it all again.' She looked at me. 'Wouldn't you?'

'Of course I would,' I said. And I meant it. Because even if we didn't win any publicity for the cause, even if no one ever knew about what we'd done, we would know. We would know that we'd taken a risk for something we believed in. And however they decided to punish us, we would know that it was worth it. Yes, I regretted going out the other night, but that was because the Ancient Hooligans and their supporters had been so awful. In a fair and just world, we would be able to go to whatever meetings we liked without fear. And that was the world we would keep fighting for.

I thought all of those things as we slowly made our way down to the drawing room. I could hear Barnaby barking on the other side of the door. I reached out to the doorknob and then paused.

'Here we go,' I said, and opened the door.

I don't know exactly what I had expected to find on the other side. Mother, Mrs. Sheffield and Grace standing in an accusatory line, perhaps, with Barnaby sitting before them, raising his paw to point at us. What I actually saw was Mother and Mrs. Sheffield sitting side by side on the sofa drinking tea, while Grace sat on the most comfortable chair with Barnaby sitting in her lap (and not a footprint on her fawn-coloured skirt, I noticed. Did he manage to keep magically clean just for her?), eating a biscuit.

Mother and Mrs. Sheffield were talking about yet another sale of work, but Mother looked up as I came in. Grace, meanwhile, was steadfastly avoiding our gaze.

'Oh, there you are,' Mother said casually. 'Did you find something for Nora to wear?'

'Yes.' My mouth felt very dry. I swallowed before I asked, 'Did you want to see us, Mother?'

'Actually, it was I who wanted to see you.' Mrs. Sheffield was all smiles.

Nora and I looked at each other in confusion.

'Don't look so worried!' Mrs. Sheffield laughed. 'You're not in trouble. But I *would* like you to help out at the special fête we're organising next week. For the pavilion, you know. The club is expanding so fast and the pavilion is far too small so we really do need to add some sort of extension …'

Mrs. Sheffield went on and on about the tennis-club grounds, while Mother calmly helped herself to a biscuit from the plate on the table, and Grace just sat there stroking Barnaby's woolly head. This couldn't be some sort of strange game, could it? I mean, Mother wasn't going to wait until Mrs. Sheffield had gone and then suddenly turn to us and tell us she knew all about our dangerous suffragette activities, was she? I was so caught up in my thoughts that it gave me quite a shock when Nora gently kicked my ankle and I realised Mrs. Sheffield was asking me a question.

'What do you think, young Mollie? Will you help Grace with the dog show?'

'The dog show?' I said stupidly. 'Sorry, Mrs. Sheffield, I think I must have got, um, water in the ear when we were out in the rain.'

'The dog show at the tennis-club fête!' said Mrs. Sheffield. 'I'm going to serve as judge. Barnaby will make a jolly little mascot for the show, won't he? And Grace has promised to make him display his tricks.'

Barnaby turned his bright black eyes on Mrs. Sheffield and barked, as if offended by her use of the word 'tricks' to describe his showing-off activities.

'Oh!' I said. And then, because I really was too worked up to think of an excuse, I said, 'I'd love to help.'

'I'm so glad!' Mrs. Sheffield beamed. 'And you too, Nora?'

'Of course.' Nora's looked as dazed as I felt.

'Wonderful.' Mrs. Sheffield stood up and brushed the crumbs from her skirt. 'Now I really must be going. Thank you so much for tea, Rose.'

'You're always welcome,' said Mother.

'And thank you for taking Barnaby home from the club, Grace,' said Mrs. Sheffield. 'It did seem a shame to take him with me when he was having so much fun chasing the balls.' She turned to Mother. 'He's quite the little ball boy.

Always running to fetch! So helpful.'

'How nice,' said Mother, but I bet she was thinking the same thing as me, which was that Barnaby was not chasing balls to be helpful, and that he probably didn't return them to the players once he'd got them clamped in his angry little jaws.

'Come on then, Barnaby.' Mrs. Sheffield held out a hand, and the Menace jumped down from Grace's lap. 'Are you going to stay with your cousin, Grace?'

'Yes,' said Nora before Grace could say a word. 'We've got something awfully interesting to show you in Mollie's room, Grace.'

'Really?' said Mother. 'What?'

'Just a book I found with some dog tricks in it,' I said quickly. My mind had clearly recovered its ability to make up excuses on the spot. 'Come on, Grace.'

And with a hasty goodbye to Mrs. Sheffield, we each took one of Grace's hands and led her from the room. We both guessed, rightly, that she would never kick up a fuss in front of grown-ups. Mrs. Sheffield and Mother followed us into the hall, and we took Grace upstairs while they continued to chat.

As soon as we were safely in my room, Grace shook off our guiding hands.

'How dare you drag me out like that!' She was not happy.

I looked at Nora in alarm. This was not a good start

to our negotiations.

'I'm sorry,' I said. 'But we really need to talk to you on your own.'

'And you didn't seem very keen on talking to us earlier,' added Nora.

'What do you want to talk about?' said Grace, though of course she knew.

'Last night,' I said. 'I know you saw what those men did to Phyllis. And I know you saw that I was with her.'

'But please, Grace, don't tell anyone about it,' said Nora.

'We are throwing ourselves on your mercy,' I said dramatically. 'Our parents will never forgive us for this.'

'We are honestly and truly begging you,' said Nora, and even Grace must have realised she was sincere. 'And in case you think this is just about us, it's not.'

'It's about Phyllis,' I said. 'She's meant to be starting university in October. But if Mother and Father find out about this, they'll probably send her off to the countryside to live with one of our horrid old aunts instead.'

'And there's Mabel too,' said Nora. 'She won't let Phyllis be punished alone. She'll tell her parents too, and then they won't let her go to college either.'

'So please don't tell,' I said. 'We'll help you with Barnaby's dog show.'

'We'll do anything you like,' said Nora wildly. 'We'll chase after the balls at your tennis matches.'

'But please, please don't tell.' I said. I felt almost breathless as I looked earnestly at Grace's impassive face.

'Is that all you have to say?' Grace's tone was stern. Nora and I looked at each other.

'Yes,' I said.

'Well, you could have saved yourself the effort,' said Grace in her most supercilious tone. 'And all the begging. I wasn't going to tell anyone anyway.'

Frances, I was stunned.

'You weren't?' I said. 'Why did you run away from us earlier?'

'I thought you were going to threaten me with menaces,' said Grace. 'I didn't realise you were just going to grovel.'

'We'd never threaten to do anything violent!' said Nora indignantly. I shot her a warning look. This was not a good time to start a fight with Grace.

'Well, I don't know what you're capable of,' said Grace. 'I wouldn't put anything past you.'

'But why?' I said. 'Why did you decide not to tell, I mean?'

For the first time, Grace looked a little uncomfortable.

'It didn't feel right, that's all,' she said.

'Really?' Nora couldn't keep the surprise out of her voice. 'After all, back in school you said …'

I tried to catch Nora's eye and give her a 'please don't

remind her of what she said back in school' look, but she kept going. 'I mean, what's changed since then?' she said.

Grace sighed.

'If you must know,' she said, 'it was those horrid men.'

This time Nora did catch my eye. She looked as surprised as I felt.

'We were crossing the bridge when the policemen had to rescue those women – I mean, ladies,' said Grace. 'I saw them knock that poor lady down. And then I saw what they did to your sister. I saw you two trying to help her.' She looked at me. 'I had awful dreams about it last night.'

'I slept like a log,' said Nora.

'Shut up, Nora,' I hissed.

'It was just because I was so exhausted,' said Nora.

'Anyway,' said Grace stiffly. 'Whatever I may think of your silly movement … well, they didn't deserve to be treated the way those hooligans treated them. They were just speaking and those men started throwing stones and saying awful things and it wasn't … it's not fair play. Miss Casey thought so too.'

So all that tennis-club talk had actually had an effect on her! I gave a silent prayer of thanks for Miss Casey.

'So that's why I didn't say anything,' said Grace. 'Can I go now?'

'Of course you can,' I said. 'And thanks, Grace. Thanks awfully. We won't forget it. Will we Nora? Nora?'

'We won't,' said Nora. She held out her hand to Grace.
'Thank you.'

For a moment I thought Grace wasn't going to take it.
But eventually she gave it a hint of a shake and turned to go.

'And I meant it about helping with the dog show,' I said,
as she opened the door. But she didn't say anything. She
just walked out and closed the door behind her.

'Well!' said Nora. And then she burst into tears.

'Nora!' I said. But I felt on the verge of tears myself.

'I'm sorry,' said Nora, wiping her nose on her sleeve in a
very uncouth fashion.

'It's all right,' I said. 'I know how you feel. Do you think
she'll keep her word?'

'I actually do,' said Nora. 'Don't you?'

'Yes.' I threw myself back on my bed and smiled. 'I do.' I
felt as though I had been wound up tightly and now I had
been unrolled. I propped myself up on the bed with my
elbows.

'Come on,' I said. 'Let's go and see if there's any cake left
over. And then we can tell Phyllis the good news.'

And that is where I shall leave this letter, because really
if I don't stop now my hand will finally fall off. I think I
need to have a little rest from writing to you for a while.
I didn't realise that capturing historic events for posterity
would be such hard work. And anyway, there is not much
more to tell of yesterday's doings. All you need to know is

that it seems that we are safe! And it's all thanks to Grace's newfound sense of fair play. I never thought she'd develop one, but I can only thank the tennis club for it. And for that, I will happily take part in their fundraising fête. Even if it does mean doing a dog show with the Menace.

Best love and votes for women,
Mollie

Sunday, 21ˢᵗ July, 1912.

Dear Frances,

I know I said I wouldn't have to write another letter in a hurry because I thought all the drama and excitement was over for the moment, but of course I hadn't told you how Phyllis reacted to the news that Grace was going to stay silent. After Grace had left us yesterday, Nora and I knocked on Phyllis's door.

'Who is it?' Phyllis still sounded rather feeble after the previous day's attack.

'It's us,' I said. 'And we have good news.'

'Come in, come in,' said Phyllis, and when we did, we saw that she wasn't alone. She was sitting in bed, propped up with pillows, and Mabel was sitting in a chair next to the bed.

'What's happened?' said Mabel. 'Did you talk to Grace? Did you persuade her not to tell.'

'Actually,' I said, 'we didn't have to.' And we told them what had happened.

'Well!' said Mabel. 'I *have* been wondering about Lily Casey.'

'The tennis-club lady?' said Nora.

'She was a few years above us at school,' said Phyllis. 'She's friendly with Kathleen's sister.'

'And whenever we meet her I've had a suspicion that she might be a little sympathetic to the cause,' said Mabel.

'She does seem to go on about fairness quite a lot,' I said. 'It seems to have rubbed off on Grace.'

'For the moment,' said Nora.

I elbowed her in her ribs. 'Don't look a gift horse in the mouth,' I said. 'We should all be jolly grateful to Grace at the moment.'

'I suppose so,' said Nora, not very graciously. 'I'll just be glad to have my room back.'

But Phyllis was still worried about the truth coming out.

'Are you sure she won't change her mind?' she asked.

'Well, as sure as we can be,' I said. 'I mean, she really did seem to mean it. And we know what she looks like when she's trying to get one over on us.'

'She gets a sort of smug expression on her face,' said Nora. 'It's impossible to miss. And she didn't have it today.'

'I hope you're right,' said Phyllis.

'And,' Nora pointed out, 'she's going home on Monday so even if she does change her mind, it would be much more of an effort to tell Mother. I mean, I can't imagine her going to all that trouble. Especially when she's got the tennis club to distract her.'

'Though won't she be leaving the club if she's going

home?' Mabel was concerned.

But Nora shook her head.

'She loves it so much she's decided it's going to be worthwhile getting the bus or the tram over for the rest of the summer season. They've got some sort of big tournament thing going on soon. Mother told me this morning. So she'll have more important things to do than tell on us.'

'Well!' said Mabel. 'All's well that ends well.'

'Are you going to stop selling magazines at meetings?' asked Nora. 'I mean, after what happened on Friday.'

I had been wondering the same thing, but Phyllis and Mabel seemed shocked at the suggestion that they might give up.

'Of course not!' said Phyllis.

'I think we should give it a miss this week,' said Mabel. 'Just because we're both still a bit bruised.'

'Yes, that's a good idea,' said Phyllis.

'But as soon as we're both fighting fit, we'll be back out there with our *Irish Citizens*,' Mabel went on. 'We're not going to let those vile bullies stop us. We're going to keep fighting, and in the end we're going to win.'

It was rousing stuff. I almost felt like applauding. If Mabel ever has time for amateur dramatics in between all the meetings and starting college in October, she would make a jolly good Henry V – you know in that Shakespeare play where he goes around giving speeches to rally his troops. In fact, I bet Mabel would make an excellent general. I'm quite sure I would follow her into battle.

'But no fighting this week.' Phyllis yawned. 'Gosh, I'm awfully tired.'

'Come on, girls, let's give her some peace.' Mabel got to her feet. 'I'll call in tomorrow, Phyl.'

We left the room, but before Mabel headed downstairs, she turned to me and Nora.

'You were both jolly brave this week,' she said. 'Especially yesterday.'

'We didn't really do anything,' said Nora.

'You came out for the cause,' said Mabel. 'You called the police for Phyllis. And what's most important, you kept a cool head. Some girls – and boys, I have no doubt – would have had hysterics when the police arrived in that room on Nassau Street. But you two didn't. And when you saw Phyllis being attacked, you could have run away. But you didn't. You ran to help her.'

I felt myself blush AGAIN. But Nora looked a bit pink too, so it wasn't just me.

'We had to do something,' I murmured.

'No, you decided to do something,' said Mabel. 'And that's an important difference. But I don't approve of you putting yourselves in danger. You are technically children after all.'

'You and Phyllis are under twenty-one,' I said.

'We're old enough to be responsible for ourselves.' Mabel fixed me with a stern gaze. 'There's a difference between eighteen and fourteen as you well know. And I know that you've earned the right to call yourselves suffragettes. But what happened to Phyllis wasn't the only attack on a suffragette last night. Women were assaulted all over the city. So I think until the general mood calms down, you should give the meetings a miss. Just for a while. Do you agree?'

I looked at Nora.

'All right,' I said.

'I agree,' said Nora.

Mabel smiled.

'Good,' she said. 'I'll give you a copy of the next *Citizen* to try and make up for it. *Courage, mes amies!*'

And with that, she was gone. I know she's right about avoiding the meetings for a while. After Nora had gone home, I looked in Father's newspaper and there were awful stories about women being attacked. Some of them weren't even suffragettes (not that that makes it any worse, but it just shows how crazed the mob were). The only good thing, I suppose, was that even the newspaper writers, who haven't always been particularly supportive of the cause, condemned the attacks in very strong language. So perhaps the public will be so shocked by the savagery of the Antis that they will be drawn to our cause? You never know, something good might come of this. I feel quite hopeful at the moment. After all, if Grace can do the right thing, then anything can happen.

I just wish things were all right between me and Frank. This time tomorrow he will be gone, and everything is still awfully awkward between us. I wish he hadn't come to stay at all – if he hadn't, he would never have seen me all red-faced in my nightie, and I wouldn't feel embarrassed every time I saw him (and he wouldn't feel embarrassed every time he saw me). But I can't bring myself to say anything that might clear the air between us, and clearly neither can he. So things will just have to stay as they are for now.

Anyway, with that I will end this letter. I'm actually looking forward to going to Skerries, just because it should be nice and peaceful there. I know that a few months ago I was complaining about how boring my and Nora's lives were, and I wouldn't like things to go back to the way they were before we discovered the movement, but I'm quite looking forward to a bit of a rest, just for a few weeks, and then we can do something dramatic again.

Best love and votes for women,
Mollie

Monday, 22nd July, 1912.

Dear Frances,

Your letter came today! New York sounds so exciting, I
really can't imagine what it must be like to walk around
such a modern city. And with so many motor cars! And
how wonderful that you have bought a copy of *Anne
of Green Gables* all by yourself. It just shows that we are
kindred spirits (like Anne and Diana) and are drawn to
the same books. I can't wait to hear what you think of it.
I bet there are lots of other books for sale that you can't
get here.

I would love to hear what American girls are wearing,
too – I bet they have lots of fashions that we haven't seen
yet. And speaking of fashion, I got a jolly nice letter from
Stella too, and she is alleviating her boredom by making
what she says is a very impressive dressing gown with
quilted lapels, which she is sure will dazzle all the other
boarders when she returns.

Anyway, I am in rather a good mood and so is Nora.
Nora is of course happy because Grace has gone. I called
around this morning, and Nora answered the door herself.

'Oh, thank goodness it's you,' she said.

'Is everything all right?" I asked. 'You look a bit …'

'I'm still worried something could happen to stop her going home,' whispered Nora. 'Like another telegram saying someone else had come down with scarlet fever. Or mumps. Or consumption.'

'You're being ridiculous,' I said, walking into the hall. 'Where is Grace?'

'In there.' Nora pointed towards her drawing room, the door of which stood ajar. 'Bidding farewell to her kindred spirit.'

I peered in and saw Grace sitting on the Cantwells' sofa with the Menace sitting on her knee. She had her arms around him. Mrs. Sheffield was sitting opposite with Mrs. Cantwell, looking fondly at the pair of them.

'Don't worry, Grace,' Mrs. Sheffield was saying. 'You can call around and see him after every tennis practice. And when you're back at school you can call over and walk him. We're not far away from Eccles Street, you know.'

I withdrew silently from the doorway. Grace looked genuinely bereft at the prospect of saying goodbye to that dreadful dog, so it felt rude to pry. I gently closed the door.

'You must feel a bit sorry for her,' I said to Nora.

'I suppose so.' Nora shrugged her shoulders. 'But I'm mostly glad she's going. Even if she did do the right thing in the end.'

We went up to Nora's room, where Grace's things had

already been packed away into a suitcase. The camp bed on which Nora had been sleeping for the previous few weeks was folded up and propped against the wall.

'What's wrong with you?' asked Nora, when we were sitting on her bed.

'What do you mean?' I was genuinely confused by her question.

'You look very … distracted, I suppose,' said Nora.

'I'm not really,' I said. I hadn't wanted to tell her about the Frank incident at all, mostly because I knew she would probably say very annoying things about it. But it really was weighing on my mind. 'But there's something.'

And I told her all. And to my surprise, she didn't make any jokes, or shriek. She just looked at me with very wide eyes and said, 'Oh dear. But I'm sure you didn't look that bad.'

'I looked unhinged,' I said. 'I saw myself in the bathroom mirror. I was bright red in the face and my hair was all over the place. I hadn't tied it into plaits. AND I was wearing that old nightie.'

'The short one with the worn out behind?' Nora couldn't conceal her horror.

I nodded miserably. 'And it's been so awkward between us ever since,' I said. 'I haven't had much time to think about it over the last few days because we've been so busy. But he's going home today and things are still so odd. And he might never want to come back to our house if things are going to be strange between himself and his friend's sister.'

'You must say something,' said Nora firmly. 'Before he goes.'

'But what?' I said.

'You've got to grab the bull by the horns,' said Nora. 'Just tell him you're sorry things are awkward and tell him you'd like to forget all about it. After all, what have you got to lose? Things are bad between you already.'

It was a jolly good point, and I was just about to tell Nora so when Grace came in. Her eyes were a little red after her farewell to the Menace. I felt sorry for her, but I had a feeling that she wouldn't be in the mood for sympathy from me.

'The cab's here,' she said, a little stiffly. She picked up her suitcase.

'Well,' said Nora. 'Goodbye, Grace.' She paused for a moment. 'Sorry about Barnaby. Having to say goodbye to him, I mean.'

Grace nodded and blinked but didn't say anything. For a moment I wondered if she were trying not to cry.

'Goodbye,' I said. 'And, well, see you on Saturday. For the dog show.'

'Yes,' said Grace. And then she walked out of the room, hopefully (as far as Nora was concerned) never to stay there again, and closed the door behind her.

Nora and I looked at each other.

'I thought,' said Nora, 'that I'd feel thrilled when she was gone.'

'And don't you?' I said.

Nora sighed. 'I just feel rather flat.'

'Oh well,' I said. 'If you're missing her, you can have a happy reunion at the tennis-club fête and invite her to come back for another visit.'

'I certainly wouldn't go that far,' said Nora, throwing a pillow at me (which luckily missed).

On my way home later that morning, I thought about Nora's advice. I knew she was right. In a few hours, Frank would be gone. And I couldn't let him go without knowing that I, at least, had tried to make things all right between us. I had to say something. So as soon as I got home, I asked Maggie where Frank and Harry were.

'Your brother's out in the garden with a bicycle,' she said. 'And his friend is up in his room, packing.'

'With a bicycle!' I was so surprised to hear that Harry had acquired a bicycle – which he has wanted for as long as I can remember – I didn't even think about Frank for a moment. 'Where did he get hold of that? It's not his birthday for ages, and Father said he wasn't going to get him one anyway.'

'It belongs to some friend of his from school,' said Maggie. 'He's going on holiday so he's lent the bicycle to Harry while he's away.' She smiled at me. 'Maybe he'll let you have a go of it.'

I hoped he would, though it didn't seem likely. I thanked Maggie, who returned to the kitchen, and then headed up the stairs to confront Frank. But just as I reached the landing, the door of Harry's room opened, and Frank appeared.

'Oh!' he said. 'I was actually just coming to look for you.'

'Oh yes?' I said, as nonchalantly as I could.

'Yes.' He pushed back a lock of hair that had fallen over his eyes. 'Can I talk to you for a minute?'

And suddenly I was quite sure that he was going to tell me he would never be able to look me in the face again, and that he thought it was better if he never came over to our house again. And I didn't want to have any sort of conversation at all. But it was too late to run away or make up an excuse. So I just said, 'All right.'

'It's about that night last week,' said Frank. 'When we … bumped into each other.'

I could feel myself getting red. Frank looked a bit flushed too.

'I want to apologise if … if I've been a bit unfriendly since then,' he said. 'I felt terrible about roaming around your house in my pyjamas.'

You can't help needing to go to loo, I thought, but of course I couldn't say that. It would only add to the general embarrassment. So I just said, 'Well, you were our guest.'

'But I just want to say …' Frank took a deep breath. 'I

hope we can forget about it and be pals again.'

I was so relieved I couldn't speak for a moment.

'Mollie?' said Frank nervously. 'Are you all right?'

'So do I,' I said, trying not to remember the moment when he nearly dropped a candle in fright at the sight of me looming over him on the stairs. 'Want to forget about it, I mean.' I held out my hand. 'Pals?'

'Pals,' said Frank. I had forgotten how nice his smile is. He's looked so uncomfortable every time we've seen each other all week. 'And now I'd better finish packing. My uncle's coming to collect me at four.'

I was still smiling when I bounced down the stairs and into the garden, where Harry was fiddling with the chain of a rickety old bicycle that was propped up against a kitchen chair in the middle of the garden path.

'What are you smirking about?' he said, wiping his brow and leaving an enormous oily streak across it.

'Am I not allowed to be cheerful?' I demanded.

'Not when I'm trying to fix this chain,' said Harry.

'Let me help,' I said, crouching down to get a closer look.

'You don't know anything about bikes,' said Harry.

'I can see that goes there,' I said, reaching out to the back wheel.

'Don't touch it!' said Harry, pushing my hand away. But, as he pushed me, his elbow hit the bike, which must have been precariously propped against the chair because the front wheel twisted around and the front of the bicycle fell on top of Harry.

'Now see what you've done!' he roared.

'Are you all right?' I said.

'No thanks to you!' said Harry, angrily putting the bike back in place.

'Well, you bashed into it,' I pointed out.

'Yes, because of you!' Harry was not pleased. 'Oh, the chain's in even more of a mess now. Just clear off, will you?'

I cleared off. But nothing could really dampen my spirits for the rest of the evening. Grace had vowed to keep our secret, Frank and I were friends again, and when his uncle came to collect him I bade him farewell with a heartfelt wave.

'See you soon, Mollie,' he said, after shaking hands with Mother and Father.

'Don't waste your time talking to her,' said Harry, who hadn't quite managed to get all the oil off himself. He can be so petty sometimes. But I can put up with him now everything else has been settled. In fact, I feel so optimistic I'm almost looking forward to the dog show. After all, now Grace has been training Barnaby, he might actually put on an impressive show for all the other dogs.

Best love and votes for women,
Mollie

Saturday, 27th July, 1912.

Dear Frances,

Good Lord. I hope you don't consider that to be taking
the Lord's name in vain, because really it is more of a
prayer. What a day I have had! We are going to Skerries
on Monday, and frankly I cannot wait to get away from
Dublin and all its excitements because just when I thought
things were getting nice and peaceful and even boring
again, today happened. And between Barnaby and Harry
and Grace and Frank … well, I don't know where to start.
But I suppose I should start with me and Nora arriving
at the tennis club to help out with the dog show at the
fundraising fête.

Neither of us had seen Grace all week, though I knew
from Mrs. Sheffield's visits to my mother that she had been
regularly coming over to this part of town for her tennis-
club practice. Strangely enough, she hadn't felt the urge
to visit her aunt and cousins. But we knew all about the
plans for her dog show, because Mrs. Sheffield had given us
detailed descriptions of our dog-show-helping duties.

'I'd like you to be there at half past ten to help Grace
put up the signs and arrange the prizes and so on,' she told

us on Thursday. 'Grace has painted all the signs already. What fun it'll be!'

'She doesn't realise what a sacrifice it is, working with the Menace,' said Nora later. 'She thinks everyone loves him as much as she does.'

It turned out there was going to be a sort of tent thing in the tennis club grounds, and they had decided it would be a good place for the dog show as the competing canines could be corralled into one place and there would less risk of them roaming free and wild around the tennis courts. (Apparently the only dog who is allowed to do this is Barnaby. Not that anyone could stop him, even if he *weren't* allowed. He is a dog who does what he wants, as today's events would prove.) As well as setting up, Nora and I were required to take the names of all competitors and usher them into the tent. Grace would be too busy wrangling Barnaby, who would be the public face of the competition, just like when you see actresses in advertisements extolling the virtues of Pears' soap and suchlike.

Harry, of course, was very amused at the thought of me helping out at a tennis-club dog show.

'Will you have to wear a little hat like a zoo keeper?' he said over breakfast, chortling at his own 'wit'.

I ignored him, of course.

'Well, I'll see for myself later,' he said, and alas this was true, because Mother had decided she had to support Mrs. Sheffield's efforts and was dragging along the rest of the family to the fête. Apart from Father, of course, who was in the office, and Phyllis, who claimed she was still recovering from being 'run over by a cab' – which was merely an excuse. I knew perfectly well that apart from a few fading bruises, she was physically in top condition. I told her this and she just laughed at me, which was jolly unfair, as I pointed out.

'The only reason Nora and I are helping at this fête is because Grace is keeping mum about seeing all of us at that riot,' I said, and Phyllis had the good grace to look slightly guilty.

'But still,' she said, 'it doesn't really make any difference to you if I don't go to the tennis club and throw a ball at a coconut shy, does it?'

'I suppose not,' I said. But I still felt she should have come along to support us.

We arrived at the club to find lots of people hurrying around carrying boxes and setting up tables. There, in a far corner, was a biggish tent, the sort they always have at fêtes and fairs and things to keep the rain off.

'Well, here we go,' said Nora. 'Let's hope she hasn't had time to change her mind about telling on us since she last saw us.'

'Don't say anything about that!' I said. 'We don't want

to give her ideas.'

But when we arrived at the tent Grace was nowhere to be seen. She wasn't outside the tent, and she wasn't inside the tent. In fact, the only thing in the tent were some stacked up chairs.

'Maybe she's behind it?' said Nora, but she wasn't. We were wondering if we would have to put on the dog show all by ourselves when we heard an all-too-familiar yapping sound and Barnaby burst through the crowd, with Grace holding onto his lead for dear life.

'There you are!' said Nora. 'Is everything all right?'

'Of course it is,' said Grace, pushing back a chestnut curl that had somehow escaped from its ribbons. She looked much more flustered than usual. 'Barnaby's just in ... in a very demanding mood today. He must be excited about his performance.'

He was always in a demanding mood as far as I could tell, but of course I didn't say that to Grace.

'So, what do we need to do?' I asked.

'Well, first of all I've got to get the signs and the prizes and things from Miss Casey in the pavilion,' said Grace. 'So you two had better look after Barnaby for a few minutes.'

I looked at Nora with dismay.

'Are you sure we can't get those things?' I said.

'I promised Mrs. Sheffield I'd look after it,' said Grace. 'No one else can be trusted with the medals.' She didn't look particularly happy about leaving her beloved charge in our care. She handed me Barnaby's lead. 'Hold on tightly and don't go anywhere. I'll be back as quickly as possible.' She ran off in the direction of the pavilion. Nora and I looked at each other, then both of us looked down at Barnaby. He barked crossly at us.

'I think you'd better hold onto his lead too,' I said nervously. 'In case he tries to burst free.'

'Let's show him the tent,' Nora suggested. 'Make him feel at home.'

And so, with both of us clutching his lead, we led Barnaby into the tent. It was a good thing we were both holding on to him, because he strained away from us in his harness as he sniffed his way around the perimeter. Then he turned around to face us, fixed us with his button eyes, and started barking.

'Calm down, Barnaby,' I said, in what I hoped was a soothing voice. 'She'll be back in a minute.'

'How does Grace put up with that noise?' said Nora, over Barnaby's barks.

'Maybe he doesn't do it when he's with her?' I said. And when Grace rushed into the tent a few minutes later, her arms full of cardboard signs, a cardboard box, and a small tin, he did calm down a bit. Of course, Grace had overheard his barking (as I'm sure had everyone in the tennis-club grounds), and wasn't impressed.

'What have you been doing to him?' she asked suspiciously, taking his lead.

'Nothing!' I said. 'He just barks like that practically all the time. Where are the signs?'

'Here,' said Grace, and she held up a large piece of cardboard with 'BARNABY'S DOG SHOW, 11.30. ALL BREEDS WELCOME. WILL YOUR DOG WIN A MEDAL?' painted on it in neat capital letters. 'This one is going to be at the entrance to the club.'

'Are there really medals?' Nora wanted to know.

Grace nodded and took a small container out of the cardboard box. It contained some tin medals with tennis rackets on them.

'Aren't they tennis medals?' I said.

'They're left over from last summer's tournament,' said Grace.

'But the dogs won't be playing tennis,' said Nora. A thought struck her and her face lit up. 'Will they?'

'Of course they won't,' said Grace impatiently. 'But they're still competing in what officially is a tennis-club competition.' When you put it like that, it did make sense to have rackets on the medals. 'This one is going up outside the tent.' She held up another sign on which was painted BARNABY'S DOG SHOW. ALL BREEDS WELCOME. AUDIENCE ADMITTANCE 1d. ENTER YOUR DOG 2d.

'Why didn't you mention the price on the first poster?' I asked.

'Is it in case it puts people off taking in their dogs?' said Nora. 'They won't realise they have to pay until they're actually at the tent.'

Grace looked slightly uncomfortable so I knew Nora was right.

'We have to charge entry,' she said. 'It's a fête to raise funds for the club, after all.'

'That's fair,' I said, before Nora could say anything. 'Come on, Nora, let's go and put up the sign at the gate.'

'And you can get a card table from the club house,' called Grace, as we set off. 'You'll need something to put the tin on when you take everyone's money.'

The club was even more full of activity as we made our way to the entrance of its grounds. We nearly bumped into a tall young woman carrying a slightly torn fire screen in the direction of the white elephant stall – or rather, she nearly bumped into us.

'Sorry!' she said, and I realised she was Grace's beloved Miss Casey. 'Do I know you two? You're not in the club.'

I hoped she wouldn't remember having seen me in my disguise just the previous week.

'You met us with Grace, the day she joined,' said Nora. 'I'm her cousin.'

'Oh, of course,' said Miss Casey. And that was when I

noticed the little badge fixed to her hat ribbon. I might not even have noticed it if I hadn't seen such badges before. It was a small yellow button and on it were the words 'Votes for Women!' Mabel had been right about her old schoolmate after all. 'Are you helping with her dog show?'

We told her we were.

'Well,' said Miss Casey. 'I may see you there. Now I'd better get this jumble over to the stall. Someone will buy it, although I can't imagine who. Or why.'

'Did you see her badge?' I said, as Miss Casey went off with her fire screen and Nora and I reached the gates of the tennis club, where a curious crowd was already gathering to look at the painted banners announcing the fête and its attractions.

'Yes,' said Nora, as we tied the sign to the bars of the gate. 'You never know, Grace might end up devoting herself to the cause after all. If only to impress her heroine.'

'Goodness,' I said. 'You might be right.' I should have known that the only thing likely to make Grace support the cause was the miracle of finding a grown-up suffragette whom she wanted to impress.

The fête was officially open by now, and the first attendees were arriving by the time we arrived back at the tent, where Grace had affixed her other sign to one of the poles.

'Here's the table,' said Nora. 'And jolly difficult to carry it was too.'

Of course Grace didn't thank us for lugging bits of furniture around the club for her.

'Put it down here,' she said, rummaging around in the box and producing a notebook. 'That's where you two are going to take people's money and write down their particulars, if they're entering their dogs. You can bring out a chair from the stacks inside after we've put the rest of them out.'

'But there's two of us,' protested Nora.

'Well, one of you will have to stand!' snapped Grace, who looked as if she were at the end of her tether. Barnaby, who is of course always at the end of his tether in a literal sense, barked crossly. 'We don't have enough chairs. Lots of the attendees are going to have to stand too.'

'All right, calm down,' said Nora. Unsurprisingly, this didn't go down well with Grace.

'Calm down!' she said. 'I can't calm down! Not with Barnaby refusing to do his tricks!'

'Oh dear, is he?' I looked at Barnaby, who did seem to be in an even more rebellious mood than usual. 'Maybe he doesn't like the prospect of sharing the stage with other dogs.'

'I don't think he does.' Grace really did look worried. 'Come, Barnaby. Please give me your paw.'

And Barnaby did hold up one woolly paw, though he did it with what looked to me like very bad grace.

'There you go!' I said, encouragingly. 'Maybe he had what do you call it, when actors don't want to go on stage?'

'Stage fright,' said Nora. 'Maybe Barnaby has tent fright.'

'Well, whether it's stage fright or tent fright, lots of actors seem to get it, but then when they're actually on the stage they feel perfectly fine,' I said. 'I'm sure he'll be quite all right.'

'Maybe,' said Grace, but she still looked a bit worried.

'Why don't you go behind the tent and practise?' I said. 'And Nora and I will set out the chairs in the tent.'

'All right,' said Grace. 'Come on, Barnaby.'

It didn't take us long to set the chairs out, not least because there really weren't very many of them. If the show was well attended, most of the audience would have to stand. When we were finished, we went behind the tent to find Grace, who was holding the paw of a slightly-calmer-looking Barnaby.

'You can practise inside now,' I said. 'We left a space at the far end of the tent for the show to take place.'

Grace didn't say thank you, but she didn't say anything else either. When she and Barnaby were ensconced inside the tent, Nora and I arranged ourselves outside with the notebook and cash tin. We scanned the tennis-club grounds, which were rapidly filling up with visitors. I noticed quite a few people with dogs.

'I wonder if they're all here for the competition,' I said. Nora had taken first turn on the chair, so I had a better vantage point. 'Look at that jolly little brown and grey one with the fluffy legs. I hope he's entering.'

And it turned out that he was.

'This is Ruffles,' said his owner, a nice-looking middle-aged lady in an excellent hat, accompanied by an equally friendly-looking young woman, whom I assumed was her daughter. 'Are we the first competitors?'

'Yes,' said Nora, taking the offered tuppence and putting it in the tin box. From the tent came a volley of loud barks. 'You're a bit early, actually.'

'Who's that?' said the young woman, pointing at the tent, where Barnaby was still barking his head off.

'That,' said Nora grimly, 'is the entertainment.'

A few minutes later quite a number of competitors and their owners had gathered outside the tent. It turned out that Mrs. Sheffield had spread the word about the competition among her dog-loving friends, and they were all eager to both help the club and show off their canine companions. I slipped into the tent while Nora sat at the table and received their pennies.

'Grace!' I whispered. 'It's nearly time to start. We've got lots of dogs outside.'

Grace turned a harassed face towards me. 'Is Mrs. Sheffield there? We can't start without the judge.'

I stuck my head outside the tent and saw Mrs. Sheffield approaching, with none other than my mother and Julia by her side. Thankfully Harry and Frank were nowhere to be seen. I didn't want to see Harry at all, and I didn't particularly want Frank to see me being Barnaby's dogsbody (so to speak).

'She's just arriving now,' I told Grace.

Grace sighed. 'Well, I suppose we'll just have to hope for the best,' she said and, taking a deep breath, she led Barnaby out of the tent. I followed them.

'Grace!' cried Mrs. Sheffield. 'And Barnaby. Oh, and Mollie.'

'We're ready to start the show,' said Grace. She looked at Nora. 'If everyone's paid.'

'They have,' said Nora. She handed Mrs. Sheffield a piece of paper. 'And here are the names of the competitors.'

'Excellent, excellent,' beamed Mrs. Sheffield. She turned to the gathered crowd, which was surprisingly large now. The competitors must have invited friends along.

'Welcome, everyone, to Barnaby's dog show!' she said. 'This is Barnaby.' She pointed at Barnaby, who was sitting at Grace's feet looking reassuringly docile. 'And he is pleased to welcome all his little friends to help support our wonderful club.'

I wasn't sure he actually was pleased, but at least he wasn't barking at anyone. For now.

'If you'll all follow me into the tent, Barnaby will give a demonstration of his skills, helped by my young friend Grace Molyneaux.'

And Grace did an actual curtsey. Inexplicably, the crowd seemed to like this, and there was a polite round of applause. With Mrs. Sheffield and Grace (and the suspiciously well-behaved Barnaby) leading the way, everyone trooped into the tent. Nora and I, of course, had to stand at the entrance to hold the tent flap open.

'Well done, Moll,' said Mother as she and Julia passed by. 'It all looks very good.'

Of course, there weren't enough seats for everyone, but no one seemed to mind too much. When everyone was inside the tent, Grace took Barnaby to what I thought of as the stage (even though it was just the chairless space at one end of the tent) and turned to address the crowd. Nora and I had stationed ourselves to one side near the front row of the audience, in order to help if the Menace decided to misbehave.

'Though I'm not sure what we could do if he did,' I whispered, remembering the time he had escaped from my clutches when I was taking him for a walk. If it hadn't been for Frank, I'd have never have recaptured him. I found myself wondering where Frank was – I knew he and Harry must be at the fête somewhere – but I couldn't think of it for long because Grace had finished her opening speech.

'And now,' she said, 'Barnaby will demonstrate his amazing skills. Sit, Barnaby!'

And Barnaby sat. The crowd clapped politely, but they didn't seem very impressed. I suppose if you didn't know what a terrible dog Barnaby was, you wouldn't realise what a significant feat it was to get him to sit on command. They seemed slightly more impressed as he performed his other tricks, and by the time Grace said, in a very theatrical voice, 'Barnaby, die for Parnell!' and he flung himself dramatically to the ground, they gave him a proper round of applause.

'I must say I'm pleasantly surprised,' whispered Nora. 'I was sure he was going to make a run for it.'

'Me too,' I said. 'But clearly he likes the attention.' Barnaby had sprung to his feet and if dogs could bow, he would have been bowing to his audience.

'Thank you Grace, and Barnaby,' said Miss Sheffield. 'And now, can the competitors please make their way over here?'

About ten dogs and their owners joined her. There were a few rather non-descript spaniels, but my favourites were the aforementioned Ruffles, along with a large mastiff who looked as if she didn't approve of the whole thing, a Newfoundland with a noble expression and a small woolly, white creature that looked worryingly like a miniature Barnaby. And we soon found out why.

'Oh, it's Archie!' said Mrs. Sheffield, as the little woolly dog pranced into place, accompanied by a boy of Julia's age. She turned to Grace. 'He came from the same breeder as Barnaby, you know.'

'Is he … are they related?' asked Grace. She sounded almost awestruck, as well she might at the prospect of another Barnaby being unleashed (so to speak) on the world.

'I believe so,' said Mrs. Sheffield. 'I suppose we would say he's Barnaby's nephew.' She looked fondly at Archie, whose beady black eyes did bear a strong similarity to those of his uncle.

As for Barnaby himself, he was still sitting at Grace's feet, but as the competitors got into position in a semi-circle I could tell that he was not impressed by the arrival of the newcomers in what he clearly believed was his domain.

'And now,' declared Mrs. Sheffield to the awaiting crowd, 'let the judging commence!' And she began to slowly walk past each dog, accompanied by Grace and of course Barnaby. The first to be judged was the disapproving mastiff, whose name turned out to be Bracknell. As the judge and her assistant paused before him, Barnaby let out a short, sharp bark.

'Hush, Barnaby,' said Mrs. Sheffield, running an

experienced hand over the other dog's sturdy back, but Barnaby didn't want to hush. He barked even more loudly at the noble-looking Newfoundland dog, whose name was Lady and who looked back at him more in sorrow than in anger. As Mrs. Sheffield and Grace went from dog to dog, Barnaby got crosser and crosser. The only dog he seemed to approve of was little Archie – at least, he didn't bark at him. But by the time they reached Ruffles, whose benign gaze only served to inflame the Menace's rage, Barnaby was yapping away like anything and straining at his lead with all his might.

'Now, Barnaby, calm down,' said Mrs. Sheffield. She turned to the crowd.

'I have made my decision,' she declared. 'In third place – Bracknell the mastiff.' Bracknell's owner, a morose-looking man with a large moustache, went up to accept his prize. Barnaby barked.

'In second place,' said Mrs. Sheffield, 'is Lady the Newfoundland.'

Lady's owners, a young couple with a small child, went up to collect their medal. As the small child happily held the medal aloft, Barnaby barked some more and strained on his leash. Grace held onto it with both hands.

'And the winner is …' Mrs. Sheffield paused for effect. 'Ruffles!'

There was a loud round of applause, and I clapped

as hard as I could. But as Ruffles's owners went up to get their prize, Barnaby burst free of Grace's grip and, barking his head off, bounded towards the newly-crowned champion. Immediately all was chaos. Ruffles, understandably, started to run when he saw Barnaby rushing towards him, and when he set off, all the other dogs joined him – apart from Archie, who raced over to his uncle's side. Within seconds, Barnaby was chasing Ruffles and the other competitors round and round the tent, with Archie prancing along at his heels. As for the human crowd, they were just gathered in the middle of the tent, mesmerized by what essentially a sort of bizarre dog race, with Barnaby driving around the runners. I couldn't help laughing, despite being a bit worried about what Barnaby would do once he actually caught hold of his prey. Though I must say that the other dogs seemed to be enjoying it all immensely.

'Barnaby!' screeched Mrs. Sheffield. 'Stop that at once! Oh you terrible dog. Catch his lead, someone!'

But Barnaby was running too fast for anyone to grab hold of his accoutrements. And then, as he rushed past the opening of the tent, someone leapt upon him and managed to grab hold of the harness. Barnaby came skidding to a halt, and his captor gripped on to the lead.

'Oh my goodness,' said Nora, 'it's Frank!'

He and Harry had arrived after all. And once more he

had utilised his impressive Menace-catching skills. His deftness hadn't totally stopped the chaos, of course, as the other dogs were still running around the tent. But once they realised Barnaby had stopped chasing them, they calmed down, and their owners quickly rushed to reclaim them. Archie, however, stayed by his uncle, gazing at him adoringly with his own little button eyes.

'My dear young man,' said Mrs. Sheffield, hurrying towards Frank. 'Thank you so much. You're a friend of the Carberrys, aren't you?'

'Frank Nugent,' said Frank, handing over Barnaby's lead. 'I'm a school pal of Harry's.' For the first time, I noticed Harry standing behind him.

'Well, I'm very grateful to you,' said Mrs. Sheffield. She looked down at Barnaby. 'You naughty dog.'

'I'm awfully sorry, Mrs. Sheffield.' Grace sounded as if she might burst into tears. 'I couldn't hold onto him.'

I actually felt sympathetic towards Grace. Barnaby had behaved himself for quite a while, but I knew only too well just how powerful the Menace could be when he decided he really wanted to get away. Luckily Mrs. Sheffield was clearly thinking the same thing.

'It wasn't your fault, dear,' she said. 'I should have known that having so many other dogs around him might … well, might aggravate him. It was my fault.'

She raised her voice and addressed the crowd once more.

'I'm terribly sorry, everyone. Barnaby just got a little over-excited by all the other doggies. Thank you all very much for coming today, and please join me in giving all the competitors and their owners a very big round of applause.'

The audience, who clearly thought they'd got their money's worth, clapped loudly and began to file out of the tent. The dogs all trotted out, none the worse for their exertions. As everyone made their way outside, I saw Harry and Frank walk out and wondered if I'd be able to find them (or at least Frank) later.

'Goodness, I need a cup of tea,' I could hear Ruffles's owner say to her daughter.

'I think I need one too,' said Mrs. Sheffield. She spotted my mother, who was leaving the tent with Julia. 'I must catch up with Rose Carberry. Can you girls tidy up here and take the table and sign back to the pavilion?'

'Yes, Mrs. Sheffield,' said Grace, who still looked a little deflated.

Mrs. Sheffield patted her shoulder.

'You gave us an excellent show earlier,' she said. 'Come and join me in the tea tent once you've tidied up here.' She looked at me and Nora. 'You too, of course, girls.'

We thanked her and watched as she left the pavilion, Barnaby trotting demurely by her side as if he hadn't just been chasing ten dogs around a tent just a few minutes earlier. It struck me that he had disrupted a meeting very successfully. Was he a little Ancient Hooligan? Or could we learn anything from his ability to protest? But I don't think Barnaby is capable of thinking of political goals. He just caused a fuss because he didn't like not being the centre of attention.

Grace walked over to the tent entrance and looked after Mrs. Sheffield for a moment. Then she sighed and started stacking up chairs. 'Your show was jolly good,' I said. 'Wasn't it Nora?'

And Nora, with what sounded like genuine sympathy, said, 'I liked the bit where he died for Parnell.'

'I suppose he did do all his tricks properly,' said Grace.

'And I have to say,' said Nora, 'it was jolly funny when he chased all those dogs around.'

And to my immense surprise, Grace stifled a smile. 'It was very irresponsible of him.'

'You can tell him so the next time you take him for a walk,' I said.

'I suppose,' said Grace. 'Come on, let's get the table back to the pavilion.' She pulled back the tent flap.

'Before we go,' I said. Grace paused at the entrance. 'I just want to say thank you. Again. For not saying anything.'

I nudged Nora.

'Yes,' said Nora quickly. 'I do mean it, Grace. Thank you.'

'I told you,' said Grace. 'I couldn't do it after seeing

those awful people trying to throw your sister in the river just for going to a suffragette meeting.'

'Going to a *what*?' said an awfully familiar voice. And Harry strode into the tent, followed by Frank. My stomach sank.

'What are you doing here?' I said.

'We were waiting outside for you lot.' Harry pointed at Frank. 'He wanted to get you all some buns. Not my idea, I might add.'

'We've got to tidy up here,' I said, trying to sound cheerful. 'We'll see you over at the pavilion.'

'Not before you tell me what your friend meant about a suffragette meeting,' said Harry. 'Who threw Phyllis in the river?'

'No one,' I said. 'You must have misheard.'

'Come on, Carberry,' said Frank. 'Let's go and get some tea and cake and wait for the girls.'

'No,' said Harry. 'There's something going on here. Is this about those riots in town on Friday? Was Phyllis involved?'

'How would I know?' I said.

'I'll just have to ask Mother, then,' said Harry. 'If someone threw her daughter in a river, she should know.' And he turned as if to leave the tent. I had to stop him.

'They didn't throw her in!' I said. 'They just held her over the parapet.'

Harry stared at me.

'How do you know?' he said. The truth was dawning on him. 'Oh my goodness. You were there too.'

I looked over at Nora, who was clearly as horrified as I was. Even Grace didn't look very happy.

'Did you go to a suffragette thing?' said Harry. 'Were you caught up in that awful riot?'

I didn't know what to say. Harry already knew that Phyllis had been there. He was clearly planning to talk to our parents about it. How could I let her get into trouble without admitting my own involvement? So I did the only thing I could do. I told the truth.

'Yes,' I said.

'You mean ... you're a suffragette?' Harry looked like he couldn't believe his eyes. 'Have you been sneaking out to meetings and marches and things?'

Grace had once told me that she knew I'd never deny my 'precious cause' if I was asked about it directly. And she was right.

'Yes,' I said. 'I have.'

'And I have too,' said Nora suddenly. 'But you can't tell your parents, Harry. Really you can't. We'd all get into so much trouble for going to the meeting.'

'And rightly so.' Harry actually looked worried. 'You should all be stopped from doing such stupid things. I can't have the girls in my family going out and getting into danger.'

'Phyllis is two years older than you!' I said.

'She's still a girl,' said Harry, priggishly. 'I have to do my duty and save her from herself.'

'She doesn't want to be saved!' I cried. 'Harry, you can't tell. They won't let Phyllis go to college if they know what she's been up to. And they'll probably send me off to boarding school.'

'It's the right thing to do,' said Harry, but he looked like he was wavering. 'You know it is.'

And then Frank said, 'No, it's not.'

'What?' said Harry.

'It's not up to you to decide what's safe for the girls,' said Frank. 'As far as I know,' and he smiled at me and Nora, 'they're fighting for the right to decide things for themselves.'

'That's a lot of rot,' said Harry. 'They need us to look after them.'

'No,' said Frank. 'They need us to stand beside them.'

And then, to my great surprise, Grace spoke.

'If you wanted to do anything for girls,' she said sternly, 'you'd tell boys and men not to behave like those awful hooligans last week.'

'You were out there too?' Harry was astounded. He didn't know Grace very well, but he knew that she wasn't exactly the rebellious sort.

'I saw it from the bridge with the tennis club,' said

Grace. 'It was utterly horrible. And if there had been more young men like Frank here, it would never have happened.'

'Come on, Harry,' said Frank. 'Play the game.'

Harry looked around at our solemn faces, and the pompousness seemed to leak out of him.

'All right,' he said. 'I don't like it. But I won't tell.'

I felt my shoulders sag with relief.

'Swear,' I said. 'On … on your honour.' I wasn't sure Harry's honour was worth very much, but I knew he thought it was.

He sighed. 'All right,' he said. 'I swear on my honour that I won't tell anyone else about Phyllis and you lot being suffragettes. Or whatever you are. I won't tell about you going to a meeting.'

'Good,' I said.

'And,' said Frank, 'to apologise for scaring you, let us help you stack those chairs and carry these things back over to the pavilion.'

And they did. Harry didn't even grumble about it. I must say that Frank really has proved to be a very good influence on him. I said as much to Frank when we were walking over to the pavilion for our tea and buns.

'He's not a bad chap, really,' he said. 'He just needs a push in the right direction every so often. I mean, so did I.'

'What do you mean?' I said.

'Well, I had never really thought about all the suffrage business until I talked about it with you,' he said. 'Maybe now he'll think about it a bit more.'

'Maybe,' I said doubtfully.

'Oh ye of little faith!' Frank laughed. 'You seem to have done something to Grace. I remember you telling me how much she despised suffragettes. But she stood up for them just now.'

I looked at Grace, who was marching along ahead of us, her arms full of cardboard boxes.

'I think that was more thanks to her tennis-club leader than me and Nora,' I said, as we passed the white elephant stall, where Miss Casey was urging someone to buy a small china dog that looked a bit like Barnaby.

'It doesn't matter,' said Frank. 'It just shows people can change their minds.'

He smiled at me, and somehow I tripped over a footstool which I presume belonged to the white elephant stall. Frank grabbed my arm in time to stop me crashing to the ground.

'Are you all right?' he said, and suddenly I couldn't think of anything to say in reply. I just stared stupidly at him for what seemed like ages but was probably just a second or two.

'Come on, Nugent!' called Harry.

The others had reached the entrance to the pavilion.

And I remembered how I had never really thought about the suffrage question myself until I followed Phyllis to that meeting just a few months ago. I hadn't thought that sort of thing had much to do with me. But once I found out more about it and really started asking questions, I changed my mind. And if I could change my mind, so could Grace. Or Harry. Or anyone really.

'Come on,' I said. 'Let's go and have a bun.'

And that, I suppose, was that. I hope this account of our adventures has entertained you on your return from the American wilds. There's not much more to tell, apart from the fact that I didn't get a chance to talk to Frank very much once we had joined Mother and Julia and Mrs. Sheffield (and Barnaby, who had calmed down after his adventures and was looking as angelic as he possibly can, which is not very) in the pavilion.

After a while Frank and Harry left the club to meet their famous friend Harrington. After eating a bun, Grace took Barnaby home to Mrs. Sheffield's house. (Mrs. Sheffield was staying on at the club to oversee the rest of the fête, but decided that Barnaby should be taken home in case he got even more over-stimulated.) Mother and Julia went to look at a tennis demonstration on the biggest court. And finally, having watched the demonstration for a few minutes, Nora and I, fatigued by the day's excitement, decided to leave.

'Well,' said Nora, as we walked along the hot and dusty road. There was a rumble of thunder in the distance. 'What a day.'

'I feel utterly exhausted,' I said, and yawned. 'What time is it?'

'It was only two o'clock when we left, according to the pavilion clock.' Nora yawned too. 'Goodness. I really am looking forward to some peace and quiet.'

'Me too,' I said. We walked along in comfortable silence for a while. There was another rumble of thunder, closer this time.

'But not forever,' I said suddenly.

'Oh no,' said Nora. 'Definitely not forever.'

'I mean,' I said, 'we need a break from all the excitement now.'

'But in a few weeks …' said Nora. 'When things have calmed down at the meetings …'

'We've still got our disguises,' I said.

And then it started to rain and we had to run all the way home.

Best love and VOTES FOR WOMEN!
Mollie

A NOTE ABOUT THIS BOOK

Mollie, her friends, teachers and family, Mrs. Mulvany and Mamie Quigley are all figments of my imagination (though Barnaby is based on a small and hilariously noisy Bichon Frise who lives very near my house in Marino, Dublin, and barks angrily at me every time I walk by).

Many events described in this book, however, really did take place. The account of the trial of the Irish Women's Franchise League activists is based on the report that appeared in the IWFL magazine *The Irish Citizen* in July 1912. An English suffragette called Mary Leigh did throw a hatchet at Mr. Asquith's carriage on the prime minister's visit to Dublin (in a 1965 interview in the *Radio Times*, she claimed she just 'put it' in the carriage) and was involved in the attempt to set fire to a box in the Theatre Royal. She was sentenced, along with fellow English suffragette Gladys Evans, to five years' penal servitude. Subsequently the two women became the only suffrage campaigners to be force-fed in Ireland. They were released from prison less than three months after their conviction.

My accounts of the yacht-based protest in Kingstown (now Dún Laoghaire), the raid on the house on Nassau Street (including the confetti) and the meeting at Beresford Place the next day, are based closely on the accounts written at the time for *The Irish Citizen*, including a piece by one of the speakers who was nearly removed from the lorry by a gang of drunk women! In her piece she thanked the police, including an Inspector Campbell, for their protection and help. I decided to make Inspector Campbell the policeman who raided the

Nassau Street house the day before. The newspaper headlines from that day that are quoted in the book are all real, and a young suffragette really was almost thrown in the river on Eden Quay by an angry crowd and was rescued by the police. I couldn't find her name in any accounts, so I let the incident happen to poor Phyllis instead.